CHRISTOPHER BUSH
THE CASE OF THE MISSING MEN

CHRISTOPHER BUSH was born Charlie Christmas Bush in Norfolk in 1885. His father was a farm labourer and his mother a milliner. In the early years of his childhood he lived with his aunt and uncle in London before returning to Norfolk aged seven, later winning a scholarship to Thetford Grammar School.

As an adult, Bush worked as a schoolmaster for 27 years, pausing only to fight in World War One, until retiring aged 46 in 1931 to be a full-time novelist. His first novel featuring the eccentric Ludovic Travers was published in 1926, and was followed by 62 additional Travers mysteries. These are all to be republished by Dean Street Press.

Christopher Bush fought again in World War Two, and was elected a member of the prestigious Detection Club. He died in 1973.

CHRISTOPHER BUSH

THE CASE OF THE MISSING MEN

With an introduction
by Curtis Evans

DEAN STREET PRESS

Published by Dean Street Press 2018

Copyright © 1946 Christopher Bush

Introduction copyright © 2018 Curtis Evans

All Rights Reserved

The right of Christopher Bush to be identified as the Author of the Work has been asserted by his estate in accordance with the Copyright, Designs and Patents Act 1988.

First published in 1946 by Cassell & Co., Ltd.

Cover by DSP

ISBN 978 1 912574 25 4

www.deanstreetpress.co.uk

INTRODUCTION

Winding down the War and Taking a New Turn

Christopher Bush's Ludovic Travers Mysteries, 1943 to 1946

Having sent his series sleuth Ludovic "Ludo" Travers, in the third and fourth years of the Second World War, around England to meet murder at a variety of newly-created army installations—a prisoner-of-war camp (*The Case of the Murdered Major*, 1941), a guard base (*The Case of the Kidnapped Colonel*, 1942) and an instructor school (*The Case of the Fighting Soldier*, 1942)--Christopher Bush finally released Travers from military engagements in *The Case of the Magic Mirror* (1943), a unique retrospective affair which takes place before the outbreak of the Second World War. In the remaining four Travers wartime mysteries--*The Case of the Running Mouse* (1944), *The Case of the Platinum Blonde* (1944), *The Case of the Corporal's Leave* (1945) and *The Case of the Missing Men* (1946)--Bush frees his sleuth to investigate private criminal problems. Although the war is mentioned in these novels, it plays far less of a role in events, doubtlessly giving contemporary readers a sense that the world conflagration which at one point had threatened to consume the British Empire was winding down for good. Yet even without the "novelty" of the war as a major plot element, these Christopher Bush mysteries offer readers some of the most intriguing conundrums in the Ludo Travers detection canon.

The Case of the Missing Men (1946)

"Oh, my God!" groaned Martin. "They're discussing the detective novel again."

"Sometimes it drives one frantic at meals," whispered Constance. . . .

Harris mopped his brow. "And it's a judgment on this house, sir, if you ask me. All this writing about murders. Nothing but murders."

--The Case of the Missing Men (1946)

IN JUNE 1947 Christopher Bush returned to American shores, virtually speaking, when his 30th Ludovic "Ludo" Travers detective novel, *The Case of the Missing Men*, which had appeared in Britain the previous year, was reprinted in the United States by Macmillan, publisher of, among British crime writers, E.R. Punshon, George Bellairs and a certain up-and-comer named Josephine Tey. The novel was well-received by American reviewers, with the result that for the next two decades almost all of Bush's many Ludo Travers mysteries were reprinted in the US as well as the UK, making the prolific author, along with the similarly fecund Agatha Christie, Anthony Gilbert and John Dickson Carr, one of the post-WW2 era's most durable writers of classic mystery rooted in the Golden Age of detective fiction. (Macmillan even reached back to publish, in 1949, Bush's 28th mystery, *The Case of the Platinum Blonde*, originally published in the UK in 1944—an excellent if belated choice!)

It is not difficult to comprehend why *The Case of the Missing Men* caught the eye of an American publisher, for it appealingly embraces classic tropes of classic mystery. In the novel we have a sort of house party murder where an amateur detective happens to be staying as a guest and the victim is a celebrated British mystery writer—one who just happens to have the initials "A.C." Before readers leap to an unwarranted conclusion based on these initials, however, let me add that the murdered mystery writer is a man, Austin Chaice, who, except in the matter of his popularity, much less resembles Agatha Christie than he does Anthony Berkeley Cox (A.B.C.), an influential though eccentric Detection Club colleague of Christie and Christopher Bush who may already have been a satirical target of Bush in an earlier Ludo Travers novel, *The Case of the Monday Murders*. (See my introduction to the Dean Street Press reissue of that novel.)

Having been invalided out of the army in the autumn of 1943 and now employed as a "haphazard sort of special consultant" to Scotland Yard (see *The Case of the Corporal's Leave*, 1945), Ludovic Travers fatefully comes to stay in September 1944 at Lovelands, the Beechingford home of Austin Chaice at the behest of not only Chaice but his and Chaice's literary agent, Cuthbert Daine. (It will be recalled by Bush readers that Ludo is the author of five books, variously dealing with economic and criminology- -*The Economics of a Spendthrift*; *The Stockbroker's Breviary*; *World Markets*; *Kensington Gore; or, Murder for Highbrows*; and *Is This a Dagger?*--and we learn in *The Case of the Missing Men* that *Kensington Gore* and another volume, presumably *Is This a Dagger?*, are still in print.) Perhaps inspired by the publication of Marie F. Rodell's *Mystery Writing: Theory and Technique* (1943), Austin Chaice is writing a "how-to" manual for budding detective fiction authors, and he would like to use some quotations from Ludo's book *Kensington Gore* and consult with him on "certain technical matters concerned with the detection of crime."

Soon Ludo is on his way to Lovelands, which upon his arrival there he finds is ironically rife with mutual suspicion and hatred. Present at the estate, besides Travers and Chaice, are Chaice's wife Constance, a "decidedly oversexed" cousin of Travers's wife Bernice, who is still away (as she has been for years now) nursing up north; Chaice's children from his first marriage, Kitty, a spirited veteran of the ATS (Auxiliary Territorial Service), and Martin, an ineffectual and neurotic Oxford student turned down by the services on account of his perpetual migraine headaches; Chaice's elder brother, Richard, perhaps just a bit barmy after having been bombed in the Blitz; Orford Lang, a failed detective novelist turned Chaice's private secretary; and an elderly butler,

Harris, attempting to run Lovelands with a much depleted domestic retinue. Also living on the estate is Cuthbert Daine, who at Chaice's invitation has transferred his literary agency, after its second bombing-out in London, to the large converted barn at Lovelands.

At Lovelands it becomes evident to Ludo that life revolves entirely around the caprices of the monstrously egotistical and even "sadistic" Austin Chaice and that growing rather restive under the mystery writer's regime are many of his subjects, such as Constance, who seems to find his merest touch repulsive; Martin, who spurns detective fiction and wants to be a modernist poet, a branch of literature his father in turn scorns; and Orford Lang, whose own fragile literary dreams have been thoughtlessly crushed by his employer. ("You know how it is," Chaice contemptuously divulges to Ludo about Lang's brief career as a crime writer, "Twelve or fourteen hundred sales and the cheapest rate. The poor devil would have starved on it. . . . Lucky for him . . . I offered him his present job.")

As Ludo perceptively puts it, after the great mystery writer is found strangled in his study: Lovelands "was completely centered round Austin Chaice and his work. His work dominated him. It was more of an obsession than work, because his very leisure was work. . . . A war on, mind you, and yet I never once heard anyone ask for the news." There is, to be sure, no shortage of suspects in Chaice's murder within his own household—yet there is also the strange matter of the missing man: an absconded individual named G.H. Preston, a next-door-neighbor and tenant of Chaice, with whom he had corresponded. Just what is Preston trying to hide, and just where has he hidden himself? Then there is a second murder at Lovelands, every bit as baffling as the first, and with it another man gone missing! Over the course of their long pursuit of ingenious criminal malefactors, Ludo Travers and his old friend, Superintendent George Wharton of Scotland Yard--with whom, we learn for the first time, Ludo plans to start a private detective agency after Wharton's retirement--rarely have been presented with a murder problem as perplexing as this one: a wickedly clever conundrum that could well have been ripped from the pages of an Austin Chaice bestseller.

Curtis Evans

PART I

CHAPTER I
TWO LETTERS

I waited for a moment at the door and gave a quick wipe to my glasses. That is a kind of nervous trick of mine when at a sudden loss, or on the edge of discovery, or faced with some unusual situation. But there was nothing nervously disquietening about that interview with Inspector Goodman. What was unusual was that I, who had assisted in the questioning of scores of witnesses and suspects in my time, was now about to be questioned. Maybe I was only wondering just what sort of hand Goodman would make of the job.

I gave a tap at the door and opened it. My eyes went instinctively to the corner by the open desk where the body had been, then they rose for another look at Goodman. He was tall—about a couple of inches less than my six foot three—but weighing a good three stone more than myself, and beneath the tightness of his coat I could see that his weight was mostly muscle. A nasty customer in a scrap was my first impression of him.

"Mr. L. Travers?" he said, and gave a quick look at his notebook. He had quite an attractive baritone voice and the tone was pleasant enough. Quite a good bedside manner, I told myself professionally.

"That's correct," I said.

"The L is for . . . ?"

"Ludovic," I told him. "Just an old family custom."

I suppose I must have smiled. He gave an answering smile in which there was a certain diffidence, and then was waving me to a chair. He seemed rather puzzled about me, or so I thought, and under some circumstances I might have been amused. The situation certainly had ironic possibilities, and yet I didn't feel the least amusement. Murder is a grim business and he'd a right to treat it seriously, and perhaps even more so had I.

"Just how do you come to be in Beechingford?" was his first real question. "I ask that because I understand your address is St. Martin's Chambers, in town."

He was peering at me with raised eyebrows, the sort of look that George Wharton would have made a whimsical one, and over the tops of antiquated spectacles.

"It's rather a long story," I began. "I'm really here killing two birds with one stone. I mean, seeing both Mr. Chaice and Mr. Daine."

"You're an author?" There was another and not unfriendly lift of the eyebrows.

"I was, some years ago."

"But not now."

"Not now," I echoed, and for a moment he seemed at a loss. Then he framed the next question.

"What exactly are you doing now?"

"That again is rather involved," I said, and not out of cussedness, but just because I didn't want to be obscure. "I was called up at the beginning of the war, then invalided out a year or so ago, and after that I carried on with certain work at Scotland Yard that I'd been doing for some years."

He looked so startled that I had to add that maybe I should have mentioned that straightaway.

"Work at Scotland Yard," he said. "Just what sort of work, sir?"

"You know how it is," I said. "They have all sorts of consultative experts, as they call 'em, on tap, and I was called in from time to time. These last few months I've been doing various jobs. They're very short-handed, you know."

The door opened and his plain-clothes sergeant came in. His name, I had been told, was Smith, and he was carrying a fat notebook and had a pencil behind his ear. Goodman was at once getting to his feet.

"Would you excuse me a minute or two, sir? There's something I should have done."

He and Smith exchanged looks. Smith took the vacated seat at the desk, and just as Goodman was at the door I cleared my throat.

"If you should happen to be ringing the Yard, Inspector, you might ask for Superintendent Wharton."

He didn't like that at first, but then he grinned. I hadn't intended to be clever or superior. I was looking after my own interests, so to speak, and trying to save time, and yet I could self-consciously tell myself that I might have done both in a different way.

"You'll excuse me, sir," said Smith, and was at once busying himself with the back pages of his notebook.

"You carry on," I told him cheerfully, and took another look round the room.

It was an airy, comfortable room. Through the window I could see the smooth lawn and beyond it the shrubbery and fringe of poplars that kept a privacy for the house from the small, if select, residential estate that lay beyond the back lane to the south. Through the open french window was coming the scent of roses from the beds that fronted the house. In the far garden corner I could see the thatch of the summerhouse that nestled in the shrubbery, and somewhere in the room itself a bee was droning clumsily. Then it found the open window and flew out, and my eyes went to the floor.

The mess had been cleared up. The chair in which I was sitting was the one that had been overturned by the body, but there were chalk marks to show just where it had been. On the same red carpet was a chalk outline of the body itself, and a smaller one for the overturned vase, and a few single scrawls that represented the rucks made by the feet of struggling men. I wondered if Goodman had noticed the queer thing about those various marks or whether it would be unprofessional conduct on my part to point it out.

Then my eyes fell on the telephone. It was an extension from the main telephone in the larger room where Chaice worked with his secretary, Orford Lang, to Chaice's private sanctum where Smith and I then were. That's why I had guessed that Goodman wanted to check up on me at the Yard. He hadn't wanted me to hear and so had gone to the other room to make his enquiries. And there was every reason to make enquiries. No one could look less like a minion of the law than myself.

That led me to wondering just what George Wharton would tell him. George and I had worked together for years, and though we could be everything from the facetious to the blasphemous to each other's faces, we were a mutual admiration society when dealing with a third party. Viewed apart we were opposites, but together we were complementary and contrived to dovetail in. George takes a huge zest in his work, relieving the boredoms with a hundred tricks of showmanship and the playing of cameo dramas in which he is the leading man. He is all things to all men: stolid or furiously impatient, wily and tortuous or guilefully direct, dignified or skittish, bland, wheedling or superbly indignant in the same minute; homely and yet lousy with snobberies and humbug. And the most curious thing about it all is that George is the more likeable because of that repertoire of tricks. And one last thing, and one not to forget, is that he is the man for his job. It's only the supermen who attain to the heights of the Big Five.

What about myself, you may say. Well, I suppose I'm the opposite of George, except that in the course of years I've acquired some of his tricks. But mine is a helter-skelter, flibbertigibbet, crossword sort of brain that works quickly or not at all. The rest of my irritating peculiarities you will know long before you reach the end of this record. Perhaps the only thing George and I have in common is that neither of us looks the part we have to play. No false whiskers could disguise my lamp-post leanness and horn-rims. As for George, his immense walrus moustache and the hunched breadth of his shoulders and that black overcoat with the worn velvet collar give him the air of a harassed if somewhat superior man from the Prudential. But, as 1 said, we get along remarkably well on the whole. I know he has for me his likings and respects, even if they are only those of an Old Master for a useful apprentice. My own likings and respects are those of the apprentice who has come to know the Old Master only too well, but who would rather change his job than be kicked out of the studio.

Goodman was the devil of a time, I thought, and just as I thought that, I heard his step outside. Smith vacated the seat and took another at the little table by the french window.

"A clear bill?" I asked.

"Absolutely," he told me, and gave an answering smile. "So if you'd be so good, sir, we'll hear all you know about this business."

"It'll be a longish tale," I told him.

"Need it be?" he asked. "I mean, can't we have the bare essentials? After all, sir, you're something of an old hand."

"Not so old as you'd think," I said. "But the trouble is to know what essentials are. My trivialities might be your highly important clues, and vice versa."

"Yes," he said, and gave a Whartonian pursing of the lips. A quick look at his watch and he was wondering if I could get through in an hour. I said it depended on Smith and his shorthand, and he said Smith was one of the fastest there were. Smith tried to look as if he hadn't heard.

Well, that was that, and I began. What you are going to read is what I told Goodman, but with many extras; in fact, your version will be ten times as long, though not so long, I hope, as to get near boredom. There are things like personal views, descriptions of people and places which he could either have guessed from my tone or which he knew already. There were also, I frankly admit, things which I couldn't very well divulge to him, since I was far from sure about them myself. And since I had no statement prepared, I had to extemporise, and that doesn't always make for clarity. The best I can say is that he was told a very few things he had no need of knowing, and I doubt if anything was left out that might have helped him solve the Case. Just one other thing I should make clear. You would hate to wade through a verbatim report as taken down by Smith, with its deviations from strict chronology, its necessary and disjointed harkings back, and Goodman's interrupting questions and my answers and explanations. What you are going to have are the very relevant facts, and in chronological order. If I describe a place or a person it will not be for the sake of padding, but because the matter contains a vital clue. You, like Goodman, have a Case to solve, and it is for you, therefore, that every single piece of the jigsaw is now placed in full view on the table before you.

As far as I was personally concerned, the whole business began with the arrival of two letters. The first was from my literary agent, Cuthbert Daine. Twenty years ago I wrote my first book, and it is ten years now since I wrote at all. A necessary word here about myself. I never was a professional author. By good fortune I had been left a reasonable income, but in those early days I took life and myself very seriously. I wanted to do something, and writing became a hobby. Not that I regarded myself as in any way superior to the professional writer—far from it. Except for the work which I am now doing for the Yard, there is nothing that would please me more than to try to write for a living. I even believe I could make a good shot at it, and maybe in my later years, when Beveridge and the Commissioners of Inland Revenue have relieved me of most of what I now possess, I may have to make that claim good.

Daine was recommended to me as a literary agent, and not only did he sell that first book of mine but it happened to go remarkably well, and it was he thereafter who endeavoured, with indifferent success, to keep my nose on the literary grindstone. Four books was my total, for I had various interests and worked by fits and starts, but with all four he did uncommonly well, though I was only a small cog in his very big machine. Two of those books are out of print, but I still draw regular small royalties from the two others, which, having gone through the cheap editions, have come at last to rest in a well-known series—the Laurel Library—published by Parsley and Branch. It contains some fine titles, and, between ourselves, I'm mighty lucky to be found in it.

Daine is one of those queer persons who may be said to possess dual personalities. Though my associations with him were almost all business ones, I rather liked him personally, even if the liking may be traced to that species of vanity that derives itself from successful sales and an agent's blandishments. But quite a lot of people didn't like him. Some went out of their way to warn me against him. In spite of his large and famous clientele, how could he keep up that superb flat in town with its lavish entertaining, and a certain even more expensive bachelor establishment he was rumoured to have in Brighton? But what Daine did with his money and his private life was no concern of mine, and an agent who was good enough for, among others, Austin Chaice, was certainly good enough for small fry like myself. All of which brings me back to those two letters.

I was surprised to see Daine's name at the bottom of the first, since I had no more books to sell and the fate of those I had written was no longer a matter of concern.

Lovelands Barn,
Beechingford.
5-9-44.

Dear Travers,

Books, as you know, are selling remarkably well, and for some time I have had your own in mind. Last week I brought the matter to a head with Harold Parsley. He has had an unexpected windfall of paper and is prepared to reprint special editions of the two now in the Laurel Library. There are varies matters arising out of all this which I should like to discuss with you before getting to work on the new contract. If you could make the matter one of urgency it would be to our mutual advantage, so perhaps you will let me know a convenient date.

In that context, you will probably be hearing from Austin Chaice. He is engaged at the moment on—among other things—a kind of manual for budding authors of detective novels, a book which we think should do well both here and in America. In the course of his research— you know his fanaticisms about verisimilitude and local colour!—he chanced on your *Kensington Gore* and would like to use quotes. He would also like your expert opinion on certain technical matters concerned with the detection of crime. But, as I said, he will be writing to you himself.

The point I want to make is that you could see both him and myself at the same time. You may remember that after my second bombing out, I moved down here with a very depleted staff into that annexe of his for which he has no use during the war, and which the Army was threatening to requisition. Am I right, by the way, in saying that Mrs. Chaice is a relation of your wife? She gave me that impression, and she certainly knows you well. That should add to the pleasure of your visit.

Kind regards as ever,

CUTHBERT DAINE.

There was something definitely pleasing about the first part of that letter. It flattered my vanity, and, in my experience, few people have an amount of money which makes them indifferent to receiving more, and especially when the receipt involves no labour in return. But the second part of that letter gave me a curious disquiet. Luckily Austin Chaice's letter had come by the same post.

Lovelands,
Beechingford.
5-9-44.

Dear Travers,

I expect you will now have heard from Cuthbert Daine what a stickler I am for absolute authenticity. In a writing career of over twenty years I have never yet had a statement or any local colour of mine called in question, a record of which to be legitimately proud, and which I should like to maintain.

To be perfectly frank, your *Kensington Gore* contains a lot of material which would be very valuable for me in a textbook I am writing for those—and they must be legion!—who think they could write a detective novel. I can hear your exclamation of dismay! But you are wrong, my dear Travers. I shall not be cluttering up the market and cutting my own throat. However conscientiously one writes books like this, it's always with one's tongue in one's cheek. And after all, if all the Schools of Correspondence which advertise themselves produced authors in proportion to what one imagines to be the numbers of their credulous clients, then both you and I would long ago have been in the workhouse.

As to the matter of authenticity which I mentioned—and boasted unpardonably about!—I should like your valuable help and first-hand advice on certain aspects of criminal investigation and procedure, for all of which I shall naturally be prepared to pay. I understand from Daine that you will be seeing him here almost at once. Perhaps you and I could settle matters at the same time.

My wife often mentions you and will, needless to say, be delighted to see you here. She sends her remembrances and best wishes, and to your wife. Please accept my own, my dear Travers, and many thanks in anticipation.

Yours sincerely,

AUSTIN CHAICE.

Perhaps you see no reason for uneasiness over the general content of those two letters. You think perhaps that I should have been highly gratified at being considered of sufficient standing and competence to be regarded as an expert by one so famous as Austin Chaice. But long contact with Wharton and the deceits and sinfulness of this wicked world have made me suspicious of blandishments. Chaice's 'My dear Travers' had even made me wince. The same detective sense had made me suspicious of the perfect dovetailing of those two letters. Why should two very important people like Daine and Chaice be so anxious to save my time? Be so keen, in other words, on my killing two birds at Beechingford with one stone. And when I came to think of it, the necessarily small reprints of my books would bring little financial profit to Daine. Why, amid all those books on Parsley and Branch's list, had mine been chosen for reprint?

So I read the two letters again and tried to make an analysis of both of them and their possible motives and of my own reactions. In the matter of the reprints, I decided that I was being too suspicious. Daine, as a conscientious agent, might consider that an author as insignificant as myself was entitled to as much consideration as the far more profitable and famous. And what about *Kensington Gore* and the use it might be to Chaice? *Kensington Gore* was a young man's book, with all the faults of superficial brilliance and a straining after wit. It was, as its punning title may imply, a discussion of certain Murder Cases in which the victims had all been blue-blooded, a theme which gave ample scope for the brand of ironic pessimism which had been so popular at the time it was written.

And yet when I thought the matter over, and the purposes for which Chaice intended to use the book, I couldn't help but think it might perhaps be useful to him for occasional quotation and illustration. After all, it was a book that had even had the guarded blessings of the Yard. As for the request for expert advice, I saw ample reason for disquiet. If I were induced to part with confidences, even with an implicit statement that they must be treated as such, then I should be taking risks, for Chaice was as unreliable as they make them. For any profit or publicity of his own he would throw me overboard with never a hint of compunction. Chaice might have a brilliant kind of one-track mind, but I had no doubts of his instability, both mental and moral.

And there was another thing—Beechingford, a town of twenty thousand people even in normal times, would have police authorities who would gladly give to a local lion all the information about police procedure and so on that Chaice could possibly make use of in his book. Why then call on me? The best I could say for him was that maybe he preferred not to be under any local obligation but to get his information from one of his own profession, so to speak, and kind.

That led me to reviewing Chaice himself. I knew him well enough, or had done in the days before the war. I had never envied him, however, which is what few authors can say, though his income must have been well over ten thousand a year. Of the detective novel he was a master, and his output was large, and without loss of quality. It must be said of him, too, that, unlike Daine, he had no interests but his work; in fact, in his case, work and Chaice were the same thing. Publicity was his life-blood and he was the showman supreme. George Wharton's tricks and showmanship were lovable and laughable as soon as you discerned the man beneath; Chaice's were irritations that left him with few friends and innumerable enemies. In enmities he seemed to revel. While he had no real or scathing wit, he had instead a perfect inability to keep his mouth shut or to halt an unpleasant truth at the tip of his tongue. He delighted in the fact that he had made himself particularly obnoxious at his town club, and even made that club the scene of one of his novels. As for his eccentricities, they took the form of self-advertisement, occasional flamboyancies of dress, for instance, and endless letters to the Press.

As for that sureness of local colour to which he referred, I thought of an example. A small army unit had its headquarters near Lovelands and Chaice helped himself to one of its typewriters. After a few days, when the local police had discovered nothing about the thief, he wrote to the local paper and to certain London ones, admitting that it was he who had taken the machine. His reasons were that all over the country there was scandalous laxity in the care of government property, and he had taken the machine to call the attention of the authorities to such laxity and the ease with which a mere amateur like himself could purloin a typewriter at will. When he was hauled up before the local beaks, he got off with honours, and then later divulged that he had also had a subsidiary motive for taking the typewriter—and that motive was that he was using the episode in a book, and had wanted his local colour to be implicitly correct! That, then, was Austin Chaice; not a man with whom I was anxious to renew any acquaintanceship, even if it would be he who was under an obligation.

I fell then to thinking about Beechingford and that place of his called Lovelands. He had had it for a good many years and had transformed it from an ancient farmhouse to a rambling structure of a place, replete, as they say, with every convenience. But a lovely place for all that, and set in some ten acres of grounds and woodland. The farm buildings had been renovated and modernised. The large barn was used for an overflow of guests, and the smaller barn was an immense garage. It was the large barn that had been placed at Daine's disposal. He had been Chaice's agent from the very beginning, and to their mutual advantage. Daine must have made well over a thousand a year out of Chaice. And Chaice made far more than that out of Daine's knack in acquiring foreign and film and serial rights, and his placing of shorts. Though the war had cut most of those, and drastically, and added as drastically to income tax, I doubted if Chaice were feeling anything of a pinch. His father—a big contractor in the last war—had left him plenty, and though he was a lavish spender he was a shrewd one, and as shrewd an investor.

Lastly I thought about Constance Chaice. She was, as Daine had surmised, a cousin of my wife, and I had known her from her toddling days. Now she would be, as I calculated, in the early thirties. As a flapper she had been definitely spoilt and decidedly oversexed, and my wife—certainly no prude—had come to avoiding her like the devil. At twenty-one she married Charlie Greene, and there was a species of agreed divorce two years later. He was very cut up about it and, I believe, would have taken her back, for she was a damned attractive woman in those days. I say 'in those days', for the last time I had seen her was just before her second marriage. That was to a man named Fanting, whom she divorced just before this war. Shortly afterwards she married Chaice.

Chaice's own marital adventures were much along the same lines, except that his first wife died, and it was the second who divorced him. By his first wife he had a son and a daughter. The daughter I hadn't met, but I knew the son, for he had been at the same school as a nephew of mine, and as they were friends, I happened at times to entertain the two of them in town. Martin

Chaice had been a curious, self-centred sort of boy, and a bit neurotic, or so I had thought. I know that he used to choose, when invited, the queerest ways of spending an afternoon.

I gave the whole matter a day's thought and then mentioned it to George Wharton. There was a week's leave due to me, though this and that had cropped up and the leave had been deferred again and again. Now there was nothing much doing in my line and he advised me to get away while the going was good and the weather not too bad. But he had to give me a backhanded remark or two about my being thought an expert. I could see he was a bit jealous.

"Expert my foot!" I told him. "If I'd thought that, I'd have referred him to you."

"Oh, I don't know," said George, with a vast assumption of modesty.

"All Chaice wants is ordinary stuff. Tricks of the author's trade."

I could see him softening, so I added that he ought to meet Chaice some time.

"Far too busy," he said, but in a tone that left open a considerable gap. "But talking about books, I might try my own hand one of these days."

"Oh no you don't," I said. "No autobiography from you, George. You and I are opening a detective agency when this war's over."

That was a project with which George and I were toying. But I took his advice about the leave and wrote that night to both Daine and Chaice, saying that unless anything happened I'd be down on the Friday by an early afternoon train.

Two days later Daine rang me to say that Chaice had been horrified at the request I'd made for the name of a suitable hotel. Chaice, he said, had thought it implicit in his letter that I should stay at Lovelands where there was ample room. I said that was very good of him and I'd gratefully accept the offer. I was hoping, I added, to be back in town on the Monday. Daine said why the hurry. There was a golf-course near if I still played, a swimming-pool in the grounds at Lovelands and a fair bus service if one wanted to view the countryside. All I could add was that we'd have to see.

That conversation took place just before I sat down to a service dinner at my flat. Two hours later the telephone went again.

"Hallo?" I said.

"Is that you, Uncle Ludo?"

I gasped for a moment, then had an idea.

"That you, Constance?"

"But of course, darling. Didn't you recognise my voice?"

"I do now," I said. It was charged with the same old ersatz seductiveness. A bit hoarse and croony and throaty, like Tallulah Bankhead's. Indeed I remembered that she had first adopted it after seeing Tallulah.

"But why the *Uncle* Ludo?" I added.

"But, darling, didn't I always call you that?" The voice now had a touch of the plaintive.

"Maybe," I said, with mock-reproof. "But you're a big girl now. Hadn't you better omit the fictitious *uncle*?"

"We'll see," she said. "But honestly, darling, I'm simply thrilled to be seeing you again. We're absolutely relying on you till Tuesday at the least."

"I doubt if I can manage—"

"But, darling, you *must*." A little throaty laugh. "Do you know, I'd actually forgotten why I really rang you up. It was for Austin, to say there'll be a taxi for you at the station if you give the time of the train."

"I thought perhaps the 2.30 at Beechingford, on Friday."

"Lovely," she said. "Simply lovely." Another little silence and then her voice changed again. It was sort of hushed and confidential. "You there, darling?"

"Yes?"

"This is desperately secret. Something I want you to do for me."

"Yes?"

"But I can't tell you now. It's simply desperately secret. Something I'm frightened about. Really frightened."

What to say I didn't know, so I cleared my throat. Constance wasn't the frightened sort. Then in a flash I wondered if she had landed herself in a mess with some man and Austin was threatening a divorce.

"Anything I can do . . . of course," I said sheepishly.

"I knew I could rely on you, darling." The voice fairly throbbed with gratitude.

"That's all right," I said. "See you on Friday, then."

That seemed to be all. At any rate I rang off before I was quite aware of it. But the following morning there was a strange sequel. Chaice rang me, and the message—taken by arrangement with the hall porter—was to the effect that he'd be glad to know the time of my train so that he could send a taxi to meet me.

In other words, Constance was up to her old games again. She had not rung me to give me Chaice's message, nor had she told Chaice the time of my train. She had rung me purely and simply to ask my help in whatever muddle, matrimonial or otherwise, it was in which she was finding herself. And that, as Shakespeare says, craved wary walking.

That early Friday afternoon found me in the train, a copy of *Kensington Gore* in my pocket for a quick review and a whiling away of those eighteen, mostly suburban, miles. One thing I had not done. I had not mentioned to my wife that I was spending a day or two at Beechingford. Women, even in my limited judgment, can put the queerest constructions on the most trivial events, and Constance's name had long been taboo. In fact I told myself that I should be back in town on the Tuesday morning at the latest, and there would be no need to mention the weekend at all. That was how I worked things guilefully out. Just how far I was wrong you will very shortly see.

CHAPTER II
OVERTURE

As THE TRAIN drew near Beechingford I began thinking about Constance Chaice, and recalling that melodramatic hush in her voice and the talk about being frightened. What it all meant I still couldn't guess, though inclined to adhere to my original suspicion of a man and a divorce both in the offing. Perhaps her vague hints had included the unspoken warning that I should find her and Chaice on pretty bad terms, and that was something which I didn't find it pleasant to contemplate, for I could see myself in a position that would be remarkably uncomfortable. There would be frigidities, and myself used as a vehicle through which the hostile pair would talk at each other, and altogether it would be a strained and trying business.

Even when I got out of the train I was still thinking about the possibly unpleasant ménage in which I was about to spend the weekend, and so occupied was I with my thoughts that I stared rather blankly at a chauffeur who asked me if I was Mr. Travers. He was a driver for a private hire service in the town, and the car awaiting me was quite a roomy and comfortable one.

There are two things about myself which I ought at once to make clear. One is that I am possessed of an insatiable curiosity, which means that I like to know what makes the wheels go round, and the whys and wherefores of this and that. The other thing, which follows as a kind of corollary, is that I take an inordinate interest in my fellow men. I like their company, to hear them talk, to know what they think and like and dislike. And all that irrespective of that particularly snobbish and British word *class*. I have no use for the strong silent men, and in my town club there is rarely an interesting specimen. A railway carriage, a bus or a pub have been my happiest hunting-grounds. That explains why, when the driver opened the door, I said I preferred to sit in front, and after that we were chatting away all the mile and a half from the station to Lovelands.

I had not been in Beechingford for years, but the town seemed to me to have changed very little. There were distant factory chimneys which I didn't recall, and the driver told me that the factory was an enormous place built since the war began. Hundreds of women and girls were employed there, and housed in a large camp south of the town. In the long High Street I also noticed a new and palatial cinema.

"There's a regular sensation on here at the moment," the driver told me.

"You mean a special picture at the cinema?"

"Well, someone might go and make a picture of it," he said, and began to explain. What he had meant was that the town was in the throes of a sensation. At nights the streets swarmed with the workers off duty, and the cinemas were crowded too. But some maniac or pervert was taking advantage of the crowds to squirt filthy liquid over women's clothes. When the cinemas were emptying was his favourite time. That would be at about nine o'clock when it was comfortably dark overhead and the black-out was in full swing.

"How long has it been going on?" I asked him.

"About a week, sir."

"And the police haven't discovered anything?"

"They will do soon," he told me confidently. "They've got a rare smart Inspector here, sir. Goodman, his name is. If he can't catch 'em, nobody can."

We were then out of the town and heading west in quite open country.

"Curious that this land between the town and Mr. Chaice's place hasn't been built over?" I said.

"Mr. Chaice can thank himself for that," he told me. "He picked up all this land during the slump, and then, just before the war, he sold it to the council. Some say there's going to be a park and a posh housing estate."

Then almost at once he was pointing out Chaice's house to me, and I saw its roof through a gap in the elms. Still a nice place, he said it was, though not kept up so well as it was before the war. But Mr. Chaice was like everybody else—he couldn't get labour. But it seemed well-kept enough for me.

The summer of 1944, you may remember, consisted of three separate weeks—Whitsuntide week, August Bank Holiday week and the second week in September, and the rest is best forgotten. This was the last brief spell, and maybe the perfect weather and the loveliness of the rare sun had something to do with my optimistic appraisal, for to me the hundred yards of drive looked spotless, the flower-beds along the house were immaculate and gay, and the lawns had those streaks of varied green that showed a recent mowing. But there was no time to peep around, for at the front door was Chaice himself. And as I caught sight of him, there came into my mind the most incongruous of thoughts, or rather remembrances—that before he had taken up writing he had been an actor.

Perhaps the thought wasn't so incongruous after all. What gave rise to it—and it wasn't hard to trace the origins-—was the wonder what his face would be like. I had known him with a sweeping moustache and small imperial, and later clean-shaven with sideburns that grew level with the middle of his ears. Now I saw that he was absolutely clean-shaven, and that gave the face a new and unexpected look.

Chaice was over fifty but possessed of the gift of perennial youth. But for a little aristocratic greying by the ears, his hair was dark and dense, though he was now wearing it inordinately short, and there was never a sign of baldness. In height he was just under the average and slimly built. Or maybe his bones had never had the time to acquire much of a covering, for of all men I have known he was most entitled to the epithet mercurial, with his perpetual and irritating restlessness, his amplitude of gesture and his impatience of quiet ease.

I could see, too, that he was wearing a perfectly normal lounge suit. He had had, as I knew, his velvet coat period, with sweeping bow necktie and Bohemian wide-brimmed hat. And there had been a corduroy trouser period with flaming red tie. Then had come a time when he was partial to outrageous checks.

"My dear Travers, what a pleasure!"

His hand had reached for mine as soon as I had manipulated my length out of the door. There was an unctuousness to make one wince. His little eyes were almost puckered with the pain of the exquisite pleasure, and his thin mobile lips, usually ironic and drooping, were stretched to a smile.

"Very nice to see you again," I said, and, "You're looking very well. Not a day older."

His hand still held mine and his other hand was patting it in a sort of Chadband approval.

"The driver," I said, and my hand escaped to my trouser pocket.

"But, no," he told me, almost horrified. "Everything's been settled." But he smiled not without disapproval when I passed over a tip. In the hall I noticed a large showcase filled with objects I couldn't identify, and then I noticed his old butler with my bag.

"You'd like to see your room straightaway?" Chaice asked me.

I said perhaps I would, and followed the butler up the stairs. We went along a wide corridor to the left and then turned sharp right, and there was my room in the wing. Quite a charming room with a fine view of the annexe.

"Harris, isn't it?" I said.

He seemed pleased that I should remember him. I told him, too, that he was looking well, though I might have added that he was looking more than his seventy years.

"The labour problem worrying you here?" I asked him.

The old boy was very depressed. His one footman had long since gone and had been followed by a procession of incompetent parlourmaids. At the moment they were lucky to have one or two old servants of the family, and a working housekeeper. As for the gardens, where there used to be three men and a boy, now there was only the old head gardener and one old man.

"Mr. Richard is a great help, of course, sir."

"Mr. Richard?" I said, and he explained. Richard Chaice was Austin's elder brother, who, I now remember, had been very much of a rolling stone. Soon after the war he came home from Canada and had since been living at Lovelands. I didn't see at the time what Harris was driving at when he had said he was a help, and I didn't like to seem too inquisitive.

Harris showed me my way about. The room had its basin with hot and cold water, and close to it was the lavatory and a bathroom. The one other bedroom in that stumpy wing was Daine's and farther from the main building than my own. Then when Harris left I had a quick clean up and another look out of my bedroom window. The thatch of the old barn annexe was a silvery blue against the hazy blue of the elms. To the right, beyond the mellowed wall, was the kitchen garden and the white of greenhouse roofs. In the air was the lovely whirr of a lawn-mower, and even the bedrooms had the faint pervasiveness of garden scents and the musky smell of roses.

I made my way downstairs to the hall, and that showcase caught my eye again, if only because of its ugliness and incongruity. As I took a look Chaice came out of the room which I afterwards knew as his private sanctum.

"I thought I heard you," he said, and was at once explaining the contents of the showcase. It was a collection of what I might call criminal oddments, and heavens knows how he had acquired it. There were articles that had been the personal property of this murderer and that, and, in one or two cases, things closely connected with the same crimes. There was a sawn-off shotgun and various knives and what can be lumped together as blunt instruments. Plenty of guns and automatics, and a small rifle or two. There was even a cigarette-end—the last that a certain murderer had smoked the morning of his execution.

"Not everybody's taste, of course," he told me, prompted maybe by the look on my face when he explained that last object. "But it all makes for atmosphere, my dear chap. And what should we do without atmosphere?"

I lamely echoed a what, and then he was saying that tea would be on in another half-hour, and why shouldn't we take a look round outside. So we went out, and through the french window of that sanctum of his. It was a cosy room with plenty of books, even if reference ones. A vase of roses filled the room with scent, and altogether it was a room that I envied him. If a man couldn't work there, as I told him, he couldn't work at all. He surprised me by saying that most of his work was done elsewhere, and at once, in that volatile way of his, he was turning back and, arm in mine, was leading me through the hall and opening the door of another room. It, too, faced south, but was much larger.

At a table under the larger window a man was typing, and he got to his feet as we entered.

"This is Mr. Travers, Lang," Chaice said.

Chaice's secretary looked about thirty. He was tall, rather sinewy in build and with fair hair brushed back from his high forehead. He had an attractive smile and I liked the look of him.

An old buffer like myself appreciates good manners, and as soon as we said the 'How d'you do's' he was moving a chair up for me and asking if I would sit down.

"Can't stay now," Chaice told him brusquely. "I just wanted Travers to see the workshop."

"And a very nice workshop it is," I said, and it undoubtedly was. It was a combination of efficiency and comfort, and Chaice hadn't spared money on it. There were even two dictaphones, and two fine typewriters besides the one that Lang had been using. The filing cabinets and stationery cupboards were expensive-looking too.

"See you some time later." I smiled at Lang as Chaice drew me out again. This time we went through the hall and out by the open front door. As soon as we got outside I said I'd been too rushed to enquire about everybody. How was Constance, for instance.

"She's always fit," he told me. "Been looking forward to seeing you, though."

We had stepped on the grass and that was why we heard the steps on the gravel behind us. Constance was at the front door, and when I turned my head she was waving. We halted till she caught us up.

"How are you, Ludo?" she said. "So lovely to see you again."

Her hand was delightfully cool and the smile frankly welcoming. When I met her eyes there was nothing in them to remind me of that brief telephone conversation of a few evenings before.

"You're looking amazingly well," I said, and she was. And I might have added that she was looking uncommonly handsome. She seemed in some curious way to have grown since I had seen her last, and she was half a head taller than Chaice. The very simplicity of her dress was a work of art, for the Worcester green skirt and the yellowish jumper went admirably with the reddish gold of her hair.

"Do you think she's been well treated?" asked Chaice uxoriously as he squeezed her arm.

"That's not for me to say," I told him, and the reason why I made a remark so fatuous was that I was thinking of something quite different—the quick drawing back of her arm when Chaice's hand went out to it and the flash of something almost like repulsiveness that was momentarily seen on her face.

"We thought of taking a quick stroll round the gardens," Chaice told her. Perhaps I had imagined what I thought I had seen, for he at any rate had noticed nothing. His look had nothing but a pride of possession.

"Far too hot," she told him, and drew a step or two back. "You two darlings run along."

We—that really means Chaice—watched her till she was back at the porch. Tea was in half an hour, she called to us, and then, with a wave, she disappeared inside. Chaice let out a kind of sigh.

"One of the best," he told me, and was taking my arm again. "Makes all the difference in a house like this. Gets on well with the children too."

"How are they?" I said, and perhaps to change the subject, for his praise of Constance had struck me as rather oddly expressed.

"Kitty's coming home tonight," he said. "Seven day's leave. She's an A.T., you know. And enjoying every minute of it."

"That's fine," I said. "I've never met your daughter. And the boy? Martin?"

"Still at home," he told me, and I couldn't miss the frown. "Turned down for the Services and . . . Still, you'll be seeing him."

We were now at the swimming-pool and he changed the subject so abruptly that I could do no more than wonder. Martin had apparently turned out as oddly as his youth had promised.

Chaice did add that nowadays one saw little of and knew still less about one's children.

"For myself, I'm up to the eyes in work. Books are selling pretty well too, in spite of paper shortage."

"You've plenty on hand?"

"Too much," he said.

"But that secretary of yours must be a great help."

"Orford's all right," he said patronisingly. "But you know how it is. Put my brain into his fingers and then we might get somewhere."

Orford Lang, I had said to myself. The name recalled something, and then I remembered.

"Orford Lang. Wasn't there a chap who wrote detective novels under that name?"

"That's the one," he said. "Never got anywhere with them." The curl of his lip wasn't pleasant. "You know how it is. Twelve or fourteen hundred sales and the cheapest rate. The poor devil would have starved on it."

"He had no private income?"

"Devil a bit," he said. "Lucky for him I saw he had something in him, so I offered him his present job. Had him for three years now. Three hundred a year and his keep, and that's twice what he ever made out of that pen of his."

There were steps and a sound like wheezing nearby, and we turned to see Harris at hand.

"Sorry to trouble you, sir," he said, and wheezed for breath again, "but you're wanted on the telephone."

"Damn the telephone!" Chaice told him exasperatedly. "Who is it now?"

"Miss Kitty, sir."

"What's she want?" The tone had definitely softened.

"She wouldn't leave a message, sir. She said she must speak to you."

Chaice clicked his tongue, but not too annoyedly.

"You carry on," he told me with a wave of the hand. "I'll probably catch you up."

I moved aimlessly on, and then the thatched roof of what looked like a summerhouse caught my eye and I strolled across the lawn towards it. It was an oblong building, built of red cedar, and large enough to contain two fair-sized rooms. There was also a veranda.

Quite a pleasant place to spend an hour in the heat of the day, I was telling myself, for it was embowered in the flowering shrubs that rose to their full height behind it like the plants of a herbaceous border, and behind that long, dense shrubbery was a double line of poplars for a shield and windbreak. Curiosity got the better of me and I decided to have a look inside, but when I turned the handle of the door I found the door was locked. Then I noticed that a Yale lock had been quite recently fitted, and I could see the filling where the original lock had been.

Don't misunderstand me when I say that I noticed these things. They remained in my mind as things of no importance whatever; things, in fact, that I had noticed only sufficiently to be able to recall them later, and that's all. As I moved off I thought no more about them, for I was wondering what way to take. Then a gravelled path caught my eye, leading through a new shrubbery that curved back to the house. In a few moments I was nearing the smaller barn which was partly converted to a garage. Through an open door I could see Chaice's Rolls, jacked up against the end of the war. At the farther end another door was open, and as I came by, a man looked out. He had the look of a superior kind of carpenter.

"Mr. Travers?" he said, and was holding out his hand. Then he took the hand back and rubbed it on his trousers. "Sorry, but I've been handling some rather dirty wood. I'm Austin's brother, by the way."

His manner had been so shy, and yet so friendly, that I smiled as I reached out for his hand. He was much older than his brother and more stoutly built, and he had an untidy straggly moustache and such gentle eyes that he had a look of forlornness.

"Doing some carpentering?" I asked, and the question was unnecessary, what with the carpenter's apron he was wearing and the sawdust and tiny shavings on his ragged working coat. "Making some seed boxes," he told me, interested at once.

I followed him inside, and under the far window he had a fine carpenter's bench, with a couple of vices, a hand-lathe and a fine array of tools. He waved a shy hand at the fixed template that held the thin boards of a box he had been nailing together.

"A lot of boxes needed here," he said. "Nothing much doing elsewhere, so I thought I'd get ahead."

He gave himself a little abstracted sort of smile and we stood for a few seconds in what seemed to him a happy vacuum. Then he gave a little start and the gentlest reprimanding smile. "You've seen Austin?"

"Oh yes," I said.

"Of course," he said, and was shaking his head. "I'm afraid my wits were wool-gathering again."

"Not at all," I told him awkwardly, and picked up a completed box. "Very well made, if I may say so."

He smiled deprecatingly and then looked like relapsing into another vacuum. I said I was on my way to see Daine, and then he came to himself again and saw me to the door. A delightful old chap, I thought him, and the same moment wondered why I should think of him as old, for he couldn't have been much over sixty.

Across the gravelled sweep before the garage a side drive led to the old barn. There was a rustic porch with steps, and on the door a brass professional plate, doubtless salvaged from Daine's headquarters in town. I gave a tap and entered. I was in the main room that had once been a lounge. The walls were lined with shelves and heaped with trays and stacks of papers. Two rather elderly women and a younger one were having tea, and from a wireless set came the whine of a wench—a croonerette sobbing out her larynx for the benefit of the troops. A door across the room opened, and Daine came in, some papers and his glasses in his hand.

"My dear fellow," he said, and stared at the sight of me. Then he grinned. "How long have you been here?"

"Only just walked in," I told him.

He handed the papers to a nonchalant typist and we went through to his room.

"A damnable noise, that," he said, nodding back at the wireless. "Can't do anything about it, though. Staffs nowadays have to be humoured."

He hadn't changed a lot, I thought, and I told him so. A bit thinner perhaps, like all of us, but very fit. I liked him, too, without his glasses, for that was when you saw the unexpected and really likeable of the two men that went to make Cuthbert Daine. In his glasses he was the shortish, sparely built intellectual; quiet, shrewd and eminently business-like. Without them you saw the rather faun-like individual of his own cocktail parties, taking a terrific zest in company, flitting drolly from this group to that, steering an impish way among the trays, and all the time his face puckered with the most surprising grins.

"A comfortable office this makes," I said, and waved a hand to include dictaphone and handsome flat-topped desk. "Didn't it use to function as a bedroom once?"

He said it had been a small games room. There were three bedrooms, and now occupied by the women of his staff. There was a little kitchen where they scratched meals, but most of their food came from the house.

The buzzer went, and, with a nod to me, he picked up the receiver. There was a five-minute conversation, with him trying most of the time to get off the line. When he hooked up, with a sigh of relief, the buzzer went again. At the same time I heard the frantic ringing of a bell.

"That'll be for you, and tea," he told me. "A terrible day for me—Friday."

"You're coming across?"

He shrugged his shoulders in humorous despair and waved at the heaped tray on the desk.

"Not a hope, my dear fellow. Lucky if I leave here much before seven."

As I made my way back to the house I was thinking that the next day was Saturday, and a holiday, and we'd have plenty of time to talk in peace. That brought a curious thought. What on earth did Daine find to do with himself in his hours of leisure? Daine, a Londoner to the very marrow of him, a sure figure at every literary gathering of the Bohemian sort, and himself the host *par excellence.* A bachelor, but very much of a ladies' man, seen at his best with that impish grin on his face as he threaded his way through the chattering groups of dilettanti and philanderers. And always, as I somehow suspected, with a shrewd eye to business. And from all that to Beechingford!

The sight of Chaice interrupted my thoughts. I told him I had had a word with Daine and I'd also seen his brother. I thought I'd dropped a brick at that last, but perhaps there wasn't a quick annoyance on his face after all. But he took my arm, which looked like confidences about to be imparted.

"Dick's quite a good chap," he said. "One of those people who can never settle down. Been all sorts of things in his time. Makes a hobby of doing odd jobs about the place, and damned useful he is, too."

"I'm sure he is," I said, and he seemed quite content to leave it at that. And one thing I did know—that whatever faults Chaice had, snobbery was not one of them. At that moment, in any case, I had never felt less like making conversation. I was anticipating tea and I was realising that not only had the weekend opened well but that it promised even better. Perhaps the weather, as I said, had something to do with that now total absence of disquiet, and the fact that the two people most concerned had been on their best behaviour—Constance and Chaice, I mean. And it had been nice to see Daine again, and I had liked Lang, and Richard Chaice, and even old Harris.

What I now know is that that afternoon had been the overture and an ironically cheerful one, for the drama that was to follow. When I entered the drawing-room the curtain rose on that drama, though no one could have been less aware of the fact than myself.

CHAPTER III
ACT I, SCENE I

THE FIRST SCENE of most plays might well be called 'Meet the Folks'. You know the sort of thing you see: a drawing-room or lounge and people discussing someone who is absent. You learn to prick your ears, and, sure enough, that someone comes in, and then, likely as not, another absent person is discussed, and there may be a foreshadowing of some dramatic situation, and so on and so on till something really happens. By that time you have met all the folks and know them, and after that it is up to the dramatist to keep things going.

What was to happen with me was much the same thing. There was this and that which made me prick my ears, and other things, far more important in the long run, which came back afterwards to bewilder and surprise me. So if I seem to you to mention trivialities, don't be too sure that they are. There was, for instance, the matter of Chaice's hat. I told you he had frequent changes of style in his dress, and I thought he'd given up that broad-brimmed Bohemian hat business and the velvet jacket get-up. But as I went through the hall again, on the way to the drawing-room, I saw on a peg outside the cloakroom door, amid an array of various garments, a hat of that same kind, and with it one of those flowing black capes.

Constance was in the drawing-room, and you can picture the scene: the low table with china and silver ware, and another low table with sandwiches and cakes. An elderly parlourmaid was just leaving, and Harris took a look in to see that everything was as it should be.

"Ready for tea?" Constance smiled at me.

"Dying for a cup," I said.

"It's perfectly unpardonable of me," she went on, as she began pouring the tea, "but I forgot to ask you about Bernice. How is she?"

I said my wife was very well indeed. She was still nursing in a hospital up north, but had had a short period of leave with me in town about three weeks before. Since association with Wharton and the law has made me a deft and shameless liar, I said we often thought about her—about Constance, that is.

"I know," she said, with an equally deft and embracing sympathy. "It'd be lovely to see her again. Sugar?"

I said I didn't take it. Chaice, who had been restlessly crossing one knee over the other and then the other over that, suddenly asked where Dickie was.

"But, darling, you know when he's working he always prefers something outside," Constance told him.

"I don't know anything of the sort," he snapped at her. I passed him a cup of tea and he was so agitated he spilt a lot of it in the saucer.

"But you do know," she told him. Her eyes had narrowed and the words came through tight lips.

"I don't like this business of Dickie being like a—well, a cheap handyman."

"But, darling, be reasonable. He couldn't very well come in here with those clothes of his. He wouldn't like it himself."

"I don't see why not." His little eyes looked very angry and he was spilling more of his tea. I passed him the sandwiches and he took one with a grunt. Then he asked where Martin was.

"But, darling, how should I know?" she told him sweetly.

"If you don't know, who does? You make an absolute fool of him." He gave an exasperated snort and began to wave a hand about. "What this generation is coming to, beats me."

"Must we have this all over in front of Ludo?" she asked him with the same exasperating sweetness. "Let's leave it like this, darling. You spoil Dickie and I spoil Martin. Now we're quits."

I plunged gallantly in. If one wanted to go to the town, how did one get there? Chaice, evidently only too glad to change the conversational trend, said there was quite a good bus service about a quarter of a mile along the road. He himself generally walked for exercise sake on the rare occasions when he went there, but if he was going to town he sometimes took a taxi. Lang had a bicycle which I might use if I felt that way inclined.

"That reminds me, darling," he told his wife. "Kitty rang up to say she was getting a lift with a friend. She won't be in till about ten."

"You've ordered a taxi?"

"No need," he said. "This friend's bringing her right here. Going on leave herself, so I gathered."

"Such a charming girl," Constance told me gushingly. "We all simply adore her."

Chaice beamed approval. Restless as ever, he had now got to his feet and was leaning against the mantelpiece, on which he had put his cup. I was wondering where Lang had his tea, and I afterwards learned that he always had it taken to the workshop, as they called that room where he worked with Chaice. Then somehow we got to talking about that small residential estate that lay to the south of the house. Chaice said it was so small and select as to have no effect on the value of his own property. Even in winter one could barely see the roofs of the few villas.

Chaice had now finished his tea. He was a gross and untidy eater, gulping his food carelessly down, and far more intent on monopolising the conversation and waving a hand around as he talked. I felt quite uncomfortable to be still eating, and then at last he could stand it no longer. When I'd finished he'd be in his room, he said, and then, with a grunt or two and a wave of he hand, he went out.

"Well?" smiled Constance enigmatically, as soon as the door had closed.

"Well what?" I countered, and blatantly passed my cup again.

"Well, what must you be thinking of us?"

"Why should I think?" I said.

She gave an elaborate shrug of the shoulders.

"Sometimes Austin is the most infuriating man in the world."

"Don't all wives say that about all husbands?"

"I wish you'd be serious," she told me impatiently. "Take Richard. Would you have him wandering about all over the house when people are here? He looks just like a tramp."

"I don't know," I said mildly, but she was cutting in again. "Then there's Martin. I know he's all nerves, but that's not his fault. That was why they turned him down for the Services. And he still has the most dreadful headaches.”

“Must be pretty rotten for him,” I said.

“It is,” she told me emphatically. “And that’s what Austin just won’t understand.”

“What’s Martin doing with himself?” I asked.

“He really wants to be an author,” she said. “Well, not an author exactly. He writes verse.”

“Does he indeed!” I said, and my eyebrows lifted.

“The trouble is he can’t get it published,” she said. “We thought perhaps you could give him some advice about that.” And there, I thought, was the devil of it. That perhaps was why Constance had been so keen on my coming to Lovelands.

“But surely Daine could give him the best advice,” I pointed out.

“You don’t understand,” she said. “Austin’s furious about it. He’s set Cuthbert against it too, we’re sure of that.” She let out a sigh. “I’m so sorry for poor Martin. I do wish you’d have a look at his work and see if anything can be done.”

“Well,” I said, “I’ll certainly do that much. I can’t promise anything farther, mind you.”

“Sometimes you’re an absolute darling,” she told me, and added would I push the bell. I’d toyed with the idea of yet another cup of tea, but I duly rang the bell and then said perhaps I’d better see Austin.

“What about a swim later?” she asked me. “We always take a dip at about six.”

“When in Rome . . .” I said, and left it at that.

I joined Austin in that sanctum of his. He had evidently been waiting impatiently, for he was prowling restlessly about the room when I entered.

“Sorry about all that backchat at tea-time,” he began, “but Constance can be very exasperating at times.”

He didn’t give me a chance to sympathise.

“Take Richard. He’s a good fellow, and, like me, he hasn’t a bit of damned snobbery in him. I admit he’s been a rolling stone in his time, and a pretty expensive one to me." He shrugged his shoulders at that. "Not that I ever worried. Richard's a good scout. And he's had some tough luck. Came over here with his wife just after the war and I found him a little place just north of town. A damn bomb dropped clean on it. Killed his wife and shook him pretty badly too. That's why he's a bit absent-minded sometimes, as he calls it. And that's the very thing that Constance keeps harping about. He's no more weak in his wits than you and I are. If anything, he's a damn sight saner than the rest of us. Come to think of it, he had to be after what he went through in the blitz."

"I must say I—" I was going to say that I'd thought him a real good sort, but Chaice only waved an impatient hand and surged straight on.

"Then there's Martin. It's hard for a parent to talk like this of his only son, but that boy's been ruined from the start. We didn't have what they call nerves in our day, did we? All damn pose and poppycock. And what do you think he wants to be? One of those snivelling damn poets that write that blasted twaddle you see in the highbrow magazines. And wanted me to influence Cuthbert to find a publisher for it." He waved his hands as if words were inadequate. "If you get a chance, have a look at it. If it doesn't make you puke, then my name's not what it is. Only one place for that sort of bilge, as I told him, and that's cut in neat little squares and hung on a hook to help out with the paper shortage."

I opened my mouth to say something, though lord knows what, and then he gave an impatient grunt.

"Let's get through to the workshop and make a start on that job of ours. Can't keep Lang with nothing to do."

He was already holding the door open, so through we went. And there we stayed till about six o'clock, with Lang editing *Kensington Gore* and making a list of quotes to submit to us later, and Chaice and I going through a host of questions that had been compiled against my visit. When we all three came to a kind of spontaneous halt, Lang asked if there was anything else and Chaice merely waved him away.

"You and I have got to settle about terms," Chaice said as soon as he'd gone. "Whatever you suggest will suit me."

I said I'd rather leave things. A token payment perhaps for the use of *Kensington Gore* and the rest would be a pleasure. He wouldn't have it, but I insisted too, and with that impasse we got to our feet.

"Always have a swim about this time," he told me apologetically. "Constance likes it. And what about you? Harris can find you a costume."

I said I'd look on. I was the world's worst swimmer and I'd rather watch the experts. So he went upstairs and I wandered round to the pool, and I was wondering just what he had meant by the phrase 'Constance likes it'. Did Constance like the swimming or for him to take a regular part in it? The latter I decided. In spite of his little rebellions, she had him well under her thumb. That was why he had tackled the question of his brother and son behind her back, so to speak, and had eased his mind on me.

A chair or two was on the concrete surround of the pool, so I took one and had a look at Constance. She hadn't seen me approach, for she was doing one of those crawl things that need a head beneath the water. When she did see me she was all heartiness. I was lazy and frowsty and heaven knows what, and why didn't I come in. But Lang appeared then and she turned her attention to him, daring him to dive in from the top of the platform. He was sheepishly protesting, and then Chaice appeared. He was a man after my own heart: stepping gingerly in the shallow end, summoning a slow courage and then dipping below for quick dampener, and then shivering again, after which he did a breast stroke monotonously and resisted all Constance's efforts to get him on the diving-board. Then I noticed someone standing by my chair.

"Martin, isn't it?" I said as I got to my feet.

"How d'you do, sir," he said, and held out his hand. It was a flabby hand, and but for the fact that its owner, standing there in a bathing costume, couldn't have been any other than Martin Chaice, I should certainly never have recognised him. He had shot up since I last saw him to five foot ten, and he was pretty heavy too, and altogether about as little like Austin Chaice's son as I could have imagined. His face looked none too healthy.

"A long while since we've met," I said amiably, and, as he was evidently hunting for words, "Let me see. How old are you now?"

"Twenty-four," he said.

"You've been down some time?" From Oxford, I meant.

"About a year, sir."

"Good," I said, for want of something better. I thought he was cold, for every now and again he gave a little shiver, and then I saw it was some kind of nervous twitching.

"You and I will have to have a yarn some time," I said.

"I'd love to," he told me.

There was an awkward silence, and then I said he'd better go in. There wouldn't be much more sun.

"I think I will," he said. He hesitated a moment as if there was something else he wanted to say, then he gave a little nod and made for the far, deep end of the pool. I noticed that he didn't look at his father. Still a bit self-centred, I told myself. He hadn't even troubled to ask me about Jack—the young nephew whom he used to accompany to town.

The pond was now divided into three distinct parts. Near me was Chaice splashing about, full of sound and fury that signified nothing, for he was never in water more than four feet deep. In the middle of the pool Orford Lang was cruising about gracefully and aimlessly, varying a breast with a side stroke. At the deep end were Martin and Constance, and I had heard her "Why, hal-*lo*, darling!" when he swam towards her.

Chaice had had enough and came shivering out. He gave me a grin that might have meant anything, stuck his feet in the plimsolls, grabbed a bathrobe and shuffled off. Two minutes later Lang came out and the process was repeated.

"You ought to have come in, sir," he told me. "The water's perfect."

"Maybe next time," I told him, and continued watching the two at the far end. Constance was sticking it out as most women can in water, and Martin was keeping near her. All the time they seemed to be talking, and so quietly that no word reached me; it was, in fact, as if they spoke out of the corners of their mouths. Somehow I knew they were talking about me.

Dinner, usually at seven, was a quarter of an hour later on Fridays on account of Daine's late working. Even then he only just made it in time. Our bedrooms, as I said, were in that comparatively stumpy left wing, and by a curious arrangement of adaptation faced each other, though not opposite. On my left was the bathroom and on his left the lavatory. I preferred my room because it looked out over the gardens, whereas his had as its principal view the back quarters of the house and that kind of no-man's-land that lay between those back quarters and the kitchen gardens. I chatted with him that evening while he finished his dressing, which was merely a changing into a darker suit.

In the dining-room I was on Constance's right, with Martin facing me. At the other end, Austin Chaice had Daine on his right, with Richard facing him, and Lang sat between Daine and Martin. I mention all that because when a certain argument started I was in a position to see the faces of both Daine and Lang. I admit that our various positions were proper and apt, and yet I couldn't help thinking, as I took my seat, that I was to be the victim of some plan of campaign hatched between Constance and Martin in the swimming-pool.

It was a good meal, but I am not going to trouble you with details. Other things are far more important. Richard Chaice, for instance. He, too, had changed into a dark suit, and with his badger hair neatly parted he had an air of distinction. Even in his working clothes he had had a natural dignity, and now the forlornness had given place to a quietness and yet an ease of manner. More than once I was to hear his voice at that end of the long table, and I couldn't help noticing that he was never interrupted, even by Austin. Perhaps that gentle voice of his had a kind of authority against Austin's rather strident cackle and Daine's frequent high-pitched laugh. As for Lang, he spoke rarely, though his attention seemed always to be on that talk at the far end.

I have said the table was a long one. It could have seated twelve in reasonable comfort, and yet when Martin came to the question of that manuscript of his, his voice lowered almost to inaudibility, and Constance's throaty drawl was lowered too. Martin was almost obsequious during the opening stages of that meal. He remembered to ask about Jack, and though Oxford himself, spoke well of Cambridge for my sake. Lang looked round and smiled appreciatively at that. He also had been at Cambridge, though he had had to come down before the end of his third year. The death of his father, Martin told me *sotto voce*, and the family affairs rather badly involved.

"Ludo wants to see your manuscript, darling," Constance said.

"That's awfully decent of you, sir," chipped in Martin. After that swim his eyes didn't look so puffy and his skin was a better colour.

"Not at all," I said, and, "Mind you, I'm no authority."

Then I tried an explanation—and hoped to God it was being as humorous as I intended—of how the position in which I found myself was a highly invidious one. I instanced a hoary old favourite of mine—Gil Bias—and what it had cost him when he had accepted the Archbishop of Salamanca's invitation to discuss certain sermons. That was when the noise at the other end of the table became only too noticeable.

"Oh, my God!" groaned Martin. "They're discussing the detective novel again."

"Sometimes it drives one frantic at meals," whispered Constance, and then the noise drowned her voice. Austin was fairly bellowing that he never made a statement of that kind—what kind I had no idea—without being able to prove it. I saw a way of escape.

"This sounds too good to miss," I imparted to my end of the table, and then, to Austin, "What's your proposition?"

"Only an old one cropped up again," Daine said. "Austin's claiming that he could write a detective novel round any single person with whom he comes into contact."

Lang was leaning sideways to listen. Richard was smiling to himself and shaking his head, as if he had been in opposition to the motion.

"Well, let's hear the proof," I suggested.

"Dammit, how can there be proof?" Austin asked exasperatedly. "Quote me persons and I'll try to give instances." He mumbled something annoyedly to himself and added that that was fair enough.

"What about those of us round this table?" I put in fatuously. It was amazing how quickly he took me up.

"Good," he told me, and spread his palms and then rubbed his hands together. "Since Cuthbert is the principal objector, I'll start with him."

He smiled ironically. "Rather like robbing a blind man of a penny. It's so obvious. All we have is the swindling agent who has to kill a client who's got wise to him."

"Damnation, Austin!" exploded Daine, and I thought for a moment he was going to push his chair back and get to his feet. His face was flushed and then as quickly he was smiling sheepishly. "What I mean is . . . Well, dammit, isn't anything sacred to you detective authors?"

"You should know," Austin told him blandly. "You yourself read personally all my stuff, and heaven knows how many others."

"But surely!" put in Lang. "Surely there couldn't be any such thing as a swindling agent. I mean, a client can check up on sales with his publisher."

"But wasn't there a recent case of an agent swindling his clients?" put in Richard mildly. "I seem to remember reading something about it."

"I'm sorry—yes," admitted Lang, and on Austin's face the irony became gloating. "All the same, the clients must have been the most utter fools, and incredibly careless. As I said, they'd only to check up with their publishers."

"Well, there we are," Austin told everybody blandly. "It seems there are swindling agents and there are fools. If that doesn't prove my proposition, what does?"

"There is still one thing you've omitted," Richard said in the same gentle voice.

"And what's that?" snapped his brother.

"Your ability to write the story," Richard told him, and we all had to laugh.

I was recognising that the meal was near its end, but I wanted to spin things out for a minute or two longer.

"And, of course," I said, "one swallow doesn't make a summer."

"You mean, another instance?" Austin said. "Well, I was coming to that. We'll take Orford here. Again a very simple instance, provided, of course"—he smiled graciously there at Richard—"that I could write the story when I'd found the plot. But about Orford. He's under contract to me for his whole time. But he thinks he'll double-cross me and make a little on the sly, so he writes a book under another name. I find out and . . ." A spreading of his palms and a shrug of the shoulders added the rest.

"But, I say, sir," Lang protested, his face a violent red.

"You must learn to take your medicine, my boy," Austin told him with a sneering tone and a patronising gesture. "Anybody else open for comment?"

But Constance was getting to her feet and we all rose. She was mentioning Kitty and how there ought to be a hot meal ready by half-past nine. Harris came in and Austin mentioned the same thing. Daine was taking my arm and whispering that coffee was always in the drawing-room.

It was cosy there with the black-out curtains drawn. Richard seemed to have a favourite remote corner, and settled at once to a book. When I blatantly went over to him he showed me the title—*The Greenhouse*. It seemed to be partly a manual on how to build greenhouses of various kinds, and he told me that he was planning an overhaul of the Lovelands houses.

Austin gulped down his coffee, refused a second cup and told me, for all to hear, that he would look through the notes Lang had made on *Kensington Gore*, and so save my time in the morning. The coffee tray was taken away and Constance said she would have to see about Trixie. When she had gone and only we five men were there, Lang cleared his throat.

"I think we missed a great chance of getting one back on Mr. Chaice."

"How was that?" asked Daine rather sharply.

"Well, we—I mean I, could have challenged him about himself." He was getting a bit flustered and involved. "I mean, we could have told him that we could have written a detective story about him."

"Oh, for God's sake!" groaned Martin.

"And how?" asked Daine.

"Well, take that summerhouse which we used to use and which he put out of bounds about a month ago. Couldn't an author make that seem rather fishy?"

"Yes, but how?" persisted Daine.

"Well, nobody is allowed to go there but Mr. Chaice, and he keeps the key. And he does go there. He says he gets a special kind of inspiration there. It sort of clarifies his ideas. I mean, couldn't an author make something fishy out of that? After all, ideas aren't the slave of locality."

He evidently thought that quite a good phrase. Daine promptly pricked the bubble.

"Footling, my dear fellow. Footling!" he told Lang bluntly. "Ideas are always the slave of locality, whatever that may mean."

Then, rather rudely, I thought, he was asking me if we might have a preliminary chat about our own affairs, and we moved to a settee beneath the large window. Lang, looking mightily self-conscious, sidled from the room. Martin lingered only a minute or two and then followed him.

Daine and I began our chat and then I had to go out to the cloakroom lavatory. When I was coming out and had switched off the light I seemed to hear whisperings in the darkness of the corridor beyond. For some reason or other I stood stock still. Constance's voice just reached me.

"I think at least you ought to watch him, darling. It may be only an excuse."

"But I can't watch him every night," came Martin's annoyed protest.

"But it isn't every night, darling." The voice was a coaxing one. "It will only be tonight and tomorrow. After that we'll arrange."

"Very well then," Martin told her ungraciously. "But it's frightfully boring for me."

"But not if anything happens. . . ."

That had been louder and I realised that Martin was coming my way. In a flash I was back in the cloakroom, but he went straight by. Of Constance there was no sound, but I waited for a couple of minutes and then made a furtive way out.

Three other things happened that night, and they won't take long in the telling. The first was after I'd finished my talk with Daine, which was just before nine o'clock. Then he said he had to look in at his office and I said I'd like to stroll outside and clear my lungs.

It was a warm fine night, but very dark. I stepped on to the lawn and breathed deeply for a bit, and then—probably with what Lang had been saying in my mind—I began dodging the elms and strolling towards where I judged that summerhouse would be. On the grass my feet made never a sound, and it was rather eerie walking. Naturally I didn't strike the summerhouse at first shot. I went far too much to the left, and so I began working back. Whether or not I actually got to the summerhouse I cannot say, but I guessed afterwards that it was from the veranda that the voices came.

"But he knows! I'm sure he knows." That was Lang's voice.

Another voice gave a "Sh!" That voice itself was no more than a dawdling murmur, but it was easy to recognise it as Constance's. It went on for a good half-minute, and then at last there were barely recognisable words.

"But, darling, there's nobody but you, and never will be."

There was a sound as of an embrace. I didn't stand on the order of my going, but took a few backward steps and then risked life and limb among the elms till I was back at the house. There was a light from beneath Chaice's door when I entered the hall. As I set foot on the stairs Martin came forward out of the darkness.

"Pardon me, sir, but the manuscript you said you'd be good enough to look at." His voice was hardly more than a whisper.

"Good," I said, and never meant anything less. A nod and a smile and I went on upstairs. In my room I had a cold splash and then I did a bit of thinking. But there wasn't much needed. Everything was far too plain. A horrible situation, one might grant, and yet, as I said, only too plain. Martin, in fact, was watching the light beneath his father's door. Keeping tag on Austin Chaice, in so many words, while Lang and Constance had their *tête-à-tête* in the darkness of the summerhouse veranda.

I chewed upon that for a bit and tried to fit it in with that telephone conversation I'd had with Constance, and her mention of fright, and finally I decided to wait for events.

It was then twenty minutes to ten, so I thought I had better put in an appearance in the drawing-room again. As I came to the head of the stairs the front door burst open, and a voice was calling "Hallo! Where's everybody?"

It was Kitty Chaice, and I'd forgotten all about her. But in a minute the hall was full of people. I heard Constance's "Darling!" Chaice's door opened and he came beaming out. I heard an "Uncle Richard!" as Dickie appeared, and then Martin trailed in from somewhere. There were embraces and chattering and laughing, and I kept well back on the landing.

"You must be simply starved, darling," Constance was saying.

"What about your friend?" Chaice was asking. "Won't she come in too?"

"Far too anxious to get home, Daddy," Kitty told him. "She just set me down and then shot off."

She picked up her bag, but Harris pounced on it. I went back to my room and waited for five minutes before coming down. The party was now assembled in the drawing-room, and I was at once introduced.

I don't think I've ever been so immediately taken by a girl as I was by Kitty Chaice. She was charming, every inch of her. And about as unlike her brother as could be. Doubtless she took after her mother, for she had fair hair, and she had a young, abounding vitality. You couldn't call her beautiful, but she had an attractive personality and a freshness and a love of life that were both enchanting.

"Didn't you use to take Martin out?" she asked me.

I admitted it.

"I used to be frightfully jealous," she told me.

"But now you've changed your mind."

She gave me a smile and a quick humorous appraisal.

"Perhaps I haven't," she said. "Do you like the pictures?"

"If that's an invitation to take you some time, then I do," I told her, and then Constance had to come fussing in and saying dinner was waiting for her, and getting cold.

I stayed on for a few minutes and then began saying good-nights and leaving apologies, for I was suddenly feeling dog-tired. But as I got into bed I made up my mind to do a little more hard thinking about the events of that night, and yet before my head had hardly nestled into the pillow I was sound asleep. It was not till I woke towards dawn that I remembered I hadn't even looked at Martin Chaice's manuscript.

CHAPTER IV
CLIMAX

IT WAS SEVEN O'CLOCK and I was wide awake, so I switched on the bedside lamp and reached for that manuscript. But I didn't open it, for suddenly I remembered something which seemed far more important—the question of whether Constance was intending to involve me in that triangle of herself, her husband and Orford Lang. I tried to recall the exact words I had heard from the darkness of the summerhouse veranda.

"But he knows. I'm sure he knows."

Those had been the words, and therefore Chaice was wise to what was going on. That was why Constance had told me over the telephone that she was badly frightened. But was it? Wasn't there something wrong with that argument? The words that

Lang had used and the tone in which they were uttered seemed to prove beyond doubt that he had only just made the discovery that Chaice knew of the intrigue! It was true that I had not heard Constance's reply. All that I had heard, except the final assertion that it was with Lang alone that she was in love, were whispers and murmurings, whereas if the news was really new to her it should have come as a terrific shock. Maybe, then, I told myself, it had been news to Lang but not to herself, and that brought me back to where I started—that Constance was frightened because her husband knew, and I had been intended somehow to become involved. And then I told myself that I was damned if I'd become involved. Constance might be cunning in her own tortuous ways, but if she involved me in any domestic mess, then the fault would be my own.

Then I thought of something else. If Chaice knew what was going on, then either he was a magnificent actor or else his conduct had been the very opposite of what ought to have been the reactions of any husband. Little things had shown me that Constance was getting very tired of Chaice and she was in the mood to snatch at any prospect of change. But Chaice hadn't shown that he was tired of her. Far from it. He couldn't change his make-up, of course. He was an egoist and splenetic and devilish hard to live with, and yet behind the little snaps of temper and the unavoidable tiffs there was on his part an uxoriousness and a fatuousness that could make one wince.

In other words, Chaice, by every sign that I had observed, was very much in love with his wife, and so much so that he had been blind to her own dislike of himself. And yet that was the man who, according to Lang, was aware of his wife's intrigue! It just didn't hold water. However good an actor Chaice might be— and I admitted that for a few years he had been on the stage—he could never have repressed his feelings sufficiently to have condoned his wife's duplicity, even for the sake of some elaborate counter-scheme of his own.

The very word *scheme* brought something else to my mind. At dinner the previous night Chaice had taken Lang as a hypothetical case to prove a theory, the hypothesis being that Lang had broken a contract and would therefore have a motive to kill the man who'd found out. But why shouldn't Chaice—if aware of the intrigue between Lang and his wife—have made the hypothesis a love affair between the pair? Wouldn't that have been the very kind of delicious irony that would have appealed to one like Austin Chaice?

I gave my glasses a polish, shrugged my shoulders and then consigned the whole business to blazes. Why should I worry my wits over a situation that was definitely not going to involve myself personally, and as a sign of that Pilate-like washing of the hands I opened the manuscript.

CONSUMMATION

POEMS

by

MARTIN FERRABY CHAICE

Not an unattractive title, I thought, though I had still to learn that the poems were a consummation of what. Then I turned a leaf and began the first poem. To my slight annoyance it was *vers libre,* so I read the one opposite, or rather began it, for it was extraordinarily obscure. I left that one and tried the next—a longer effort that occupied two pages of the manuscript.

A quarter of an hour later I was closing that manuscript with a curious kind of furtiveness which had nevertheless two recognisable origins. One was a distaste of its contents and the other, closely allied, an awareness of the embarrassing position I was about to be in when Martin Chaice asked me, and probably all dewy-eyed, what I thought of it.

Mind you, I'm not bigoted about modern painting, music or verse. Critics, especially the only partly informed like myself, have made such fools of themselves in the past that it behoves us to choose our words. When I'm asked what I think of this and that, and it's something utterly incomprehensible to me or even loathsome, I merely admit that it's a bit beyond me and perhaps I'm too old-fashioned. If pestered further I may instance what the critics thought of Galileo and Wagner and Keats and Whistler. But when Martin Chaice asked for my views on that manuscript I could hardly take that line. What I had read was the most extraordinary collection of bilge that had ever spoilt paper. Not as incomprehensible as Joyce or Gertrude Stein perhaps, but even more infuriating, because it had lines and even stanzas that seemed to have some sense in them if only one had a few months' leisure to ferret it out.

Just then I thought I heard a noise in the corridor outside. But it was not coming from the bathroom, so I hastily got into a dressing-gown and tried the bathroom door. Half an hour later I was ready to go downstairs, and I could hear Daine stirring in his room. It was still short of nine o'clock, but the front door was open, and when I took a look out the air was fine and it looked like being a marvellous day.

Chaice and Kitty were at breakfast in the dining-room. "Hallo, young lady," I said. "Why aren't you celebrating leave by having breakfast in bed?"

"Leave's far too precious to waste in bed," she told me. "And I'm like daddy. He simply has to get up early."

Chaice wanted to know how I had slept, and I told him.

"The air here's wonderful," he said, and as if he generated it personally. "London's all very well for people like Constance. Give me a place like this."

I agreed politely, and then asked what had happened to everybody.

"Constance always has breakfast in bed," Kitty told me. "So does Martin, sometimes."

"And your Uncle Richard?"

She smiled. "He's up at dawn. Probably built half a greenhouse by now. Don't you think he's a darling?"

I said I did, and then Martin came in. At least he just looked in and as quickly disappeared. He was obviously avoiding a meal with his father, for Kitty flushed slightly and Chaice scowled.

"And what's your work in the A.T.S.?" I asked Kitty. I liked her even better in the jumper and skirt than I had in the uniform.

We were talking about General Duties, which seemed to be her line, and how she was hoping for a job as technical officer, when Daine came in. Then we talked about the capture of the Flying Bomb sites and wondered if we'd get any more missiles. Then Chaice left with the reminder to me that we were to get down to business when I was ready. No hurry, though. There'd be any correspondence to go through first.

"What about Lang?" I asked Kitty.

"He'd finished just before you came in," she told me, and at that moment in came Martin. At least he sidled in, giving me and Daine a subdued good morning as he made for the sideboard. But nothing there seemed to have suited his appetite, for he came back empty-handed and toyed with toast and marmalade. Kitty was eating a terrific breakfast, and I didn't feel like being left ultimately alone with Daine and the owner of that manuscript, so I brought my own meal to a quick conclusion, said I'd be seeing everybody later, and then made my way upstairs. Ten minutes later, when I was just going downstairs, Martin came up and we met on the landing.

"Did you sleep well, sir?" he enquired politely.

"Superbly, thanks," I said. "Just had time for a dip into your manuscript and no more."

"You . . . er . . .?"

"Exactly," I said. "That sort of stuff wants really serious consideration. Nothing worse than snap judgments."

I gave him a smile and a pat on the shoulder. As I went on my way downstairs I thought my evasion had been masterly. Then, with far less elation, I realised that it was only a temporary one.

And there, at half-past nine in the morning, the whole of the Saturday can be virtually dismissed. I spent most of the morning with Chaice and Lang, and after lunch a brief talk with Daine settled the matter of my reprints. At about three o'clock we all—except Martin—went to the swimming-pool. There we had tea, and after that Constance and Kitty went in again while the men smoked and gossiped. By six o'clock a party of us—Constance, Kitty, Lang and myself—went by taxi to the cinema, where there was quite a good show. I noticed nothing untoward between Lang and Constance, though having no eyes in the dark. I had wished to take the party out to dinner but was told that Beechingford was impossible for a meal, so we took the bus as far as it went and finally got in well after nine o'clock. Daine and Richard were still at their cold supper. They said they had waited for us and then thought they had better begin.

"Where's Austin?" asked Constance.

Daine shrugged his shoulders. All he knew was that he had had supper and had gone out. And that was all for the day, except perhaps that since we'd been to the cinema there was a discussion on that liquid-squirting about which my driver had told me the previous day. Constance said it was a horrible thing to talk about, and when Daine persisted she reprimanded him, and unnecessarily sharply.

"Cuthbert, please! I'd rather you talked about something else."

"Not like you to be squeamish," he told her mildly, but the conversation was changed nevertheless, and Constance tried to be specially gracious. Then, just after ten o'clock, Chaice came in. He looked a bit tired and said he'd been taking a walk. Lastly Martin appeared. I was watching him closely. Constance caught his eye and he distinctly shook his head.

The Sunday was very much a day of rest. Breakfast was later and then everybody lounged about to read the Sunday papers till after midday, when some of us had a swim. I spent that hour with Richard in his workshop, and he was telling me some of his experiences in South America, the States and Canada. He was a first-class storyteller in his quiet way, and it was my fault that we were both late for lunch. Constance frowned at the sawdust on his trousers and I realised that there was some on mine.

After lunch Chaice disappeared, but I spent an hour with Lang, and we settled all our business. The rest of the day was spent round the pool. I'd expected another cold supper, but

there was a normal dinner. Chaice and Daine excused themselves after it, and when they'd left the drawing-room Constance
did an extraordinary thing.

"What are you doing, Martin?" she asked him.

"A spot of reading, perhaps," he told her.

"I think I'll read too," she said, and then, unmistakably di-
rectly to Kitty and Lang: "Why don't you two go out for some
fresh air? It's a lovely night."

Kitty blushed to the eyes.

"It might be a good idea," Lang said, and afterwards I knew
he was part of the plan. "I mean, if Kitty'd like to go."

"Do you both good," said Richard from his corner. We'd forgotten all about him, and for some queer reason his sudden in-
tervention made us laugh.

"Right-ho then," said Kitty, and, with a last expression of
freewill: "Only I do hate being ordered around."

Well, she and Lang went out and we heard them laughing in
the hall, and then the door closed on them. Martin began looking up from his book as if he were trying to mesmerise his uncle
into leaving the room. Richard must have sensed something, for
after a few minutes he said he was feeling a bit sleepy and with
our permission he'd be getting off to bed.

The door closed behind him. I felt at once a strange difference in the room. It was a kind of hostility, and then I knew that
that was absurd. What I didn't know was that the second act was
about to begin, and the second act, according to my vague ideas
of drama, was the one that brought the climax.

The two looked at each other as if asking which was to begin.
Constance moistened her lips and fidgeted with her fingers.

"You show the letters," she told Martin, and, to me: "We'd
like you to see them, Ludo."

I raised polite enquiring eyebrows.

"This is the first one, sir," Martin said, and produced it from
his pocket. It was in an envelope that bore the Beechingford
postmark, and the date, as a moment's reflection told me, was

the day before that evening when Constance had rung me in town. This was the letter:

Beechingford.

Dear Mrs. Chaice,

I write to you as a friend, to beg you most sincerely to watch your husband's movements. The activities he is engaged in will otherwise bring disgrace on yourself and every member of your family. As a test of my sincerity find out when he is absent from the house after dark and if that night there was a recurrence of the liquid-squirting, as it is called, that has been disgracing the name of the town.

P.

So flabbergasted was I that for a moment or two I lost all power of thought. Then I found myself polishing my glasses, and Martin retrieving the letter where it had slithered to the floor.

"Do you mind if I have another look?" I said.

I read the letter again and had another good look at it. The writing was extremely neat and upright. Every letter was so carefully shaped, with a hint of thick down strokes and thin upward ones, that I knew it for a perfect disguise, and far ahead of the hackneyed method of writing in crude block capitals. But it argued a person of some taste and culture.

"Did I gather there were more letters?" I said.

"Only one," Martin told me as he passed it.

It bore the same bare Beechingford heading, and again no date. The writing was the same meticulous kind.

Dear Mrs. Chaice,

I now have irrefutable proof that your husband is primarily if not wholly responsible for the outrages. Unless something can be done, and very quickly, I shall have to take action myself. Perhaps you had better burn this letter. If your husband knew of it, there might be danger to yourself.

P.

I gave a Whartonian grunt and handed the letter back. When I looked up it was to find the eyes of the two embarrassingly fixed on mine.

"Any idea who wrote the letters?" I asked.

"None whatever," Constance said, and gave a kind of shudder.

"You have plenty of friends in town?"

"Quite a lot. Not in the town perhaps, but near it."

"There *is* an idea, sir," Martin cut in. "Something that happened between the two letters. A man came to see father one morning when he was out. Lang saw him instead, and this fellow was most damnably angry about something. He said he insisted on seeing father, and if not it'd be the worse for him. Lang got rid of him."

"Did he give a name or address?"

"That's what I was coming to, sir. When Lang first saw him he gave the name of Preston. Naturally Lang didn't ask him for an address, and after that he got so angry and abusive that there wasn't a chance, as it were, to ask for his address."

"Preston," I said. "You think he was the P. of the letters?"

"Well, sir, it's an idea."

"You're right," I said, "And what was this man like?"

"Shortish and stout. He had what Lang called a choked sort of voice and a faint foreign accent."

"Anybody you've ever run across?" I asked Constance.

"Never," she told me emphatically. "I know nobody like that."

"Anything else about him?" I asked Martin.

"Well, he looked a bit of a crank. I know it was a wet day, but he had on a muffler and overcoat. He had weak eyes, because he screwed them up when he took off his glasses. Oh yes, and he had an untidy sort of black beard."

"Any suspicion of disguise?"

"Not the least, sir—I mean, according to Lang. And, by the way, this is highly confidential. Lang never should have mentioned it."

"Did Lang mention your father's reactions when he was told about this man Preston's call?"

"He said father laughed like blazes. All he said was, 'Oh, him!'—just like that."

"In other words, he knew this Preston."

"Well, sir, it certainly looks like it."

"I see," I said, and began giving my glasses another polish. A minute of that and I knew the line I would take.

"My own opinion is this," I said, "and I'm taking it that you want an opinion. I think this first letter should have been shown to your husband with no reservations. That would have been the honourable thing. Mind you," I added hurriedly, "I can see you were in a bit of a dilemma. I think P. knew you would be in that dilemma, and that's why the second letter distinctly warned you against it. That, by the way, is something that needs careful thought.

"But we'll leave that for a moment," I went on. "The really vital thing is this. You must—both of you—have believed the allegations in the letters. Do you mind telling me frankly why?" Constance took charge, leaning forward, and her husky voice even more husky with a passionate intensity.

"Because it's just the thing he would do. You've only seen him on a visit like this. You know nothing. I tell you there are times when he's positively mad. He's an egomaniac."

"Did you read about that typewriter business, sir?" cut in Martin. "That's the sort of thing he does." He shrugged his shoulders in a helpless sort of gesture and let his hands fall. "I know it sounds a rotten thing for a son to say about his father, but I do believe he's going mad. Let me tell you something," he went on hastily as I was about to speak. "He's been a kind of Jekyll and Hyde for years. That typewriter case was a mild example. He's got that mania for verisimilitude, and that encouraged the Hyde in him. Now it's got too much for him, and I believe he's mostly Hyde."

"You're suggesting that he *is* responsible for these outrages and that he's committing them for the purpose of using the atmosphere in a book?"

"I know it sounds far-fetched," he said, "but that's what I believe. We both believe it."

"That's that, then," I said, and shrugged my shoulders.

"You don't believe us?" asked Constance, and with a touch of temper.

"Oh yes," I said. "I believe you. What I don't trust is the evidence of these letters."

"But there *is* other evidence," cut in Martin. "He was out last night well before you got in. I rang the police this morning, and there *was* more liquid-squirting last night, and at about a quarter to nine."

"That may be a coincidence," I pointed out. "But how did you know your father was out?"

"Because I've been watching him," he said frankly. "I had to watch him."

"And were you able to follow him?"

"I wasn't. I'd see him come out of the house and then I'd lose him almost at once. And what's more, I believe he knew I was following him. I knew it from something he said yesterday afternoon, You know the way he sneers at you when he wants to say something meant to hurt. Well, this was something Lang said at the pool. Lang asked me if I was doing anything in the evening. What he wanted was for me to make one of the party for the cinema. I said I was. Father overheard, and what do you think he said? 'I understand Martin's got a job as a sleuth.' You ought to have seen Lang stare! I didn't want to talk, so I just swam away."

"I see," I said. "You've been trying to follow your father and he knew it."

"There's more than that," Constance said. "He's been queer during the last three weeks. He hardly ever left the house, as Martin knows. He'd read a book after dinner or do what he called research work with Orford, or he'd play chess with Cuthbert."

"Tell him about the chess," broke in Martin eagerly.

"Yes, the chess," she said. "Just about three weeks ago the chess-board and men disappeared. We couldn't find them anywhere in the house. Cuthbert hadn't seen them or touched them and Harris was nearly frantic. The whole house was searched and there wasn't a sign of them."

"Interesting but hardly relevant," I said. "But what you want in all this, I take it, is my advice."

"Yes, sir, we do. Something's got to be done. If it's true, then it's damn serious. If it isn't—well, we still ought to find out."

"My judgment is limited," I said. "I was tempted to say straight out that the whole thing is rather a nasty hoax and your father would never do anything of the kind. My advice is that you, Constance, show him the letters and pin him down before a witness. By the way, I should make it perfectly clear that I have no intention of being that witness."

Martin looked disappointed.

"We wouldn't dream of asking you," Constance said, and with no trace of malice. "We thought of the same thing, and we know what would happen. He'd simply deny the whole thing and make a terrific scene. And then suppose the—er—happenings went on? What then?"

"And suppose he was ultimately caught?" added Martin. "He'd be absolutely ruined, and so should we—socially, that is."

I nearly said, "Socially be damned!" I could see his point, and I began getting to my feet.

"Well, that's the best I can do. I repeat I'm still very sceptical about the whole thing, but I grant that you two know him and the circumstances better than I do."

Constance took my arm and made me sit down again.

"Ludo, will you do something for us?"

"Maybe."

"Just this," she said. "Martin's trouble is that he can't follow his father alone. If there were two of you, you'd stand a better chance."

"You mean?"

"Constance means, will you watch him with me tomorrow night, sir. Just the one night."

I smiled.

"I see. I'm a guest in this house and you're asking me to spy on my host."

"But if it's for his own good?"

"You're not his guest, Ludo," Constance told me sharply. "You're my relation, in a way, and you're my guest."

It was a plausibility, and I hated the idea of it. Then I saw a way out.

"I'll consider it and let you know in the morning," I told them. "But I won't even do that unless you give me those two letters."

"You're not going to take things into your own hands?" Constance looked genuinely frightened.

"That was neither nice nor necessary," Martin told her sharply. "Mr. Travers wouldn't do a thing like that."

"All I want the letters for is to have a thorough examination of them," I said, and to my surprise Martin was handing them over.

"That's that, then," I said, and got to my feet. "First thing in the morning I'll give you my decision."

I was just in time. There were voices in the hall, and Kitty and Lang appeared.

"Why, you're wet!" Constance said.

"Only a heavy shower," Lang told her, and then cocked his ear. The voices of Chaice and Daine were heard, and a couple of minutes later they joined in.

"The weather's breaking again," Daine announced dismally.

"You're all wet, daddy," Kitty said. "Where've you been gallivanting off to?"

He grinned impishly and he flicked her cheek with a finger.

"Wouldn't you like to know!" Then he looked owlishly round. "Quite a lot of people would like to know. But all in good time, my dear. All in good time."

"Keep that for your mystery stories," she told him, and he frowned.

"Not at all, my dear. I'm a mystery story, as you call it. You're a mystery story. We're all mystery stories."

"Oh, my God!" muttered Martin audibly, and moved towards the door. I followed him out.

"About tomorrow," I said. "I think you can count on me after all."

CHAPTER V
CATASTROPHE

I'M NOT GOING to bore you with a long account of why I made that sudden decision to watch for one night the movements of Austin Chaice, though in fairness to myself I would say just this: that when Chaice struck an attitude and made that high-falutin statement about all of us being mystery stories, he happened to direct the remark full at me, as if it were some sort of challenge. Pose and poppycock can rile me at any time, and if Chaice had been aiming at getting my goat, then he certainly succeeded.

Also I hate an unsolved problem of any kind. It gives me no rest and gnaws at me like an aching tooth, and in that house was more than one thing of which I needed an explanation. The fact that I had been wrong about Martin Chaice in thinking he was watching his father for the purpose of furthering the intrigue between Constance and Lang, wasn't, for instance, an explanation of the intrigue itself. As for the business of the liquid-squirting, either the whole thing, letters and all, was hocus-pocus, or else it had in it the material for a pretty nasty scandal, and somehow I had to find out the truth.

I came down to breakfast that Monday morning to find Chaice and Kitty alone again. Chaice at once said that something ought to be done about me. Business was over and we ought to have some sort of a holiday. Was there anything I could suggest? Anything I would like to do?

I said I wasn't going to be a nuisance to anybody and I was perfectly capable of making a holiday for myself. I did add that since the weather was reasonable again, I'd rather like to borrow Lang's bicycle and go to Leavenmore, where I'd have lunch. Or if Chaice wouldn't be bored, and could spare the time, we might have a car.

"I'd just love to go," Kitty said. "There's a bus too. Let's make a party of three, daddy."

"You and Travers go," Chaice told her. "Churches and abbey ruins aren't much in my line."

"A great idea," I said. "Sure you won't come, Chaice?"

He said he was a bad walker and wouldn't spoil our fun. As a matter of fact he *was* a bad walker, but not in the sense he intended to convey. His walk was typical of himself: an absolute furious pace and with such short steps that it was quite impossible to adjust one's pace or steps to his speed. But we decided in any case that Kitty and I would have the day out. We'd take the ten-thirty bus from the stop down the road, and we'd lunch in Leavenmore. We might be home for tea and we might not.

When I went out to the hall after breakfast Chaice hailed me from the lawn where he was smoking a post-prandial cigarette. "Sure you don't mind going with Kitty?"

"It's an enormous pleasure," I told him. "It's a pity you can't come too. I think she'd have liked it."

"My dear fellow, I'm simply up to the eyes," he said, and took my arm and began leading me away out of earshot of the house. "You know what contracts are."

"A lot of work in hand?"

"That book you and I were working on, and trying to run two detective stories at the same time. And—keep this under your hat, by the way—something more important still."

"Really," I said, for he had paused as if he expected surprise.

"I'm bucking the stage, my boy. A play of mine will be on in town before Christmas."

"But how splendid!" I said. "I always wondered why you didn't try your hand at it. The play is written?"

"Not a word," he said, and his lip drooped in an ironic complacency. "But it's here"—he tapped his skull—"and it's going to be good."

"I'm sure it is," I said. "The detective type, is it, or straight?"

"Mystery. A case of—" Then he broke off. "But you'll know when the time comes."

"Won't you give me a clue?"

"You're too shrewd," he told me, and yet I could feel that he was itching to let out more. "All I will tell you is this: that there's a bit of Jekyll and Hyde in it."

I remembered what Martin had said, and before I knew where I was, I was polishing my glasses. He was giving me a queer look, as if he was expecting some comment or a pat on the back.

"It always was a good plot," I said, "and you're the one to handle it differently. An adaptation, is it, or something quite new?"

"Absolutely new, my dear fellow. Absolutely new."

"What does Daine think of it?" Daine was the best judge of a play in town. He gave me another quick look.

"But I told you it wasn't yet written."

"Of course," I said apologetically, though I didn't see how that mattered. He could have talked the whole thing over with Daine. Or was he writing the play under another name, and so doing Daine out of commission? Just the sort of trick Chaice would be capable of. And then I had doubts. If the play was a winner, Chaice would never keep the secret.

"Is one permitted to ask the title?"

He shook his head, then changed his mind again.

"You'll keep this implicitly to yourself?"

"Most certainly," I assured him.

"Then the tentative title's *Mr. Polegate*."

He looked up for approval.

"*Mr. Polegate*," I said. "It's unusual, and it's snappy."

He had been drawing me towards the house again, and that was all the talk we had. He tapped the barometer in the hall and said he thought there wouldn't be rain. Then I saw Martin hovering round, so I dodged him by going upstairs. When I came down he had gone.

It was a lovely ride on the bus-top, and by the time we had reached Leavenmore we had had a fine gossip. It began when I pulled her leg about paying for the fares. I said she must be getting a very wealthy person with all the pay she was getting.

"I'm getting frightfully mean," she told me. "I'm saving up like billy-o."

"But not for your old age," I said.

"What does that imply?" she asked me laughingly.

"Well, unless the young men of this generation have lost all powers of perception, you'll be spending someone else's money some fine day."

"I'm only a plain Jane," she told me, and blushed nevertheless. "Still," and she sighed—"money's awfully useful. Daddy was frightfully sporting about my allowance, by the way. When I was twenty-one he made me an allowance of a hundred and fifty, the same as Martin's, and he wouldn't make any deduction when I got a commission."

"And how does Martin get along on his allowance?" I asked brazenly, and she didn't seem to notice anything outrageous in the question.

"Martin was just furious when Daddy made my allowance the same as his. He never seems to have a penny. Says he's saving up."

"A girl in the offing?"

"Heavens, no!" she said. "Something very different. You won't mention this, will you, but he's written a book of poems—well, it's not exactly a book yet. I think they're the most frightful bilge, but he's trying to find a publisher, and if not, I think he'll pay to have them published."

I let out a whistle.

"That would cost him a packet in wartime."

"I know," she said. "There's only me and Constance who might help. I don't want to help, because I think it's silly."

"And Constance?"

"He's playing up to Constance now. Hanging round and trying to get her in the mood."

So much for relevant chatter. As for the rest of the trip, we saw the few sights and then had an excellent lunch. We lingered out our coffee, and then, as it was still an hour and a half before a return bus, we decided to start walking back. We took it fairly steady, and when the bus did overtake us we were mightily relieved, for it was trying its best to rain. By the time we reached home it was coming down pretty smartly, and we were both out of breath from the run. As it was, we were dangerously wet, and I thought it best to change.

Official tea was long since over, so Kitty and I had tea by ourselves. Then Constance came in and was asking us about our trip. When the meal was over, I could see that there was something she wanted to tell me confidentially.

"Those photographs I was going to show you, Ludo," she said at last. "Would you like to come and see them now?"

I said I'd be delighted and followed her up the stairs to her room. As soon as I was inside, she locked the door.

"Ludo, something awkward's happened. Martin can't go tonight."

My eyebrows lifted.

"Don't look at me as if I could help it," she told me, and her hands were trembling with nervousness. "It's one of his bad headaches. He's absolutely prostrate."

"But why doesn't he take something for it?"

"He has," she said. "But it takes hours to go. Even then he's utterly useless for a day or two."

"Only one thing then," I said. "We must call it off."

"But you can't!" Her hand went out to my arm. "You've just got to go through with it, Ludo."

"But surely," I pointed out, "if Martin wanted me to help him because he was useless by himself, then I should be useless by *myself*."

"You must get someone else to help you," she said. "You must get Cuthbert."

"Cuthbert!" I couldn't believe my ears. "I thought you wanted this business kept secret."

"Well"—she smiled rather feebly—"it isn't like telling a stranger. Besides . . ."

"Yes? Besides what?"

"Well, when the first letter came I confided in Cuthbert." Her hand went out in what she doubtless meant to be a gesture of appeal. "That was before I rang you up. I just had to tell somebody. And I knew Cuthbert could be trusted."

"And what did he say?"

"He wouldn't believe it," she said. "He told me to throw the letter on the fire."

"I see," I said, and probably ironically. "And now you want me to induce him to change his mind. But that's not part of the bond. All I did was promise to accompany Martin."

"But you will see him, Ludo, won't you? I tell you, you've got to see him."

I turned away and was mentally consigning the whole business to hell. She was following me, hand on my sleeve again.

"All right," I said. "But you've got to understand this. I'm not going to do any persuading. If Daine refuses to have any hand in it, then I throw my own hand in. You agree to that?"

"But of course I do," she told me, and I thought a bit too relievedly.

That was how we left it, and I'm afraid my leave-taking was far from gracious. If you don't understand why, then all I can say is that contact with Constance always left me with the feeling that she regarded all mankind as specially designed to serve her own particular ends. And there seemed something definitely fishy about the whole thing. In fact, a minute's quiet reflection told me that I had never been intended to accompany Martin. Martin would have contrived to drop out, just as Daine would certainly refuse to take part in anything so mad, and I was to be left holding the baby. But why? Why was I to be alone responsible for the exposure of Chaice? The other side of the picture didn't matter, for if Chaice's possible walk that night proved quite innocuous, then I should be unaffected. *Unless*—and there I paused. Was there some reason why Constance should wish me out of the house that night? Was that the reason for all the hocus-pocus about liquid-squirting? Was it not to matter what Chaice did, provided I was got out of the house?

It was an uneasy thought, and one that could be the product only of a mind as suspicious as my own. But just after half-past five I went across to the barn. Five o'clock was the official closing time, but I found Daine in his room. He had been talking to the dictaphone, but said he had just finished for the night.

"Something very private I'd like to talk over with you," I said. "We can't be overheard here?"

Confidences were nothing to Daine. In his time he must have had many a peep at family skeletons, but he did give me a quick, enquiring look. As I said before, I'm always a bit uneasy in the presence of a Daine wearing glasses. They give me the idea that he can read not only my thoughts but what lies behind them.

"It's nothing about books," I said, and then began telling the story.

"A second letter, was there?" he said. I passed it to him, and he was shaking his head as he handed it back.

"Sorry to interrupt you. Do carry on."

I told him of the original arrangement made with Martin, and how it had fallen through, and Constance's suggestion about himself.

"I wouldn't dream of it," he told me with a brusque finality. "I gave Constance my advice, and I still adhere to it."

"That settles that, then," I said. "But, strictly between ourselves, will you answer a plain question? *Could* Chaice be guilty of doing what the letters accuse him of?"

"Could he?" he said sharply. Then he hesitated, and began fidgeting. "Do you know, I'm not so sure."

"You believe he's mentally unstable?"

"Damned if I know," he said. "I own there are times when I think he's absolutely mad. Not mad enough to lock up, of course. In fact, mad is rather too strong a word."

"Another question, then. Assume he *is* doing this liquid-squirting. *Why* is he doing it?"

"God knows, my dear fellow. Exhibitionism run mad; that's all I can suggest."

"He couldn't be doing it so as to incorporate it, or something like it, in a book?"

His mouth gaped at that.

"He couldn't be such a bloody fool as that! If he were found out he wouldn't get away with it as he did over that typewriter business." He shook his head and frowned as he rubbed his chin. "I wonder." Then he shook his head again. "I can't think he's as mad as that. Mind you, if he is and he's caught, then it's the end of him. His sales would flop—just like that."

The gesture was expressive enough. I added something.

"Wouldn't it cost you a packet too?"

"Well, yes. I suppose it would. Not that I'm thinking over-much about that. It's the scandal and the family that I'm more concerned about." He clicked his tongue annoyedly. "It puts me in a hell of a quandary."

"Well, I leave it to you," I said. "I go away tomorrow, and after that it's no pigeon of mine. If you like to come with me, I'm prepared to keep an eye on him tonight, if he goes out. Whatever happens, I shall have an easy mind."

He took off his glasses and blinked for a moment or two.

"I don't like it, Travers. There's something just a bit under-hand about it."

He hooked on the glasses again and got to his feet.

"Dammit, you've got me in a hell of a fix. If I refuse, then I'm in bad with Constance—if I know her."

He began prowling about the room, and then suddenly whipped round.

"I'll do it on one condition. I'll go with you tonight, if Chaice goes out, but understand this. Whatever happens, Chaice is to be shown those letters tomorrow morning. There may be a hell of a row, but that's the only decent way of settling things. If Constance doesn't agree, then I wash my hands of the whole matter."

"Sounds reasonable," I said. "Perhaps I'd better see Constance again."

He gave a pretty grim smile.

"*I'll* see Constance. You've had quite enough bother as it is. That young woman can do with a little straight talking to."

We left it that he was to report at my bedroom just before dinner. Everything was arranged, he told me then. Constance had had to agree. Then we fixed up about ourselves, and by that time we were a bit late. I thought it best that he should go down first, so as to avoid any suspicion of a palaver.

Two minutes later I went down. Or rather I got to the head of the main landing, when I saw a maid approaching from the direction of the servants' staircase with a large tray. A sudden suspicion seized me, and I managed to meet her as she turned right into that other short wing where Martin had his room.

"Somebody ill?" I asked her with an amiable kind of talk-making.

"Only Mr. Martin, sir," she told me, and smiled unconcernedly. "He often has his dinner up here."

It seemed a pretty useful dinner too, and, for a man prostrate with a headache, a perfectly staggering one. In fact I decided that Martin's headaches were a fake. For some reason of her own, and of his too maybe, Constance wanted not only myself to be out of the house that night, but she wanted Daine absent as well. When I knew that I almost decided to change our plans—to take Daine into my confidence and get either him or myself left unsuspected in the house while the other followed Chaice. Then I shrugged my shoulders and let things go. Maybe all Constance wanted was to have the coast thoroughly clear for something special in the petting line between Lang and herself. And then the whole thing struck me as so cheap and sordid that I cursed myself for a fool for letting myself be drawn into it at all.

There was nothing unusual during dinner, unless that with the presence of Kitty it was quite a merry meal. Both Constance and Daine had themselves well under control, but Lang seemed to me to be definitely nervous. Then, as soon as the meal was over, Daine excused himself as having work to do, and the rest of us went into the drawing-room for coffee. There was a fire in the grate, and very cheerful it looked. Harris said there had been one or two heavy showers, and it was a dark, unpleasant night.

Kitty said she'd run up and see how Martin's headache was. She was down almost at once, and reporting that she hadn't disturbed him as he was asleep. Richard was sitting in his corner near the door, so I had a word or two with him and then made an unobtrusive exit. The front door closed gently behind me, and I tiptoed to the grass and towards the front gates. Across the road Daine was waiting, and he had my waterproof and hat.

"I suppose there's no other way he might use?" I asked Daine.

"I don't think he'd use any other way tonight," he told me. "Between ourselves, I rather think we're on a fool's errand. He didn't say a word at dinner about going out."

We stood there in the lee of the hedge with our eyes on the entrance gates. At first I could see no more than a few yards, and then the clouds must have lifted, or else my eyes were more accustomed to the dark, for I could just discern the gates themselves. A pedestrian came by and I watched him till he disappeared, and that was a good thirty or forty yards on. And then, with a suddenness that was startling, there was Chaice. Though he was only a sort of greyness that moved, I could clearly make out his Bohemian hat and the dark flowing cape.

He moved off to the left along the gravelled path. At our side of the road there was no path and the grass of the verge made our movements soundless, and Daine, in addition, was wearing rubber-soled shoes. Then Daine whispered to me to move on where I was, and he himself moved across the road.

On went Chaice. He crossed the road where it cut the avenue in two, and then in a few moments he was turning sharp left, or so it seemed to me. I nipped across to Daine's side.

"Isn't it near here where you take the bus for the town?" I was whispering. "What shall we do if he takes it?"

There was no reply, but he was nudging me and moving cautiously on, and then, just faintly in the greyness ahead of me, I saw Chaice again. Now we were on the hard pavement, and when we stopped I could hear Chaice's steps ahead. Daine's feet made no sound and I was trying awkwardly to tiptoe. I noticed, too, that we were in a street of quite nice houses, if one judged their size and that of their gardens by the distance they lay apart. And then suddenly there was the sound of a gate, and Chaice had disappeared.

"What's happened?" I was whispering.

"Don't know," Daine whispered back. "Unless he's going to somebody's house."

He moved cautiously on with me at his heels. We heard the sound of a door-knocker, and when Daine drew me to a halt in the shadow of a garden shrubbery I could see Chaice standing at the door of a house. Then the door opened and he disappeared. There was the sound of the door as it closed again.

"What now?"

"Damned if I know," Daine whispered back. "Might as well wait for a bit and see what happens. Or shouldn't we?"

"We might give him a quarter of an hour," I said, and then I thought of something else. "What road are we in, do you know?"

"I believe it's the road just back of the house"—Lovelands he meant. "Why?"

"Is there another way out?"

"My God, yes," he said, and clicked his tongue. "If Chaice is up to mischief, that's just the cunning trick he'd think out."

He clicked his tongue again and then had an idea.

"You get inside and step into this shrubbery. I'll nip along to the back door."

We opened the gate quietly and I nipped into the shrubbery about a third of the way along its thirty-yard length. Daine moved on, his rubber-soled shoes soundless on the gravel of the drive. I could just see him as he went by what seemed a lean-to garage, and then he was out of sight. I drew back farther into the shrubbery. A strong scent as of honeysuckle was somewhere near me, and as I disturbed a bough raindrops went down my neck. A minute or two and the honeysuckle was over-poweringly strong, and in that rain-sodden air it had a sweetness that was almost too sickly. Then, as I moved my hand to guard my neck from the wet again, I somehow discovered that there was no honeysuckle after all. It was a tall weigela bush among whose low straggling branches I had forced my way, and one of those slender branches that lay by my neck was heavy with its second bloom.

"You there, Travers?" came an urgent whisper.

I revealed myself.

"He's still there," whispered Daine. "I listened at the kitchen door and I could still hear voices."

"You get back and keep an eye on that door," I told him. "I'll stay here. Whichever way he goes out, the one who sees him follows him."

"What about the other?"

"If he hears steps he can follow on behind," I said, and we left it at that. Daine disappeared again and I wriggled back among the weigela.

I must have stood there for a quarter of an hour before anything happened. Indeed I knew that the agreed quarter of an hour was up and I was wondering if Daine would come back and say we might as well go home, and that was something which I somehow didn't want. And then all at once I heard Chaice's voice at that barely visible door. There was just the sound of it, and as if he had said a good night, and there was the quick flash of light from a door quickly opened and as quickly shut. I heard his foot on the gravel and once more I drew back. My heart began to pound as I waited.

The steps ceased, and I didn't know why. Then something black was going by me a few yards away and I knew Chaice had taken a short cut across the grass of the lawn. He was opening the gate and turning right, and then his steps were on the pavement. Along that shrubbery ran a grass verge, and my feet were soundless as I made for the gate. As I went through I could just see Chaice ahead. He seemed in even more of a hurry, and with his short steps he was getting over the ground at a pace as good as my best. So I gave up the attempts at tiptoeing and strode on. If Chaice halted or turned back, then, I told myself, I would cross the road.

And just then something peculiar happened again. Chaice stopped, and before I could make a move he was entering another gate. I could just faintly hear his steps on the gravel of a new drive, and when I drew cautiously up I could just discern him before he disappeared in the darkness that was the deep shadow of yet another lean-to garage.

I waited for a good ten minutes, and then was telling myself that this was the very devil. What on earth was Chaice up to, with this round of evening calls? And then I had an idea. Chaice must have discovered that he was being followed, and he was amusing himself by leading his tracker a pretty lively dance. In the same moment I realised that the house where he now was had also a front and back way out. In other words, he might have used that house as a convenience and have gone straight through to whatever road it was that lay behind.

"To hell with it!" I told myself angrily, and whipped round on my heels. As near as I could judge, I was two houses from the original one, and when I got there I knew I was right, for I had left the gate open. Now I went along the clipped grass by the shrubbery till it ended by the garage.

"Daine! . . . You there, Daine?"

In a moment or two I saw him coming.

"Better not talk here," I whispered, and moved on to the road. I crossed it, he at my heels.

"Might as well get back home," I told him, and I didn't even trouble to lower my voice.

"What's happened, then?"

When he knew, he cussed a bit. In fact we both cussed a bit. Then he was saying that he'd heard never a thing away at the back of the house, and he was wondering why Chaice had gone to the house at all.

"I think we'd better get home as soon as we can," I said. "We'll look a couple of pretty fools if he really was wise to us. We'd better think up some yarn to satisfy him."

"He may not be home," he said. "He may have dodged us and gone down town after all."

"To blazes then!" I said annoyedly. "Let's get back home and forget the whole thing. We might go to the barn first. Then it won't be a lie to say we've been there."

"Wait a moment," he suddenly said, and drew me to a halt. "This doesn't seem right. I think we must have taken the wrong turn when we crossed the road."

I had been too busy talking, and in any case I might as well have been in Philadelphia for all I knew of my surroundings. But then we heard steps, and it was laughable how we drew back and cowered, as if the steps were those of Chaice. But it was a stranger, and he told us we'd taken the wrong road for Love-lands. What we'd better do was go back a hundred yards and then turn sharp left.

Three minutes later we knew where we were, and after that it was easy going to the house.

"Shall we go to the barn or just not give a damn for any-body?" I asked Daine.

"Damn the barn," he told me peevishly. "Let's go straight to the house. My feet are wet, and I'm not getting pneumonia for Chaice or anybody."

We were about twenty yards from the front door when it suddenly opened and a dazzling beam of light ran across to the lawn.

Harris was at the door, and I remembered I was thinking, most inanely, that he must have heard us coming.

"What the devil's he doing with that light showing?" growled Daine, and at that moment Harris caught sight of us. He made a step or two towards us, then stopped.

"Mr. Daine, sir. Is that you, sir?"

"Yes," called Daine, and then we had come up. "What's the matter, Harris? . . . *What* the devil's the matter?"

I can't describe old Harris. He was gesturing and making un-intelligible noises, and then he somehow blurted out that it was Mr. Chaice. Lang appeared in the hall as we went through the door, and he looked scared to death.

"In there!" was all he could say, and he was pointing.

Daine gave him a kind of glare and went through the open door of Chaice's room. Then he drew back.

It is strange how little things stand out in one's mind in mo-ments of danger or crisis—little things that have apparently no real significance. I know that I was most aware of Lang, and how he closed the front door and switched off the hall light. It was as if he wanted a spotlight focused on that open door at which Daine now stood.

I looked over Daine's shoulder. Beyond us Chaice was lying, head against the desk, and by him an overturned vase of ros-es. As I pushed Daine gently aside and took a step nearer I saw a something round Chaice's neck—the cord with which he had been strangled.

PART II

CHAPTER VI
G. H. PRESTON

BEFORE I RESUME I should like to make perfectly clear what things I omitted, by accident or design, to tell Inspector Goodman. I didn't mention the intrigue between Constance Chaice and Lang because there was just an element of doubt, and by that I mean that when I came to think the matter over I was not dead certain that it was Constance's voice that I heard. That it could have been any other woman's seemed impossible, but what I decided was to prove or disprove the matter by making certain unobtrusive investigations of my own.

Naturally, too, I didn't give Goodman a complete character study of Chaice. All I told him was sufficient to justify the fact that Daine and I had thought it desirable to check up on his movements. I saw no reason to tell him about Martin's manuscript or that I suspected the genuineness of the headache, for if he was worth his salt he'd find out that later for himself. I was glad, too, that he seemed to take it as a natural thing that we should have come to suspect Chaice of the liquid-squirting. Obviously he thought Chaice capable of pretty nearly anything, for it wasn't hard to deduce from certain of his remarks that he'd been involved in the enquiries into that typewriter business, and was still pretty sore at the trick Chaice had played.

* * * * *

I had stopped dead short when I came to the moment of seeing the cord round the neck of Austin Chaice. It seemed a logical place at which to stop, for, except in the things I had just been relating, I was not concerned with the murder except as a kind of Peeping Tom who had had a look at the body. And Goodman had interviewed Harris and Lang overnight. The interviews had taken so long—for there had been all the fingerprint and photographic routine beforehand—that Daine and I had gone to bed. We were both half asleep as we waited by the embers of the drawing-room fire, and we hoped rather guiltily that we should have an undisturbed night. I had slept like a log and had not woke till seven o'clock. Then I had come down early and had had the breakfast table to myself, except for the occasional potterings of old Harris, who entered every now and again and peered round like someone gone weak in his wits. Then Daine had come in, and just as we were wondering if and when Goodman would be seeing us, in came Sergeant Smith with the request that I'd see the Inspector for a minute or two.

As I've said, I came to a full stop at where I had seen the body. I could have added that Lang had told me from somewhere behind me that Chaice was dead.

"And then you rang us, and that was that," said Goodman.

"More or less," I said.

His eyebrows lifted and I explained. When Lang said Chaice was dead, Daine asked him if he'd rung the police. Lang said he hadn't had time. He'd only just discovered the body.

Daine then lifted the receiver but nothing happened.

"What the devil's wrong with this phone?" he asked Lang.

Lang didn't know. He was all of a dither in any case, and wondering, so he said, who was going to break the news to Constance and Kitty.

Daine went through to the workshop, but was back in a couple of minutes. That telephone was out of order too, and it wasn't hard to guess that the murderer had put it out of commission.

"What about your telephone in the barn?" I said. "That's on a line of its own."

Daine went off again, and with a torch that Harris found from somewhere. It was over half an hour later before I saw him again, and that was when he joined me in the drawing-room. We'd got Richard out of bed and he'd broken the news to Constance and Kitty. Constance had fainted and everything was at sixes and sevens. Kitty seemed more stunned than distraught and we had got her to go to bed. By *we* I mean Richard and Lang and myself. Then, as I said, Daine came in.

He'd had the devil of a time. His telephone had been out of order too, and he'd wondered what on earth to do. Then, to save time, he'd not come back to the house but had hurried off as fast as he could in the drizzle and the dark to the nearest house where there might be a telephone. He had had to go almost to the end of Harcourt Avenue before he could find one.

"But the telephones were in order when we got here?" Goodman pointed out to me.

"I know," I said. "A wire in the workshop had been cut, and Richard—Mr. Richard Chaice—did some quick repairs. He's a very knowledgeable man at all that sort of thing. When you got here he was repairing the annexe telephone. That had been cut too."

He grunted for a bit and pursed his lips in thought, and then was asking if there was anything else I could think of. If there wasn't, then he'd get my statement typed out.

"Make enough copies for me to have one," I told him. "I like to know how I look in print."

He grinned at that as he told Smith to get going. When Smith had gone I had something else to say.

"I suppose I can get back to town this afternoon?"

"I'd rather you didn't," he said. "If you could stay on for only a day it might help to clear things up."

"We'll see," I said airily. I didn't feel like making promises just then, though I knew, and he knew, he could hold me there. "But what about answering a question or two of mine? It's about my turn."

"What sort of questions?" He seemed just a bit suspicious.

"Well, I haven't had a chance to talk to anyone in the house—to Mr. Lang, for instance. Just how did he happen to discover the body?"

"Well, it was like this," he said. "Mr. Lang was tired and was thinking of going to bed. Harris came into the drawing-room and brought him a glass of hot milk which he'd requested. Then Mr. Lang asked him if Mr. Chaice had returned. Harris said he had—at least he'd seen a light from under the door there. So Mr. Lang sipped his milk and said good night to everybody, and Mr. Richard Chaice said he'd be going up too, and the pair of them went out to the hall together. There wasn't a light then under this door, so he went along to the cloakroom. When he came back there was still no light, so he took a peep in here. As soon as he switched on the light he saw the body. Harris happened to be coming through the hall, and that's all there was to it."

"What was Harris doing in the hall?"

"He thought that, since Mr. Chaice was in, everybody was in who'd be likely to use certain rooms, so he was on his rounds to see all windows and doors were shut. He was waiting till you and Mr. Daine were in before he fastened the front door."

"What about alibis?" I asked brazenly.

"Well, I haven't been into them fully," he told me, and I knew he was hedging.

"But those you *have* checked up on?"

"To be perfectly frank, I haven't," he said. "A son—Martin—was in bed most of the day with a bad headache—"

"That alone might take some checking," I cut in.

"How do you mean?"

"Well, if you're in a bedroom, that doesn't say you can't get out of it, especially in the dark."

"Know any motive?"

"Now you're getting ahead of me," I told him. "Besides, I thought I was asking the questions. What about the other men? Lang and Richard Chaice?"

"All I've got so far is a kind of general post in the drawing-room," he said. "Mr. Richard Chaice spent the whole evening there. Didn't budge at all, so I'm told. The others were in and out." Then he gave me a sideways look. "You're pretty sure it was an inside sort of job?"

"What else could it be?"

He shrugged his shoulders.

"A prowler. Burglar, if you like. That french window there was open—not locked, that is to say. He came in, Chaice surprised him, and—"

"And, as they say in the music-halls—Bob's your uncle."

I nodded with what I hope was a straight face. "The burglar had his usual strangling apparatus handy, and that's that."

"All right, sir," he said, and laughed. "You needn't rub it in. I know I stuck my neck out with that one. No casual burglar would have known the whereabouts of the telephones, especially that one of Daine's in the annexe."

"Well, I wish you luck," I said, and got to my feet and stretched myself, for my backside was pretty near numb. "Anything else I can do I'll be only too glad to do." And as he made no comment, "Like me to send anyone else in?"

"Yes," he said. "I think I'd like to see Mr. Daine. But wait a minute first. One or two things I've got to do. I ought to see Mrs. Chaice, if she's well enough. Then there's an alibi I'd like to go into rather specially."

"Whose?"

"Don't tell me you've overlooked it!" he told me, and looked quite pleased. "It's the alibi of the gentleman Mr. Chaice went to see last night."

"Of course!" I said, and clicked my tongue annoyedly.

"That's why I'd like to see Mr. Daine," he went on. "You and he can show me which house it was, and I'll do the rest."

"And leave us on the doorstep? You wouldn't be so heartless," I said.

He grinned as he got to his feet and told me he'd see.

Daine was far from pleased about being routed out. Monday was another busy day for him. All the crankiest of his clients, he said, spent their Saturdays and Sundays worrying about their damned books, and the Mondays always produced shoals of letters. I asked him to show me where his telephone wire had been cut, for I'd been wondering how an entry could have been made. But none had been necessary. The roof of that old barn sloped down to within eight feet of the ground, and the wires had a fastening on the wall before entering just above Daine's window. In other words, to cut the wire from outside was the easiest thing in the world.

Goodman sent for us sooner than we expected. He had a police car, and I sat alongside him with Daine at the back, and we drove slowly towards the bus stop.

"Which road now, sir?" Goodman asked when we came to that multiple crossing.

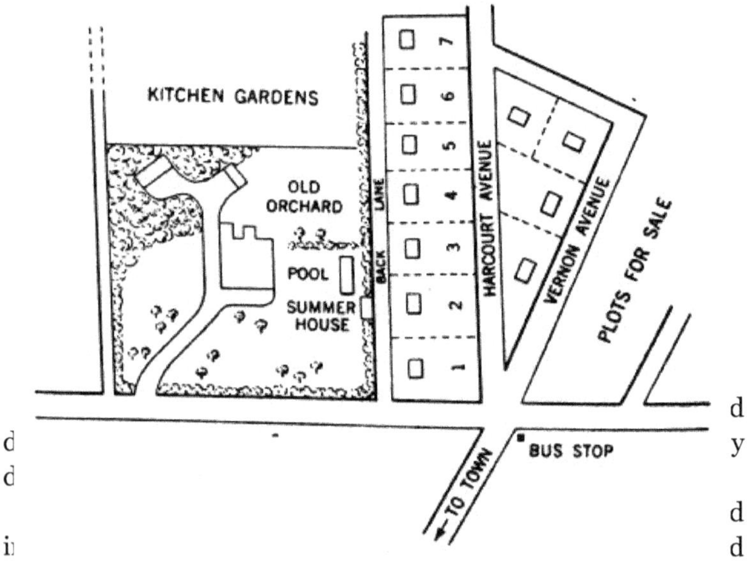

size and well screened from each other. They were not all alike, though each had a garage on its left.

"I'm practically sure this is it," I said, but Goodman drove on, and turned right into Vernon Avenue and so to the bus stop again. "It certainly wasn't Vernon Avenue," Daine said. "Too few houses."

"Then we'll try Harcourt Avenue," Goodman said. "How many houses along as a rough estimate?"

I thought six or seven and Daine agreed.

Goodman said he'd leave the car outside No. 4 and work along. We got out, too, and waited. In a couple of minutes he was coming out again. Nobody had called there the previous night. As for Chaice, they knew him by name, of course, but not by sight.

At No. 5 the husband was in town, but the woman of the house made much the same statement. At No. 6 there was nobody at home. At No. 7 a friend had called, but he was nothing to do with Chaice.

"That's very curious," Daine said.

"I don't know, sir," Goodman told him. "If you two gentlemen are correct there's only one thing for it. He must have called at No. 6."

So back we went to No. 6. Daine and I were supposed to wait at the gate, but I spotted something and called Goodman's attention to it. It certainly was my weigela bush in that narrow shrubbery, and there were the marks of my feet where I had waited.

"Now we're getting somewhere," Goodman said. "We might as well have a look round."

We went by the garage, where a gravel path led to a side door. Goodman knocked and listened, but there was never a sound. Daine had been casting round and he found feet-marks where he had trodden on the edge of the little kitchen garden.

"No telephone here," Goodman said, giving a look up.

"Wait a minute," Daine said. "I think it must have been No. 5 that I telephoned from. You know, when I called the police. If it's called Rosebank, then it's the one."

"Which way did you come then, sir?" asked Goodman.

"The same way we came just now," Daine told him. "There is no other way."

He was looking puzzled, so Goodman explained. Hadn't there been a telephone at one of the lower numbers? Maybe, Daine told him rather huffily. But what he'd done in the dark and drizzle was to overshoot No. 1, and even perhaps No. 2—enquiries would prove which—and at the houses at which he had enquired there had been no telephone, but they'd told him there was one at Rosebank just along the road.

No. 5 was Rosebank right enough, and the three of us went to the door. The woman remembered Daine asking to use the telephone.

"What about the people at No. 6?" asked Goodman. "Do you know them at all?"

She shook her head. No. 6 was a house which was let furnished and the present tenant had been there only about three weeks. It actually belonged to a man who was in the Army, and his wife and two children had gone to live with a sister of hers. That was why the house had been let furnished.

"You don't know the name of the present tenant?"

"It's Preston," she said. "That's all I know."

"Married, is he?"

"No, he's a single gentleman," she said. "I *have* seen him once or twice in the mornings, but I think he works down the town. Now I come to think of it, he told me so himself."

"You've spoken to him?"

"Only the once," she said. "He came to ask me about his newspaper which hadn't come, and I told him mine hadn't come either. That was when he said he wouldn't have it come any more. He'd get it of mornings when he went down town."

"A shortish, stout man, was he?" I cut in.

"Yes, he was rather," she said.

That was all she knew. The houses of Harcourt Avenue, as I said, were well screened from each other and it took a good time to get really acquainted with a neighbour unless one walked with him of mornings to the bus stop. She didn't know, for instance, if Preston had a woman come in to do housework or if he fended entirely for himself. Her husband had never seen him in the back garden. She did think he spent most of his nights indoors, because on one or two occasions she had seen chinks of light through the black-out curtains.

That was that, and Goodman didn't say a word till we were back at the car. I wasn't at all sure that he'd remembered G. H. Preston.

"A bit of luck that, Inspector," I said.

"You mean about Preston?"

"Who *is* Preston?" broke in Daine.

"A man called to see Chaice one day," I said. "Didn't you hear about it? Lang saw him and got rid of him. A rather objectionable person, I gathered."

"So *that* was Preston," he said, and then frowned. "Didn't Chaice tell Lang he knew him or something?"

"Well, he acted as if he did," I said, and then Goodman was motioning for us to get in the car. He drove a few yards and then pulled up.

"Now then, sir," he said to me, "you said you followed Mr. Chaice for two houses back and then he went in at a gate. Wouldn't that be this one—No. 3?"

"I wouldn't be positive," I told him.

"Well, if he actually called at another house, then it wasn't No. 4, because we've already enquired there. You gentlemen wait here and I'll enquire at No. 2."

"Nothing doing," he told us when he came back. Daine and I were out of the car again, and we followed him to the door of No. 3. A woman opened it. Goodman told her his name and said a burglar had been operating in Harcourt Avenue. Had she heard or seen anything?

She hadn't, and she had had no visitors the previous night who might have seen anything either. Goodman said his information was that the man had been seen entering the gate of No. 3, and might he have a look round at the back in case there were signs of an attempt at an entry?

The woman was mightily relieved when there was never a sign. Goodman said we'd look along the back garden in case there might be suspicious footprints. We followed him along a concrete path to a back gate that opened on a narrowish, unmetalled lane. Just across it was the boundary fencing of Lovelands, and the polled, interlaced poplars that backed the shrubbery. So dense was that shield that there was nothing to be seen of the house. But in that fencing, and almost opposite the back gate of No. 3, was a door. Goodman tried the handle and the door opened.

"There we are, gentlemen," he told us. "That's why Mr. Chaice went right through at No. 3. He took a short cut back to his own house."

"Rather a brazen sort of thing to do?" I said.

"Not for Austin Chaice," said Daine cynically. "But what's that, Inspector?"

He was pointing to the lock of the door. Plainly enough it had been forced back, and the marks of the forcing were fairly recent.

"Maybe Chaice didn't have a key on him," I suggested. "He forced the lock to get through."

"Might be that," Goodman agreed. "Let's have a look inside."

Inside the door a weedy gravel path cut back to our left and came out at the summerhouse. The path actually branched, with its main part going right round to the summerhouse veranda. The other branch led to the back, where there was a door in the summerhouse with steps that led up. There was also an Elsan closet that seemed to have been cleaned out some time ago and hadn't been used since. Up against it was propped a rubber-tired wheelbarrow covered with a piece of tarpaulin.

Goodman looked across at the house from the veranda.

"Was there a tennis court in front of here?"

"Before the war—yes," Daine told him, and then I saw the faint difference in the colouring of the grass. "Then balls were difficult to get, so Chaice had the surrounding posts taken up and the whole thing incorporated in the ordinary lawns."

"Locked, I see," Goodman said, trying the handle of the front door.

"No real use for it now," Daine said. "Chaice used to come and browse here sometimes, that's all."

"He had a new Yale lock fitted."

That was obvious, and we neither of us made any comment. Then Goodman was having a look at the grass, and taking a few steps and trying to see what impressions his own feet made. From the shrug of his shoulders it was easy to tell that the comparatively light rain of the last twenty-four hours had softened the lawn but very little.

He stood there for a minute or two rubbing his chin and looking about him.

"I don't think I need trouble you gentlemen any more," he said. "Unless Mr. Daine has anything he can think of."

Daine said he couldn't think of anything, but he'd be glad to answer any questions.

"I don't know that there are any," Goodman said, and then was giving a somewhat quizzical look. "Unless you have any ideas about who could have killed Mr. Chaice? In strict confidence, of course."

Daine's lip pouted, then lapsed to a cynical smile.

"I can't go into details, but I think I could tell you the names of quite a few who'd have been—well, not inconsolable at hearing the news of his death."

"He wasn't popular?"

"He had a fine collection of enemies."

"Maybe," said Goodman dryly. "But any of them in the house itself?"

"Sorry, but I can't answer that," Daine told him tersely. The quick frown went and he began to hedge a bit. "You know how things are. There isn't a family that hasn't its tiffs and rows. Or that doesn't take sides. And people's nerves get a bit frayed after five years of war."

"You mean?"

"Only this," said Daine and shrugged his shoulders. "If I told you about little family squabbles, you might magnify them into something serious. I'd rather you got such information from somebody else—not that I want to seem rude."

"I understand, sir," Goodman told him. "No need to trouble you any longer, I think. And if there's anything I should want, I'll know where to come."

Daine shot him a look at that ambiguous remark, gave me something of the same look too, and then moved off towards the house.

"Think I'll go back and get the car," Goodman told me. "Mind if I come?" I said. "Rather awkward spending one's time in the house. Intruding on people's grief and all that."

"Mr. Daine didn't seem any too grieved," he remarked as he held back the fence door for me to go through.

"If it comes to that, neither do I," I told him bluntly. "In our job, speaking well of the dead doesn't get one very far. Chaice was an irritable and an irritating man. Even when he had his genial moments you suspected they were unreal. And Daine was his agent. He couldn't dodge him or get away from him."

"I rather gathered a lot of that from your statement," he said as I got in the car.

He had to watch for traffic at the road junctions, so I kept my mouth shut. It was as we neared Lovelands that I again mentioned my going back to town that night.

"I'd rather you didn't, sir," he said. "My Chief will be back early this evening, and I know he'd like to see you."

"Very good of him," I said, and didn't mean it as ironically as it sounded.

"He's in town on one of those periodic conferences," he went on. "You know this morning when you thought I was going to ring the Yard? I was actually ringing the Chief."

"Good," I said. "A pretty piece of deduction wasted."

"Oh, I don't know," he said, and grinned. "I thought the Chief might as well do the enquiring as he was on the spot. And something else he's doing, sir, between you and me. Seeing the solicitor about the will."

I'd forgotten all about that. Goodman was a much smarter man than I'd been prepared to believe.

"That's a good move," I said. "But what about fingerprints? Did you find any anywhere?"

"Never a one," he said. "Not even on the cord that strangled him."

"Medical report all in order?"

"Absolutely. He'd been dead about a quarter of an hour when he was found. And he'd had a blow on the skull that stunned him first."

"No sign of the weapon?"

He shook his head.

"Anything missing from his pockets?"

"Possibly some papers from his wallet. And his keys."

"His keys," I said, and then suddenly I had to smile. We were standing then outside the car which he'd parked by the garage, and he spotted the smile.

"Something funny about the keys?"

"No," I said. "Only about you and me. You're making me stay on here because you might want me to lend a hand, of sorts. Yet you're not telling me a damn thing except what I get out of you with a pair of forceps."

"Oh no, sir," he said, and shook his head. "After all, I've answered every question you put to me." He grinned again. "Unless you'd like *me* to make a statement."

"I was just pulling your leg," I told him. "But what's the programme now?"

"Seeing Mrs. Chaice," he said. "She wasn't quite ready for me before. And I've got to interview the rest of the family." Then he thought of something else. "And I'll send a man along to wait for that Mr. Preston."

"Well, I'll be around somewhere if you should happen to want me," I said, and we went our separate ways. I didn't like the idea of going into the house, so I went back towards the garage. Richard wasn't in his workshop, but he'd evidently been there, for a glue-pot was boiling on a little primus stove.

I strolled in to wait. The bench was thick with shavings, and some planed lengths of wood were standing as if ready to be glued. Shavings always fascinated me as a boy. I still love their resinous smell, and as I stood there with my back against the bench my fingers were feeling the crispness of the shavings that lay heaped by my elbow. Then suddenly I was aware that I was fingering something that wasn't a stout shaving, and as I looked at it I saw it was a piece of cord. I pulled at it and there seemed to be yards of it. Something about it seemed vaguely familiar, and then all at once I knew it was just that sort of cord that had been drawn tight round Austin Chaice's neck.

CHAPTER VII
TALKING IT OVER

THERE WAS NO concealment about that cord: it was only that the accumulated shavings had covered it. It was in a neat coil too, and there was just a possibility, it seemed to me, that one might be able to check if a length had been cut off. Whoever had bought it—and that in all probability would be Richard Chaice—would know the original length and the amounts which might have been subsequently and legitimately used.

I was wondering about that and thinking that Richard was a long time coming back to his boiling glue-pot. I thought I'd like to have a look at that jacked-up Rolls, so I went through. At least I went to the door and was about to go through when I saw Richard. He was sideways to me and he neither saw me nor heard me, for my feet had made no sound on the shavings that strewed the floor. What he was doing was just nothing. He stood there, eyes on the wall ahead, hands tightly together against the pit of his stomach, and altogether absolutely motionless. As I watched him I saw his lips move once or twice, and he nodded to himself. It was as if he was debating some urgent problem, and then, after a minute or two, it began to be something quite different and rather uncanny. Even when I had first met him I had noticed his fits of mental abstraction, but this was something different and prolonged. In another minute, I could stand it no longer. I backed to the workshop, made a bit of a din, coughed loudly, and suddenly there he was at the door. He gave his usual friendly smile at the sight of me.

"I think the water in your glue is boiling away," I told him.

He had a look at it.

"Very strange," he said mildly. "The stove hasn't been alight a minute."

It was no business of mine to tell him otherwise, even if he now seemed his normal, gentle self. As he put in more water from a bottle standing on the bench, I asked him if he often had visitors. He smiled.

"A workshop to a man is like a kitchen to a woman, Mr. Travers," he said. "Everyone comes in here. And they like to do little jobs. A bit of planing, perhaps, or sharpening a chisel."

"What about finding me a job?" I said.

"Well, you might hold these boards for me," he said. "Then we needn't use the big cramp."

So I began holding boards while he glued and fixed the mortices, and all the time I was keeping him busy with talk. I said it had been a bad business about his brother, and all he could say was that he still couldn't believe it was true. He added that Austin had been the best brother in the world.

"He had his faults, Mr. Travers, I won't deny that, and if I said otherwise I shouldn't be speaking the truth." Then as suddenly he changed the subject. "Let me see, sir. You're going away today, I believe."

I said that had been the arrangement.

"You've enjoyed your little stay with us?"

A queer look had accompanied the question. I said I certainly had enjoyed my stay, until the events of the previous night.

"We're not everybody's company," he said. "Everything isn't always as it should be. I could have made mischief myself if I'd liked to speak. Now perhaps I wish I had."

There seemed to me to be only one meaning to be attached to that, and I was wondering how to put a question. I couldn't very well ask if he meant that he knew who had done the killing, and then it struck me that he might have been referring to that intrigue between Constance and Lang.

"But Kitty's a good girl," he was saying.

"A charming girl," I added, and waited.

"Martin's a good boy too," he said. "Queer sometimes, but a good boy at heart."

"And how do you get on with Constance?"

It was a tricky question. He stood for a second or two, the glue-brush unmoving in his hand, and then, when I was wondering if he were going off into one of those fits of abstraction, he was nodding his head.

"I'm not much of an ornament these days, Mr. Travers. Young people have young ideas—ideas that would have shocked our fathers and mothers."

I was doing some quick thinking about how to make use of that obvious opening, when there were steps outside and in came Harris with a tray. The old boy was looking more himself.

"Your lunch, Mr. Richard," he said, and set it down on an upturned nail keg.

"Thank you, Harris," Richard told him mildly. "We've just about finished."

I could see Harris regarding the job with a professional eye, so I asked him if ever he tried his hand.

"In a way, yes, sir," he told me judicially. "I often spend an hour here with Mr. Richard. I find a little manual work a great comfort, sir."

I didn't ask what miseries needed comfort, for I was realising that I was late for lunch. Harris said it didn't matter. Lunch was a very scratch meal that day. That Inspector Goodman had been interviewing various members of the family. Indeed, Mr. Martin was still in the master's room with him then.

"Do you mind if I ask you a very confidential question?" I said when we were out of earshot of the workshop. "Mr. Richard: does he suffer from . . . ?" I had to think for a moment. "I hardly know how to put it. It's not exactly amnesia. Fits of abstraction, shall we say? Even hallucinations?"

Harris stopped in the lee of that shrubbery that shielded us from both workshop and house.

"You're quite right, sir," he told me. "The master didn't like it referred to, sir. He was very fond of Mr. Richard, sir, as Mr. Richard was of him."

"I noticed that," I said.

"Madame didn't like it at all, sir. It made it awkward when there were guests present. All I mean, speaking quite respectfully, sir, is that that was her attitude."

"But he only seems to have those fits when he is alone."

"I agree, sir. In company—even with myself, if I may say so—he behaves as normally as you or me, sir, if you'll pardon the liberty. Sometimes, sir, he can make a very shrewd remark."

"Exactly," I said. "And what caused the trouble?"

"The trouble, sir? Ah, I see what you mean. It was the death of his wife, sir."

"Of course," I said. "That bombing—"

"Pardon me, sir—but no," he said. "I think the master would have approved of you knowing, sir, and that's why I tell you. His wife died in Canada, sir, just after war broke out. The master persuaded him to come home and he found him a nice little place in London. Then there was the bombing, sir. Mr. Richard had severe shock and it left him with the idea that his wife had been killed in the bombing. That's why the master brought him down here."

"A pretty tragic story," I said as we moved on again. Then I heard the wireless as we neared the kitchen, and the sound of the pips that preceded the one o'clock news. When I came down from my room, where I had had a quick wash and brush-up, Goodman was in the hall, looking at that showcase of crime souvenirs.

"It's unlocked," I said, "if you should want to handle anything."

He gave a bit of a start, for my steps had been unheard on the thick carpet of the stairs.

"Heaven forbid," he told me hastily. "A pretty gruesome collection, don't you think?"

"I knew a man who collected matchboxes," I told him. "Had lunch yet, by the way?"

He said he'd be having some sandwiches later, and Harris was bringing coffee. But first of all he was completing his interviews by seeing Richard Chaice. I drew him quietly outside and mentioned the cord.

"Thanks for the tip," he said. "I'll see what I can find out."

I told him to go carefully and explained in confidence why. Then I went on to the dining-room.

"Good morning," I said, and with what I hoped was just the right amount of cheerfulness.

Kitty smiled a good morning. Martin was looking on good terms with himself. Lang murmured something inaudible. He wasn't looking at all happy.

"You don't think we're wrong, eating like this?" Kitty said.

"Of course you've got to eat," I told her severely. "Morbidity is silly."

"Just what I was telling her," Martin said.

"How are you this morning, Martin?" I asked him.

"Much better," he said, but was putting on an expression decidedly lugubrious.

"Not such a bad turn as usual."

He gave me a quick look at that and then agreed that perhaps it hadn't been such a bad turn. Then he gave me a real facer.

"What train are you going by, sir?"

It had sounded to me as if he'd be damn glad to see the back of me, but I explained how Goodman thought it necessary for me to hang on—perhaps even for the night.

"I liked that Inspector," Kitty said. "Go on telling us what he was like with you, Martin."

So that was the conversation I had interrupted. Martin wasn't too keen on its resumption.

"There isn't anything to tell," he said. "I did put him in his place, though, when he started enquiring into my movements. I told him that if he was hinting that I had parricidal tendencies, I'd rather he said so straight out."

"What nerve!" said Kitty. "But you hadn't any movements. You were in bed!"

For some reason or other—and it was one at which I could make a shrewd guess—he looked a bit nonplussed.

"No need to tell me what I know already," he told her stiffly.

"Nothing to get huffy about," she retorted. "I'm only trying to protect your own interests."

"I'm quite capable of protecting my own, thank you. And better, perhaps, than some other people will be able to look after theirs."

The remark seemed directed at Lang, for his face flushed and he was nervously wiping his lips with his napkin.

"What a horrible thing to say!"

"If you don't like the truth, of course—"

I cut in there.

"How's Constance this morning, Kitty?"

"Much better," she told me. "She hopes to come down for tea."

"A dreadful shock," I said. "And a bad business all round." There was a silence then and I was the one who broke it. "How's all this going to affect you?" I asked Lang.

"He's going to be a frightfully important person," broke in Kitty. "He's got to finish Daddy's two books."

"Really?" I said politely.

"That's only Mr. Daine's idea," Lang told me diffidently. "He's to be the literary executor, you know."

"And a very good choice too," I said. "And you too. You're the very man for the job."

He blushed a bit and gave a tentative smile. I said it was quite exciting. Rather like Edward German taking over from Sullivan, and Quiller-Couch from Stevenson.

"Let's hope Orford makes a better hand at it than that bloke—I forget his name—made of the Unfinished Symphony," was Martin's highly superior comment.

"Don't be so priggish, Martin," flashed Kitty. "Of course Orford will make a good job of it."

"Priggishness, my dear, like beauty, is in the eyes of the beholder," he told her with a sweet acidity, and then he was turning to me. "Have you by any chance finished with that manuscript of mine, sir?"

"To tell you the truth, this wretched business quite put me off it," I said.

"That's all right sir," he told me. "It will be published now in any case."

"You've found a publisher?"

"Ways and means," he said vaguely, and there, if I'd only known it, was the solution of a good deal of mystery.

"I think that's a horrid thing to say, with Daddy lying . . . Well, it's horrid, anyhow."

"You're implying what?"

"I'm not implying anything," she flashed back at him. "I'm pointing out that everyone knows that you'd have to have it published at your own expense, and now you're just boasting that you'll have the money."

"And what if I'm not paying for it?"

"Of course you are!"

"Very well," he said, and gave a shrug of his shoulders. "I'm open to bet you that the book's published within the next six months, and it doesn't cost me a penny. And I get a good royalty rate."

"It would be ghoulish to bet about that."

"Oh, my God!" he groaned. Then he gave me a look that invited sympathy. Then he slapped his unfolded napkin on the table and stalked from the room.

"You must excuse his frightful manners," Kitty told me. "The exit wasn't so frightfully effective after all. He'd already finished his meal."

"Don't you think you were just a bit of a nag?" I pointed out.

"He just gets my goat," she said.

"But you were, you know."

That was Lang. Kitty looked as if she couldn't believe her ears.

"You say that! After my sticking up for you!"

"Go on," I said. "You've finished your meal, so why don't you stalk from the room."

She laughed at that.

"As a matter of fact, I *was* just going," she said. And go she did, though the look she gave Lang was a venomous one. In a couple of minutes Lang mumbled an apology and went out too, and I finished my lunch alone.

I lighted my pipe and made my way upstairs for no particular reason. Martin, I saw, had helped himself to the manuscript, and when I came down again he was in the hall.

"You didn't mind my taking the manuscript, sir?" he said. "Not in the least," I said, and added the palliative that I'd be seeing it in print.

He went on up the stairs, and then Goodman was looking out from the door of Chaice's sanctum.

The man who was on duty there had gone and he was alone. The weather had turned fine again and I couldn't help thinking what a delightful room it was.

"What was that about a manuscript?" Goodman asked, and added that he couldn't help overhearing.

I told him all about it.

"A poet, is he?" he said. "A friend of yours?"

"Not in the least," I said. "Say what's on your mind."

"There's nothing much to say," he said, and shrugged his shoulders. "Only if that's the sort of product Oxford turns out, then I'm glad my boy's never likely to go there."

"Speaking as a Cambridge man, thanks very much," I said. "But about that cord. How did you get on?"

"It's the same stuff," he told me impressively. "I've sent off the cut end to see if it tallies with the end of the cord that did the trick."

"Good," I said. "And how did the cord get there?"

"Richard bought it himself to repair sash-cords with," he said. "He's used some, but he doesn't remember how much."

"Sash windows?" I said. "I didn't remember there were any in the house. Those in my room have leaded lights."

"All the back of the house has them," he said, and added that he hadn't noticed any signs of abnormality about Richard Chaice.

"I don't wonder," I said. "Ninety-nine hundredths of his time he's a perfectly charming and normal man."

"What you'd call a natural gentleman."

"Exactly," I said, and then he said that that reminded him, and he was handing me a copy of my statement of that morning. "There you are, sir," he said. "Like to check it up?"

"Inviting insults?" I said, and put it in my pocket, and just then Harris came in with coffee on a tray. He said he'd fetch another cup for me.

"Did you hear the one o'clock news, gentlemen?" he asked us when he came back, and we said we hadn't.

"A very kind reference to the master," he told us. "It spoke very highly of his work and how he'd be missed."

"It's a queer thing," I said to Goodman when he'd gone, "but I haven't heard the wireless since I've been in this house."

"Meaning what?" he asked me over his cup.

"I hardly know how to put it," I said. "It just seems to illustrate something—how this house was completely centred round Austin Chaice and his work. His work dominated him. It was more of an obsession than work, because his very leisure was work. And this whole house revolved round his work. I know it got on Martin's nerves," I said, warming to the job of showing him just what I meant. "A war on, mind you, and yet I never once heard anyone ask for the news."

"But aren't most authors like that?"

"I doubt it," I said, and I was wondering why he didn't seem to regard that peculiar feeling of mine as important. Then it struck me that I should find it hard to put into words the impression that had suddenly been made on me by a realisation of that complete subordination of the house and its occupants to the work, or should I call it the obsession, of Austin Chaice himself. In any case, I changed the subject, for I was anxious to know if anything had happened about G. H. Preston.

"He isn't back yet," Goodman told me. "He'll probably come off one of the evening trains from town. All the same, I think he's going to be a bit of a mare's nest."

I must have looked hopelessly disappointed at that.

"This is the position," he said, "and I think you'll see what I mean. He took the house on a monthly tenancy, and the business was handled by Morlands, the local agents. Mr. Chaice. I should have said, is the ground landlord. All those houses are on long lease. Mr. Preston applied personally to Morlands for the tenancy. Said he'd heard it was going, and he gave Mr. Chaice as a reference. Naturally that clinched the matter. Morlands rang Mr. Chaice, who said he'd be a good tenant. Now do you see, sir?"

"Afraid I don't," I had to admit.

"Well, then, that visit Preston paid to Mr. Chaice. That morning when he was very angry and Mr. Lang got rid of him. Why should he have been angry with Mr. Chaice? Because something was wrong about the house. You know how tenants are, so he came to complain to Mr. Chaice personally." As I still didn't show signs of comprehension, he went on. "Remember that Mr. Chaice said to Mr. Lang, 'Oh, *him*!' That shows he'd already approached Mr. Chaice about his grievance and Mr. Chaice had got fed up with him. And if Mr. Chaice hadn't known him before, he wouldn't have recommended him for the tenancy."

"But surely," I said, "a tenant doesn't approach the ground landlord? The ground landlord has nothing to do with matters. The contract was between the owner of the house and Preston. Morlands were the agents who drew up the contract and made the inventory, and in the absence of the owner they would deal with all complaints by the new tenant. Mr. Chaice didn't even get his ground rent from the tenant. He still continued to get it from the owner."

I rather fancied he hadn't thought of that, but he found a good enough answer.

"All right, sir; we'll take that as agreed," he told me patiently. "So when Preston did approach Mr. Chaice, he was almost certainly told he was wrong. But Preston was a bit of a crank perhaps, and pig-headed, and he approached—wrote, I should have said—Mr. Chaice again, and then came to see him personally. Hence Mr. Chaice's 'Oh, him!' Don't you think that's it?"

I said it probably was, though it didn't satisfy me by a long chalk. Then, as he seemed in such a coming-on disposition, I thought I'd try to get further information generally.

"By the way, about the clothes Chaice was wearing. Naturally I touched nothing in the room, but he was wearing his cape and his hat was on the floor beside him. Were his clothes at all damp?"

"Not in the least," he said. "Should they have been?"

"They shouldn't," I said. "There actually wasn't any rain at all while Daine and I were out. Rain before and drizzle after, but no rain then. But about the hat. Was Chaice wearing it when he got that crack on the skull that knocked him out?"

He rubbed his chin for a moment or two before he answered. Only a man of absolute integrity could have given that answer, and at once I had for him a vastly increased respect.

"To tell the truth, sir, it was something that escaped my notice altogether."

It wasn't his fault, and I told him so, and that I wasn't trying to be superior. With his Chief Constable away, and short-handed in any case, he had had everything on his hands. I had had little to do but think.

"Any chance of checking up on the hat now?" I asked. "There ought to be hair adhering to the inside of the crown."

He clicked his tongue, then gave a sheepish grin.

"That hat's at my office. The last I saw of it was when I went in, and there was the man on duty at the telephone passing the time by giving it a good brush."

I had to laugh. It was easy to guess the kind of man he had to make use of in wartime.

"After all, it doesn't matter so much," I said. "But do you remember if the hat was at all damp or dirty?"

"Wait a minute," he said, and was picking up the receiver. When he was through he was asking for the man who'd been upset at the sight of a dirty hat.

"No mud or dirt on the outside? . . . Only a bit dusty? . . . Yes, that's all."

"There we are then, sir," he told me as he put the receiver back.

"That complicates matters," I said.

"Just what was in your mind?"

"This," I said, and paused. "Mind if we approach it from another angle?"

"Any angle you like, sir."

"Then don't take this question wrongly," I said. "But this room when you first saw it. Did anything strike you as odd about it?"

He rubbed his chin.

"Can't say there did."

"Maybe it wasn't there," I said. "But I thought those rucks on the carpet there were a bit too regularly placed." I pointed to the chalk-marks. "Practically all lateral, so to speak. None of them criss-cross as they should have been if he put up anything of a fight. And the room gave the impression of a struggle."

He had got to his feet and was having a good look down.

"But there wasn't a struggle," he said. "He was knocked out before being strangled!"

"Then why the impression of one?"

"I get you," he said. "It was faked."

"Let's look at something else," I went on. "Here's where the vase of roses fell, and here's where the water spilled out of it. Anything peculiar about that water?"

"Looks all right to me . . . at first glance."

"But the water made a regular pool, and just in front of the mouth of the vase. Is that what should have happened?"

"Good God, no!" he said. "The vase was knocked over. Therefore the water started spilling before it hit the ground. If not, the jar would have splashed it everywhere."

"What were the roses like?"

"Just scattered around."

"There we are, then," I said. "Chaice wasn't killed here at all. His body was dumped in here and the room was arranged—and it had to be done damn quickly, mind you—to give the impression that he'd been attacked here."

"Yes," he said, and then whipped round. "Where was he killed, then?"

"My guess is as good as yours," I said. "For what it's worth, mine is that he was struck on the head by someone who followed him back to the house here. Perhaps he was struck just outside the door here. If his hat fell off it would have been on wet grass or wet gravel. That's why I asked about it."

"I'm sure you're right," he said, and frowned to himself for a minute. "But who could have followed him here?"

"Maybe we'll have to change our ideas about Mr. Preston," I told him.

And that was when the telephone bell went. I didn't listen to the conversation more than I could help, but from his respectful tone I gathered he was talking to his Chief Constable. My name was mentioned, and about my being present at something. It was a good five minutes before he hung up.

"The Chief's coming back by the six-ten," he told me. "He's got the details of the will and he wants to read them to all those concerned. I've got to round them up, and we'd like you to be present."

"What's the idea?" I said. "Hoping to gather something from their reactions?"

"That's it," he said, and grimaced. I gathered he hadn't been wholly in favour.

"What's your Chief like?" I asked unconcernedly.

He gave me a quick look, then smiled rather enigmatically.

"Well, sir, he's not quite so modern as some. A real gentleman though, and one of the best to work with . . . or under."

I gathered a good deal from those last two words, but before I could pursue the subject further he was getting to his feet.

"Well, thank you very much, sir, for what you've done. I'll see that you know the time of that meeting about the will. Oh, and one thing you might do for us. Make out a list of times for you and Mr. Daine last night. As near as you can get them." I said I'd have to consult with Daine about that. He said he hated to hurry me, but he'd like to get to work on them before the arrival of his Chief. That was why I at once went across to the annexe, and why I happened to see Daine and Martin parting in the vicinity of the garage.

CHAPTER VIII
THE WILL

"Hallo, young fellow," I said to Martin. "Taking a bit of fresh air?"

"That's the idea, sir." I'd never seen him looking so pleased with himself. Then he added that he was expecting to be busy for a day or two.

"Writing?"

"Yes," he said importantly. "I've had one or two ideas. I don't know how it struck you, sir, but I think that volume of mine might be on the short side. Perhaps another half-dozen poems might give it just the length."

I agreed hypocritically enough. I didn't care how many of those damn poems he added provided I didn't have to read them first. So we parted friendlily enough and I went on to the annexe. Daine was in his room, and he was purple with fury.

"What do you think that damn conceited young puppy is up to now?"

"Lord knows," I said.

He waved me fussily to a chair and his voice lowered.

"Not a word about this, but this is what he had the nerve to tell me. That he'd seen his father yesterday and he'd agreed to have that blasted book of poems published! Can you beat it?"

"You mean it's all lies?"

"Lies? Of course it's all lies." He had realised he was shouting, and his voice dropped dramatically, though his hand was still gesturing fiercely. "Austin loathed the sight of those damn poems. Mental abortions was what he called them. I'm absolutely sure he never changed his mind."

"Well, I think Master Martin quite capable of a little sharp practice," I said. "Obviously he thought that now his father was dead you, as literary executor, could be hot-stuffed into anything."

"Literary executor be damned!" exploded Daine. "I must have been a fool ever to have told Chaice I'd do the job. I only agreed because I knew I'd never have to do it. Look at me"—and he waved at the trays on the desk. "And look at the staff I've got."

"It's going to be pretty tough," I said. "But about Martin. What was your attitude?"

A cautious look came over his face.

"You're keeping this to yourself?"

"Didn't I say so?"

He grunted a kind of apology and asked me if I considered him a business man.

"I consider you a super-business man," I told him. "And quite capable of handling Martin."

"Good of you to say so. But this is what I've done. And what I'm proposing to do. I've given him my O.K. . . . . I'll find a publisher, and if I can't, then the cost of publication will be borne by the literary side of the estate."

"But you can't do that?"

He gave his impish grin.

"I know I can't. All I'm doing is stringing him along. And this is why. He's got Constance behind him. If I antagonise her, then she will probably have the power to get me out of here. I'm not ready to go yet. But I shall be. This war isn't going to last much longer, and I'll get another place in town. Then I'll calmly inform Master Martin that there's a snag about paying for the publication out of the estate. I'll say there has to be written evidence that that was his father's explicit orders."

I grinned too.

"Didn't I say you could handle him?"

"You think the idea's a good one?"

"It's superlative," I said. "But I've got to waste some of your valuable time."

He took it philosophically enough, especially when I assured him it wouldn't be a matter of more than ten minutes. As a matter of fact it took us a quarter of an hour, and these are the times at which we arrived.

Chaice leaves Lovelands   8.45
Chaice knocks at door   8.57

I thought I remembered hearing a distant clock in the town strike the hour, which was why I was so sure about that last timing.

Chaice leaves house   9.35
Chaice enters gate of No. 3   9.38
Travers returns to No. 6   9.53
Travers and Daine see Harris   10.12

The latter was proved by the fact that I happened to glance at my watch just after I'd glanced at the body, and the time then was ten-fifteen.

Goodman was in Chaice's room and Sergeant Smith with him. He thanked me for the list of times and said Harris had been looking for me. Harris was in the hall when I came out.

"Here you are, sir," he said. "The mistress's compliments, sir, and will you have tea with her in her room. She doesn't feel equal to coming down."

"Delighted," I said. "How long will tea be?"

"Now, sir," he told me. "As soon as you're ready."

I didn't realise how quickly the afternoon had gone. By the time I'd had a quick polish it was well after four o'clock.

The room looked cheerful with the afternoon sun lighting the bowl of roses and gay curtains and chintzes. Constance was reclining on a settee under the big window and she was dressed, and by that I mean she wasn't flopping around in a dressing-gown. Not that she'd have looked floppy in anything.

"Dear Ludo," she said gushingly. "I'm so delighted you're staying on for a bit. You're such a support."

"Anything, provided I'm not a nuisance," I said.

"You couldn't be that," she told me, and then Harris came in with the tray. It looked as if we were going to do ourselves well, what with hot tea-cake, sandwiches of two sorts, and a delicious-looking sponge sandwich cake.

"The chess things have been found, madame," Harris announced dramatically as he removed with a flourish the cover of the tea-cake.

"Really! Where did you find them, Harris?"

"In the drawer of the hall table, madame."

She stared.

"But that's preposterous! I looked in there myself!"

"I'm sorry, madame, but that's where they were."

"But it's absurd." She looked at me for confirmation. "There was nothing in that drawer, Harris, but a duster."

Harris bowed an agreement but said nothing. She frowned and then told him that he might go. Then she rounded on me as if I'd touched the damn things.

"Perhaps it was the fairies," I suggested.

"The fairies!"

"Just a little private joke in our flat," I said. "If Bernice or I have lost anything, we say those damn fairies have been at it again."

"I see. Just like household gremlins."

"You've got it," I said, and changed the subject by asking how she was.

"Just a bit limp," she said. "Perfectly ghastly, wasn't it? I wouldn't go through it again for worlds."

"Yes," I said. "A bad business. And likely to be worse for the one who did it."

"Who was it, Ludo?" Her hand touched my sleeve. "Could it have been some tramp? Or a soldier? One does read the most dreadful things about soldiers."

I told her I hadn't the faintest notion, but that Goodman would probably know in a very short time. I said that to get her in the right state of perturbation for the next question.

"Tell me, Constance, strictly between ourselves. When you told me on the telephone that evening that you were frightened, had you any idea of what might happen?"

Then she *was* frightened. That hand that held the tea-cake was trembling and she was gaining time by putting it back on the plate and wiping her mouth with the paper napkin.

"But, my dear, how could I have had any idea!"

"All you were frightened about, then, was that anonymous letter mentioning the liquid-squirting?"

"But of course." Then she had to say too much. "Perhaps I did feel a something. You know, like when people say they feel something in their bones. Perhaps I'm psychic."

"Maybe," I said. "But for God's sake don't tell Goodman so."

"And why not?"

I sighed and then tried a more direct approach.

"When I came in just now you told me I was a support. I'll put that a different way. I'm trying to be a cushion between you and the police."

For a moment she was badly scared again. To hear Constance stammer was an experience.

"But why . . . I mean . . ." Then she managed to smile. "But what have I got to do with the police?"

"Goodman has questioned you, hasn't he?"

"In a polite way—yes. He's a very charming man."

"Exactly. That's his first bedside manner. The first turn of the screw. Wait till he gets nasty."

"I don't understand you."

"Well, as soon as things don't begin to explain themselves, he'll be questioning you and everybody else again. He'll want details of your movements and he'll ask you to tell him about other people's. He'll go into every detail of your life, present and past. If you refuse to answer, then he'll put you in the witness-box at the inquest where you'll be made to answer in public."

"But what questions could he ask?"

"Anything," I said. "Whether you were thinking of marrying again, perhaps."

Her lips parted at that. I went ruthlessly on.

"He'll probably deduce from what he gathers from other people that your feelings towards Austin had changed, so he may even ask you if you were already carrying on an intrigue with some other man."

Her face went a sudden and violent red. Then she was coughing into her napkin and explaining at last that a crumb had gone the wrong way. Then once more she could smile, if only feebly.

"You're being ridiculous, Ludo. You're not a cushion. You're a bogey man."

"An apt retort," I said. "Let's talk about something else."

We talked about all sorts of things while she toyed with her food. Then she told me that at six forty-five we were all to assemble in the drawing-room to hear the details of Austin's will.

"I thought it was always done after the funeral," she said sadly, as if she didn't know. "But perhaps that Inspector knows better. But I know I shall make a fool of myself," she went on, and tried then and there to summon a preliminary tear. Then she sighed instead and said, "Poor Austin!"

That was about all, except that when I was leaving she thanked me warmly.

"You always were a darling," she ended. "And do go on being a cushion."

I'd have liked to have a key-hole peep when the door closed on me so that I could have seen her face and watched her reactions. But when I got downstairs I lurked in the cloakroom till I heard Harris upstairs. Then I sprinted quietly up again and managed to waylay him as he took the tray towards the servants' stairs. Perhaps he wondered what I was doing there, but if he did he gave no sign. What I noticed was that Constance had had quite a good meal after I left. That she knew a good deal about Austin's death was plain enough, at least, as I had seen things. That she was immediately concerned seemed to me better than an even-money bet.

The Chief Constable—Colonel Marney-Hope—didn't take a deal of summing up. He was a man of well over sixty: the type so popular with Watch Committees not so long ago, when fine figureheads, well in with the County, seemed far more desirable than working policemen who had learned their jobs in the hard and only school. When Goodman had called Marney-Hope a gentleman he had certainly been right. He had delightful manners, urbanity and obvious tact; in fact the best type of Army officer and definitely an anti-Blimp. Goodman had been even more right when he had said his Chief was a good man to work *under* as opposed to *with*. It didn't take long to discover that Marney-Hope would leave his senior subordinates to their jobs, if only for the plain reason that his knowledge of those jobs was little more than sketchy. That he should himself suggest and undertake that business of reading Chaice's will was no interference with Goodman; it was merely an indication that he *was* Chief Constable, officially in charge of the Case and always to be taken into consideration.

Goodman introduced me to him in Chaice's room, and, as I said, I found him perfectly charming. He thanked me for what I had done, said that Wharton had most strongly recommended him and Goodman to make use of me, and then he began searching his mind for various Traverses he had known. When he mentioned at last one who had been Commandant at—in his young days, and I said that was my father, he was positively delighted, and I was at once a member of that Inner Circle in which blood has no relation to brains.

Goodman cut across those initiation ceremonies with the remark that he feared that time-list of mine wouldn't be much help after all.

"Impossible to pin the other people down," he told me. "That drawing-room seems to have been a kind of cloakroom from all I can make out. A regular sort of popping-in-and-out place, and nobody can give me any reliable times. The only fixture was Richard Chaice. Whenever anybody went in, he was there, and when they went out they left him there."

"All the same, an inside job. Don't you agree, Travers?"

"There's every indication of it," I said warily, and hoping Marney-Hope wouldn't pursue the question farther. But he did. "And only a man could have done it."

"On the face of it—yes," I said. "But that isn't to say a woman mightn't have been behind it."

He gave me a sharp look at that and then nodded genially. "Ah, yes, of course. *Cherchez la femme* and all that."

Then Harris came in to announce that everything was ready. Marney-Hope fussed a bit over his papers and then had to make a final speech before we adjourned to the drawing-room.

"I think you and Goodman will get on admirably together," he told me. "I've known the Inspector for years and he knows my opinion of him. In fact, between ourselves, we hope to be calling him Chief-Inspector very shortly."

That was handsomely said and I didn't know what to add. I did manage to get out that I was sure it was a promotion well deserved, and what little I could do I'd be pleased to do.

"You can't say more than that, my boy," he told me, and gave a preparatory clearing of the throat. "Better make a move, I think. Can't keep people on parade."

So off to the drawing-room we went. It seemed a sparse audience for that large room, and yet everybody concerned was there except the chauffeur, who was absent on service. A table had been placed for the Chief Constable, and Goodman and I sat somewhat to the side—or should I have said on the flank? I imagined the job of Goodman and myself was to watch the faces of the fortunate legatees.

I won't go into details, but here is my own summary compiled that night for future reference. The will, by the way, dated from 1942, and here are the main provisions:

(a) £10,000 pounds to Constance, together with the house and contents. Reversion of house, etc., to Martin or Kitty or their heirs at her death or on remarriage.

Poise of Constance perfect. Her eyes remained downcast and she finally dabbed at them with her handkerchief.

(b) £10,000, in trust—trustees Daine and Richard Chaice—for Martin. The principal to revert to him either at age of thirty or when he had for three consecutive years earned by his own efforts an amount of not less than five hundred a year.

Minor sensation in court. All eyes discreetly on Martin. Martin, arms folded and slightly Napoleonic, quite unmoved. Thought I caught, however, a superior smile.

(c) £7,500 to Kitty. No reservations.

Kitty smiled, then realised the lack of decorum and looked grim. Her eyes puckered and she began quietly to cry. Constance put her arm round her and in a moment the crying ceased. Martin gave the same superior smile.

(d) To Cuthbert Daine the sum of £10,000. Provisions for the literary executorship and for suitable payment for those duties and remuneration through royalties on a sliding scale.

No reaction on the part of Daine except that he buried his face in his hand at the mention of his name. Marney-Hope added that further details were with the solicitors.

(e) £1,000 to Orford Lang if still in his employ.

Lang also cupped his face in his hand, but I could see that his cheek was flushed. Constance's head turned his way and as quickly turned back.

(f) £1,000 to George Arthur Harris, or, if not in his employ, a pension of £150.

Perfect poise on the part of Harris.

(g) £1,000 to the chauffeur, or, if killed on service, the same sum to his widow and/or children.

Lastly came Richard Chaice, and why he came last I did not know, unless it was because the original provisions had stood and his peculiar circumstance had meant additions that had then demanded a new will.

(h) An annuity of £250 to Richard Chaice. If he so wished, the estate would convert the rooms above the garage into a flat for his use, and the workshop should be his property for life or until he chose to relinquish.

Richard's eyes were squinting as if he couldn't hear very well, but at the end he nodded to himself once or twice. I missed Constance's reactions, but Kitty turned and smiled at him.

That was that, except that the estate would probably amount to about £75,000. Remainder, after payment of legacies and duties, was Constance's for life. Reversion on death or remarriage to Martin and Kitty in equal shares, or their heirs.

I must say I admired Constance's self-possession as she left the room. She must have been feeling rather exultant, and yet the only thing visible on her face was a noble grief. One felt that money could not bring back a loved one; at least, that must have been what Marney-Hope thought, for he shook her solemnly by the hand, though I didn't catch the murmured words. I was following the general exit towards the dining-room. Daine turned off towards the hall and so did Lang. Richard disappeared in the direction of the servants' quarters.

"Rather rough on you, Martin," Kitty was saying.

"How do you mean?"

"Well, I don't want to sound cattish or anything like that, but it will be jolly rough if you don't earn that five hundred a year."

"I should worry," he told her flippantly. "Five hundred a year's chicken feed."

"Not out of writing poetry it won't be."

"Like to bet?" he asked her sarcastically. "Like to bet I don't make five hundred in the next twelve months?"

"I think you're hateful!"

That was all I heard, for they were entering the dining-room, and to have followed on their heels would have been a bit too obvious. What I did was to go back to Chaice's room. Marney-Hope was just preparing to leave, and I gathered that Goodman hadn't given too promising a report on the watching of reactions. He shook hands with me warmly and said he'd be seeing me again, and that when everything was cleared up I must have dinner one night.

"What now?" I asked Goodman when we'd returned to Chaice's room.

"Calling round at No. 6," he said. "Preston ought to be home at any minute now. After that I'll have another go at those timings. Something might emerge."

I asked him to let me know what happened with Preston, and that again was that. I dressed for dinner and had a chat with Daine while he finished dressing. The talk was mostly about the will. He was glad about Richard and Lang and Kitty, and very sceptical about Martin's chances. Constance wasn't mentioned, but we did agree that Austin Chaice had never been a piker. Considering what the death duties would be, it was a very liberal disposal of the estate, and pretty fair to all.

Nothing happened at dinner. Constance preferred to dine in her room after all. Martin wasn't there. Kitty said disapprovingly that he had gone down town to celebrate. As he hadn't struck me as anything of a tippler, I wondered what form the celebration would take. Daine was at the head of the table and I and Lang were with him. Richard was at the other end with Kitty. I couldn't hear what they were talking about, though they seemed cheerful enough. We were talking mostly about Chaice's unfinished novels, and that manual for detective-story writers that had brought me to Lovelands.

After dinner, which was quite late, Daine went back to his office to dictate some stuff, for the day's interruptions had left him badly behind, and the next morning he had to go to town. It wasn't always possible, he said, to get clients and certainly publishers to come down to Beechingford, so he had set aside Wednesdays for the purpose. Lang had work too, so after coffee there were three of us in the drawing-room. Richard, I noticed, hadn't got very far with his book, and while I was talking with him Kitty disappeared. Then I thought I'd get a breath of air before turning in.

I lighted my pipe in the hall, and as a light was coming from under the door of Chaice's room, I took a look in. The door was locked, but one of Goodman's men opened it and told me he was sort of night-watchman there. So I went on outdoors. The sky was a bit cloudy, and but for the sound of distant planes the air was very still. I took a few steps on the grass and then had the idea of taking a peep at that summerhouse.

That boundary line of shrubbery and pollarded poplar was nothing but an unbroken blackness, and once more I failed to hit it plumb. This time I didn't know if I was to the right or left of the summerhouse, so I turned left and by chance found it in a matter of twenty steps. It was very unnatural somehow in that darkness, and there was nothing either to see or to hear. Then as I was turning away I caught a quick flicker of light, and it was coming from inside.

It went so quickly that I thought I must have been mistaken. I listened too, and there was never a sound, and then, just as suddenly, there was the flicker again. It was coming through a window, and all those windows, as I had seen in daylight, were boarded up as a kind of permanent black-out and for protection of the glass. Once more the flicker went, and again it returned in that momentary flash. Then I knew what was happening. Someone was in that summerhouse with a torch.

I pressed my ear against the wall and listened, and there was at once a faint sound like the shuffling of feet. A moment for thought and then I gingerly hoisted a foot on the veranda and clutched a pillar to raise myself up by the most direct route. If a light could come through a window, then my eye could see inside by the same black-out crack. That was what I thought.

It was a nail that the damp had made project above the flooring of the veranda that ruined that scheme. My toe caught it as I moved forward in the dark and, though I didn't fall, I went out with a kind of lurch and my arms struck the match-boarding at my left and steadied me. But inside those empty rooms the thud of it must have been very much of a warning. I know my cheeks flushed as I cursed myself for a clumsy fool, and then I was holding my breath and listening. Almost at once there was a sound, and at first I couldn't locate it. It went, and then there was another sound—the faint squeak of a door on rusty hinges. Then I knew. Whoever it was that had been in that summerhouse, he had now nipped out by the back door and the door to the lane, and it would be hopeless for me to try to follow him.

I listened again, but there was no sound of steps. Then I tried the handle of the front door and found the door locked. Then I made a very careful way to the back door and found that locked too. And then I had an idea. Maybe it was Goodman who had been in that summerhouse, and for some reason or other he hadn't wished the fact known. What that reason was, or why he should have considered a nocturnal search desirable, was something I couldn't arrive at, though doubtless the reasons were something that had occurred to him earlier in the day when he and I and Daine had come through that splintered door from the back lane.

I tapped at the door of Chaice's room and the plain-clothes man let me in.

"Inspector Goodman been along recently?" I asked him.

He told me the Inspector had left at eight o'clock and as if for the night. I asked if he'd mind calling the station and finding out if he was there. Inside a couple of minutes I had Goodman on the line.

"It wasn't me," he said. "I've been here since about half-past eight."

"Then it was somebody who was up to no good," I said. "Might be worth an inspection in the morning, don't you think?" He said it certainly might.

One other thing happened that night, or rather in the morning before it was properly light. I was sound asleep when I was awakened by a tapping at my door. I called a "Come in!" and grabbed my glasses with one hand and switched on the bed light with the other. It was Harris.

"Sorry to disturb you, sir, but you're wanted on the telephone."

"The hell I am," I said peevishly. "Who is it, Harris?"

"Inspector Goodman, sir."

"I'll be right down," I said, and got into a dressing-gown. My wrist-watch said it was a quarter-past six.

"Travers here," I said into the receiver.

"This is Goodman, sir. About our friend Preston. He hasn't been home all night."

"The devil he hasn't!" I said. "What are you doing about it?"

"Going along now to have a look inside. I wondered if you'd like to join us. In, say, half an hour's time."

As a matter of fact I was there before Goodman arrived.

CHAPTER IX
MORE ABOUT PRESTON

GOODMAN HAD ROUTED out a member of the staff of Morlands, the agents, and now had a key to No. 6. We went in by the front door. There was quite a decent entrance hall with a cloakroom and lavatory to the far right. Doors opened to a lounge on the right, a dining-room on the left and a kitchen and scullery in the rear. Wide stairs led upwards to a landing. The first thing we noticed was that no clothes whatever were hanging on the hooks in the cloakroom.

We had merely peeped into the downstairs rooms and Goodman suggested we should go upstairs and have a look at the bedrooms. There were four of them, and a bathroom with separate lavatory. Only one room appeared to have been used. The double bed had not been made, and though there wasn't a window open, the room hadn't the smell one associates with a bedroom that has been consistently used. But we found the door ajar and Goodman thought enough air would have circulated to offset the closed windows. But the main thing we noticed at once was that drawers were left open in a couple of chests. What was more, the chests were absolutely empty, and so was the wardrobe. From a general air of untidiness it was plain that the exit had been a hurried one.

"Looks as if we're on to something at last," Goodman said. "A thousand to one he's bolted."

The other bedrooms had never been used and the furniture was covered with dust-sheets. In the bathroom was nothing but a dirty towel, still slightly damp. The toilet roll in the lavatory had been very little used, but the seat was free from dust.

"It's been a long while since a woman did any cleaning up here," Goodman said, and I agreed. Someone had gone round with a duster and had given what my old nurse used to call 'a lick and a promise'. Things like chairs, hand rails, picture rails and the pictures themselves had good coatings of dust.

Goodman called up Sergeant Smith and set him to work on fingerprints, and we made our way downstairs. The kitchen was fairly clean, but with plenty of dust in the less visible places. A couple of cups and saucers and one plate had been washed and stood on a drying-rack. In the pantry was never a sign of food except an opened tin of coffee and a couple of tins—one opened—of household milk.

"He must have had all his meals out," I said rather obviously. "Just had a cup of coffee of a morning before going out."

"It's the feeling of bareness that gets me," Goodman said, and frowned as if he didn't understand it. "It doesn't give you the idea of a house that's been lived in."

"You're a married man and Preston was a bachelor," I said. "You expect home comforts. All he wanted obviously was a place to sleep in."

"But he might have had a woman to keep the place a bit more clean."

"Women are hard to come by," I pointed out. "I'll bet every available woman in Beechingford is working at that factory."

"Well, let's have a look at the lounge and see if he put his feet on the mantelpiece," Goodman said, and in we went.

There was a distinct smell of tobacco and there was ash on the carpet, and those were the only signs that the room had ever been used. Goodman drew the black-out curtains, and at once we could see the dust in odd corners. With his gloved hands Goodman was opening the top of an unlocked desk that stood by the window. It was empty, with not even a scrap of paper or a stub pencil. Then we did find something—four letters on the mantelpiece behind one of those bronze equestrian ornaments that flanked an old-fashioned marble clock.

"Here's one thing he's missed," Goodman said, and spread out the letters so that we could see the envelopes. All were addressed to G. H. Preston, Esq. But nothing could have been more uninteresting than the contents. The first we looked at was from the Electric Light Company and giving terms for hire of electric kettles; the second from a firm in town in reply to enquiries that had evidently been made about greenhouse glass, and the third was from a Beechingford firm of stationers saying that they had heard from their agents and could entertain no more subscriptions, on account of rationing, to the *Philatelist*.

"Collected stamps, did he?" was Goodman's comment. "That is the first what you might call human thing about him discovered."

The last letter was a winner. Whom should it be from but Chaice himself!

My dear Preston,

I do *not* know of any woman who'd be likely to come in and clean your house.

As I informed you recently, I have nothing to do with your house, and if you will take all your worries to the right people—the agents—it will save you trouble and me further pestering. I am a busy man, and the sooner you appreciate the fact, the better for both of us.

Yours faithfully,

AUSTIN CHAICE.

"Very interesting," said Goodman.

"Looks as if you were right," I said, "and he been pestering Chaice about the house after all."

"Don't know yet," he said. "One thing these letters will give us, though."

He called up the stairs to Smith.

"Any luck up there?"

"Nothing at all, sir."

"Well, come down and have a shot at some letters."

Smith came down and began testing them for prints.

"You mean to say there wasn't anything on the door-handles or anywhere," Goodman interrupted him.

"Everything was wiped clean," Smith said. "Someone had been round with a duster."

"All to the good," I said. "When we do get a print, the Yard ought to be able to tell us a few interesting things about G. H. Preston."

Smith tried a couple of letters and envelopes and soon had a fine collection of prints. Chaice's was probably one of them, and from a corner of the letter he had signed. Goodman said he'd check it up at the mortuary.

"Won't the Yard have a job sorting these out, sir?" Smith said.

"What do you mean?"

"Well, there'll be the typists' prints, perhaps the sorters' and the postman's, and the people who signed the letters, like Mr. Chaice."

Goodman sighed heavily.

"It doesn't matter if there're a hundred different prints. Either the Yard's got them or it hasn't. If it's got one of them, and it's a man's print, it's a thousand to one it's Preston's."

Smith smiled sheepishly, and then there was a knock at the front door. Goodman looked at me, and then we moved off together.

"You Inspector Goodman?" asked the man who'd knocked. He looked like a professional man, and from his dark clothes and neat leather portfolio was probably on his way to catch a train to town.

"I'm Pymme, from No. 5," he said. "My wife told me you'd been enquiring there about this house and the other night."

"Come in, Mr. Pymme," Goodman said, but Pymme said he hadn't a minute to spare. Besides, what he wanted to say wouldn't take a minute. But he did step into the hall.

"A rumour's got round about burglars," he said, "and what with that and my wife telling me, Inspector, about your call, I thought I'd mention something that happened on Monday night. We've got a puppy for my little girl and I'm training him to use a cinder patch near the top of my back garden. I'd just taken him up and was waiting for him to be clean when I saw someone go running past my back gate."

"I see," said Goodman gravely. "But, pardon the question, Mr. Pymme, why did you sound surprised at anybody running?"

"You know that road?" asked Pymme. "It's never been made up and it's all potholes and puddles—or was. Whoever this fellow was, he must have been in the devil of a hurry."

"Did you actually see him?"

"Well, I saw what you might call the back of him as he went by. And I distinctly heard him pant."

"I don't suppose you could tell us where he went to?"

"I couldn't," Pymme said. "He seemed to come and go, just like that, if you know what I mean."

"You didn't hear his footsteps receding?"

"That lane isn't like a hard road," Pymme pointed out. "You wouldn't hear steps."

"And the time, Mr. Pymme?"

"Now that I can give you," Pymme said. "It would be about five or ten past nine. I always take the dog out then."

He was already moving towards the door. Goodman thanked him and said he wouldn't detain him, but if anything else cropped up he'd be glad to hear it.

"Can we fit it in anywhere?" he asked me.

I said I didn't see how. After all, anybody might have been running along that lane, and for anything. A man late for an appointment, for instance.

We had a look in the scullery and opened a cupboard or two, and by that time Smith had gone over all the letters. Goodman told him to take the car and ask the Chief to get into touch with the Yard and have the letters sent up by motor-bike. Then he told him to wait a minute.

"At what time did Preston bolt?" he was asking me. "Heaven knows," I said. "There was nobody watching this house till yesterday morning. Any time, therefore, after Chaice left the house on the Monday night and the time you put a man on watch."

"And how did he go?" He answered his own question. "The first bus leaves the corner here at six o'clock in the morning. The last at ten-thirty at night. Or he might have had a taxi."

"Or a pal might have met him with a car," I said.

"For God's sake don't make it more difficult," he told me with a grimace. "But you get to work, Smith, as soon as you've seen the Chief. See the bus people and the taxi services. You've got that description of Preston that Mr. Lang gave us at Lovelands."

"What about the railway station?"

"Fine!" said Goodman. "That'll be a short cut. Put on every man you've got."

*　*　*　*　*

"What now?" I asked when Smith had gone.

"The summerhouse," he said, but still seemed reluctant to go. He stood looking round and sniffing, and then gave a bit of a grin when he caught my eye.

"I can't make out the atmosphere of this house," he said. "There seems something wrong about it somewhere." He shrugged his shoulders. "Perhaps it's what you said about me being a married man."

"But we're getting somewhere."

"Most decidedly, we are. Preston took care not to leave any prints, and he wouldn't have done that if he hadn't been scared of his prints being found. And he wouldn't have been scared if the Yard hadn't his prints."

The relief had arrived for the man who'd been on duty all night. Goodman told him to carry on downstairs trying to find prints, and then we left. Just short of the front gate Goodman turned back.

"Let's have another look at the back garden. I've been wondering why Preston made enquiries about glass."

I'd remembered that there was a tiny greenhouse at the far end of the garden, and when we had a look at it we found quite a few panes missing.

"Probably blast," Goodman said. "We had a bomb or two about a quarter of a mile away. And now we've got so far we might as well use this back gate."

The lane was as Pymme had described it, though the puddles had mostly dried up. It wasn't a bad morning and it looked as if it might be a better. I was feeling most damnably hungry, and the sight of Lovelands as we came through that smashed-in door made me hungrier still.

"How are we going to get in?" Goodman said, surveying the summerhouse door.

I said it wouldn't take five minutes to fetch Richard Chaice, but it took longer, for I finally ran him to earth at the green-houses. He said he'd fitted that Yale lock but he hadn't a spare key. Austin had taken the two keys. The best way to get in would be to break a pane of glass and move a window catch. I asked him to go and supervise, and to tell Inspector Goodman I would be there in a couple of ticks.

I don't think I've ever gulped down a breakfast so quickly. Luckily it was well after nine o'clock and I had the wolfed meal to myself. From the time Harris set the hot dish before me till I was out of the house again was under ten minutes. But it shows the kind of detective I am, with my stomach well before duty. And it would have served me right if Goodman had gone.

As a matter of fact he was already waiting to go. The forcing of a catch hadn't taken two minutes, and there'd been nothing to see inside the summerhouse. But he did ask me if I'd like to look in.

It was a fine large summerhouse with a match-board lining. There was a tiny hall with hooks for garments, and a couple of doors that opened left and right to two quite large rooms. That on the left was a ladies' dressing-room with a lavatory. The men's room had a few chairs of the tea-room, hard-backed type and a table. The other room had a carpet that almost covered the floor, and it had four wicker easy chairs. There was a better-class table under the back window and on it stood a Victorian dressing-mirror. On the walls were few photographs of nothing in particular.

"No sign of the intruder?" I asked Goodman.

"Not that I can see," he said, "but I'll have it gone over for prints."

"What can he have been looking for?" I said. "Or if he found it, what the devil could it have been?"

"Don't know," he said. "The whole set-up's perfectly innocuous. Just a couple of dressing-rooms."

I had a look at that mirror at which many ladies must have powdered their noses, and then I saw a something on the floor. I picked it up, and it was a stoutish stick of rouge.

"One pre-war relic," I said.

He smiled. "Rather hard to come by now, so my missus tells me."

"It might be Kitty's," I said, and slipped it into my inside fob pocket. "If it isn't, she might be glad of it."

"Easy to see you're not too much of a married man," he told me with a grin. "Women are rather particular about lipstick. Depends on the clothes they're wearing and the colour of their hair."

There wasn't anything else to see, so he closed the door again and we stood for a moment on the veranda looking towards the house. Just as I was going to put my usual, "What's next?" I remembered something.

"That 'P' of the anonymous letters; do you think it might stand for Preston?"

"Don't know," he said, "but it's an idea. Chaice had choked him off, so he thought he'd be a bit spiteful. But how does it help?"

"It doesn't," I said, "except that someone had to write those letters. By the way, what *are* your people doing about that liquid-squirting?"

"We have patrols out at night," he said. "What we want is a man with his hands in his overcoat pockets. The stuff's probably squirted from a syringe through a slit in the pocket. Hardly the sort of thing you'd think a man like Chaice would have done. It doesn't seem quite in line with what I've heard of him." He sighed. "Still, there's no accounting for that kind of sex brainstorm. All sorts of men of his age make fools of themselves."

I was thinking that any man who had Constance wouldn't need to get any sex brainstorms, but I didn't put the thought into words. Then he was asking me if I felt like a job of work. What about seeing the house agents and whatever man of theirs had interviewed Preston, and so getting a more complete description? Since he was an important witness, the B.B.C. might broadcast it. I said if he'd stroll as far as the house, I'd tell them I'd be out for lunch, and then we could take a bus together.

As a matter of fact we got a ride down. Goodman hadn't told me, and there was no reason why he should, that the inquest on Austin Chaice was at eleven o'clock. Lang was attending to give evidence about finding the body, and Martin to make formal identification, and the two had ordered a taxi which we shared. The whole proceedings, Goodman said, would not take more than a quarter of an hour, and there would be an indefinite adjournment. He warned Lang and Martin that there'd be sure to be a good attendance of the Press, but he'd take steps to keep them out of the way of questioning.

"When's your father's funeral?" I asked Martin. It was a purely family affair and I hadn't liked to make enquiries.

"He's being cremated," he said. "On Friday. Daine is settling details today. Constance wanted to avoid any fuss."

He seemed very subdued that morning; possibly, I thought maliciously, because he was egg-bound with a poem. Lang was his usual reticent self, but just a bit on edge, and he owned that he wasn't anticipating that inquest with anything but alarm. Perhaps he had something very much on his conscience. A man whose trade was murder and corpses should have welcomed a little gratuitous local colour. Still, as George Wharton once re-marked to me, many a lusty baritone who bellowed 'King of the Deep am I' would be horrified at the thought of diving off Southend Pier.

I'd arranged with Goodman that we'd have a late and quick lunch at the Wheatsheaf. I had that description of Preston ready for him, and I surprised him by saying that in addition to getting details from Morland's man I'd also nipped back to Harcourt Avenue and No. 5 and had got more information from Mrs. Pymme.

This was our final draft of the broadcast message.

> In connection with the death of Mr. Austin Chaice, the police are anxious to interview a George Herbert Preston, recently of 6, Harcourt Avenue, Beechingford. He is about sixty-five years of age, five feet six in height, stoutish of build, of florid complexion, with a slightly hooked nose, and with a shortish, straggly black beard. Hair dark and grey at temples. He may also be wearing tortoise-shell rimmed glasses. Speaks as if suffering from catarrh and has a slightly foreign accent. Last seen wearing a bowler hat, muffler, dark clothes and black overcoat. Any information about this man should be communicat-

ed to either the Chief Constable, telephone Beechingford 321, or to New Scotland Yard, telephone Whitehall 1212.

The Chief Constable, Goodman told me, would at once get in touch with what Wharton would call The Powers That Be, and probably that broadcast would be put out as early as six o'clock. And that seemed all that could be done about G. H. Preston.

"One thing struck me as very peculiar when I was making those enquiries," I said to Goodman. "Not so much the limited range of people with whom he came into contact, as the fact that the range *was* so limited."

"You mean . . . ?"

"Well, take the average person who might take a furnished house here or anywhere. There's rationing and a ration card, and that means an identity number. There'd be things off the ration like a newspaper and milk and fuel."

"I get you," he said. "He went out of his way to dodge the whole lot. Didn't have a paper, got all his meals out, and used an electric fire."

"As against that," I said, "we must set the fact that he was largely driven to it. If he'd been able to get a woman to do for him—and we know he tried—then he'd probably have changed all that."

"Well, for better or worse, he's our sheet-anchor," Goodman said resignedly. "I'd give a ten-pound note to have him here."

"All the same," I said, "he must have been an ingenious devil if he killed Chaice. Take the facts as far as we've been able to prove them facts. No. 6 was under observation from me in the front and Daine in the back. When Chaice left, Preston was still there, *but he couldn't have got out.* I followed Chaice, and if he'd come out of the front door and followed me, then I'd have seen him pass me while I waited at No. 3. If he came out at the back, then Daine would have seen him. Therefore he didn't come out till after both Daine and I left. If Harris's evidence is correct, that there was a light in Chaice's room at that very time, then Preston couldn't have done the strangling."

"Wait a minute," Goodman said. "What about that man that Pymme heard running past?"

"He was running the wrong way," I said. "If he'd been running towards Lovelands, and not away from it, I admit we'd have had a good case for thinking the runner was Preston. And another thing. The time was wrong. Work it out and you'll see that the house was still under observation when Pymme heard the runner."

"Yes," he said slowly, and then brightened up. "There is, of course, one other thing." He brightened still more. "In fact I think we've got something. What about this? Preston knew the lay-out of all those houses and gardens. He knew that if you went in the front gate of any of them you could walk right past the garage and on to the back gate. Chaice knew that and nipped through the gate of No. 3. But why shouldn't Preston have come behind you and nipped in at the gate of No. 4 or 5 and so got to the back lane at the same time as Chaice? All he had to do then was follow Chaice across the lawn, hit him on the head, put his body in the room, fake the room and get back to No. 6 at his leisure. Then he packed up and made his getaway."

"Yes," I said, my tone an agreement, though there were holes in that theory that made a slab of Gruyere look solid by comparison. Knowledge of the house and the habits of its occupants, for instance, and the cutting of the telephone wires.

"Let's look on the worst side," I said. "Suppose we don't get Preston or he can prove himself in the clear. Then who's our man?"

He gave me a cautious look and asked if it need necessarily be a man.

"Kitty's definitely not a suspect," I said. "Mrs. Chaice, perhaps. But do you honestly think she could have strangled her husband?"

"Frankly, I don't," he said. "As for the men, Harris couldn't. He hadn't the strength, even if Chaice was hampered by that cloak he was wearing."

I didn't point out that no great strength was needed. To strangle a conscious Chaice—yes. But Chaice had first been knocked out by a crack on the skull, and Harris could certainly have been capable of that.

"I think we can leave Harris out," I said. "That legacy of his wasn't a motive. If Harris hasn't got far more than that salted away, then I'm a Dutchman."

"Lang doesn't strike me as the type either," Goodman said, but still as if inviting comment.

"You never know," I said. "That legacy might have come in handy too. It mightn't be a bad idea to find out his financial circumstances."

"And the brother—Richard. A harmless, inoffensive-enough old gentleman." Then he frowned. "Unless, of course, he's liable to brainstorms. There seems to have been a considerable amount of hushing-up about his mental condition."

"True enough," I said. "That's a line that might be followed. You can be in the company of people like that for months and never suspect homicidal tendencies."

"That leaves Martin," he said. "Plenty of motive in his case." He leaned forward.

"You think he's a little . . .?" He tapped his skull significantly for the rest.

"If you want my candid opinion," I said, "I think all those— what shall I call them?—symptoms of egomania are nothing of the sort. Oxford abounds with poseurs, attitudinisers, and young fools who think the *outré* is the only wear."

"You mean it's a disease of the young and he'll grow out of it." Then he grinned. "And what about Cambridge?"

He certainly had me there. In any case we didn't do any more speculating. He had a busy afternoon before him, and as I didn't want to go back to the house, I proposed spending the afternoon at a cinema. In fact I wasn't actually to see Goodman again till the next afternoon, and then under circumstances so extraordinary that if the Archangel Gabriel had revealed them beforehand I'd have told him to go and swallow his trumpet.

CHAPTER X
EXIT A SUSPECT

I would like to tell you, extremely briefly, the general lay-out at Lovelands on that Thursday morning. Kitty and Constance were in Constance's room with Mrs. Edwards, the housekeeper, and the three were busy over the adapting of certain black or dark-coloured garments to be worn by the two women at the cremation service the following day. Daine and Martin were to go too, but Richard was definitely not going.

Lang had told me that he would be spending all his time in near future in the workshop, and that's where he did spend that morning. Within a month, according to the terms of Chaice's outstanding contract, the publishers had to be in possession a manuscript. Doubtless they would have waived their right in view of the special circumstances, but Lang didn't want that and neither did I, for if a right can be waived, then a privilege can be claimed, and in less than no time a wagon and horses might have been driven through a contract. Moreover, Lang was on his mettle. He thought he could complete that unfinished novel on time, and if not he was prepared to kill himself in the attempt. As far as he was concerned, a lot depended on it, as he told me at breakfast.

Daine spent the morning in his office, for with the cremation due the following day, and the previous day having been spent in town, he had work to anticipate and arrears to overtake. Richard spent the morning putting glass in one of the greenhouses that had been damaged by blast. It was an urgent job, for chrysanthemums were going into it, and nothing spoils the blooms more quickly than the dripping of rain from gaps in the glasswork.

Martin was busy upstairs over his additions to that volume of poems. He broke off for a swim not long before lunch. I was there in time to see him come out. It hadn't been much fun, he said. It was an overcast morning and the water had been a bit cold. But his brain had been a bit tired, he told me wearily, and as he was proposing to go on working all day, he thought a spot of swimming might help. He also told me in confidence that composing was like concentrated chess, only worse. I said I could very well believe it.

I thought for a bit that morning, then I wrote up some notes on the Case and then read one of Chaice's own books. I found I'd read it before and yet I enjoyed it the second time. Chaice, I thought, was certainly an ingenious devil and the last word in mastery of suspense. In fact I stopped reading because I didn't want to finish that book too quickly, so I saved it up in case of a lazy afternoon.

Then I got Goodman on the telephone and asked if there was any news. He told me—what I already knew from Harris—that that broadcast had been put out at nine o'clock the previous night and had since been repeated. He also told me that nothing whatever had been discovered about the kind of transport Preston had used for his getaway. Questioning had also revealed that Preston had no season ticket, nor did anybody at the booking office remember a man of his description. He added that he'd be seeing me at Lovelands some time in the afternoon.

One other thing remains to do—to show you the lay-out of some of the upstair rooms. The sketch is a very rough one made for my own use, and, I should guess, considerably out of plan. But good enough for its purpose, which is to show you where various people slept, or where they happened to be spending their time that vital afternoon.

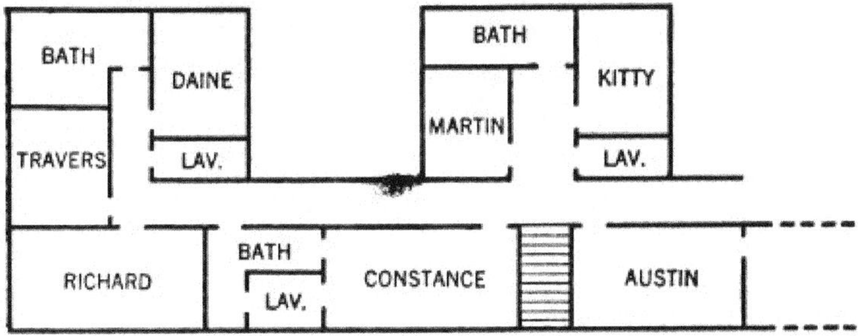

And so the afternoon itself. Daine came into lunch, and very tired he looked. He had had a harassing day in town, he told me, and that further business of the cremation had made him late. Martin had lunch upstairs and Lang had his in the workshop. It was a cold meal in any case, and so there wasn't all that extra work. Constance and Kitty made the four at the table, but they went upstairs again as soon as the meal was over, and I gathered that the dress alterations weren't going any too smoothly. One other thing I remember is that the sun chose to come out, and as Daine and I sat over coffee it felt positively hot, and even Daine seemed suddenly to become more cheerful. He had had a twinge of sciatica that made him limp slightly, and I told him, I remember, that he ought to have a short swim and then treat the sciatica to a sunbath.

What was to happen was such a bolt from the blue that I can bring the suddenness of it home to you only by telling the trivialities that preceded it. As Daine and I got up from our coffee, he remarked that he'd seen Parsley the previous day and perhaps I'd like to know what had already been done about the reprints of my books. There was also the agreement which I might as well sign, and that would save posting it to me in town.

We went up the stairs together and Daine said he wouldn't be a minute, and he wasn't. I had thought of nipping into the lavatory, but he beat me by a short head.

"Carry on," I told him, and went into my room till he should emerge. Then I went in and he waited for me. It was less than half a minute later when I heard the shriek.

A woman was shrieking and I heard the quick patter of Daine's feet and his startled, "Hallo! . . . Hallo!" as if he expected some answering explanation. I couldn't move for a moment or two, and all the time I was trying to puzzle out the direction from which that shriek had come. It had seemed curiously near and yet away from the house. And there had been no identifying of a voice, for it had been no more than a shriek, and then another, and then nothing.

It was perhaps half a minute before I was out of the door and making my way back to the stairs. Then Daine appeared, and he looked scared out of his life. He beckoned frightenedly and disappeared just round the corner. The door of Martin's room was open. Kitty was on the floor and Daine was hoisting her in his arms. Sprawled out in a chair by the window was Martin.

"Good God, what's happened?" I said.

Daine nodded back at Martin as he picked up Kitty.

"He's dead," he said. "You'd better try and get hold of that Inspector."

I wriggled by him as he went through the door. Martin lay in that chair, one hand loosely across his body and the other drooping by his side. At the angle of his forehead, just above the left temple, was a neat hole and round it a tiny seepage of blood. The window at his left was closed and fastened, and that shot must have come from the door through which Daine had just carried Kitty.

I looked round the room. There was a companion window farther back, but that was closed and fastened too. Then I saw something on the carpet beneath it, and at the foot of a huge old-fashioned mahogany wardrobe whose doors were partially ajar. It was a rifle.

I moved carefully across and had a look at it, and then I knew where I had seen it before—in that showcase of crime souvenirs in the hall. It was of French or Belgian make: a wicked-looking weapon with a stubby barrel, the whole thing not two feet in length. And then I saw something else. A string was tied round the trigger and ran back through a swivel attached to the bottom of the butt, and that string ended not far from the hand that flopped by the side of the chair.

I heard Daine calling, and the call was coming from Kitty's room. She was on the bed, propped up with pillows, and he had been bathing her face.

"She's just coming to," he said. "Do you think we ought to question her?"

Then we heard voices coming from the direction of the hall. Constance and someone were coming up the stairs. I nipped out and closed Martin's door. Constance looked surprised at the sight of me. I recognised the housekeeper, though I'd seen her only once before and at a distance.

"It's Kitty," I said. "She's fainted. Daine is looking after her in her room."

"Fainted? What on earth for?"

The housekeeper turned back to Constance's bedroom. Constance went on towards Kitty's room. I nipped into Martin's room and closed the door.

It was suicide then, I told myself, though why the devil he should have wanted to make away with himself was utterly beyond me. For the last day or two nobody could have been on better terms with life and himself than Martin Chaice. And under the window was a table on which was paper and his manuscript. There on the carpet was a pencil and an old magazine. What was the magazine for? Then as soon as I moved it carefully I saw a sheet of paper beneath it. That magazine had been used as a writing pad. He had been sitting at that window, the light well behind him, trying to compose one of those poems he had wanted for the completion of his volume.

I used my handkerchief for a glove and gently drew that sheet of paper out. It was a poem, as I had thought. Your ideas about poetry and mine may differ or coincide. Perhaps you will think I was generous to call it a poem.

REQUIEM

Grass and flesh
grass
effulgent, horrific.
flesh
voluptuous, abhorrent.
Life's integer and element.
the ultimate of death.
me and my own element
logic and illogic
and then nothing.
noth . . .

I frowned over it for a moment or two and then put it care-fully back. Maybe my lip had a slight ironic curl. What it all meant I had only the haziest notion. But if what it all amounted to was that all flesh, as the Burial Service has it, is grass, and life ends in nothingness, then Martin Chaice had ended his career as a poet in a way that was not only singularly macabre, but also uncommonly apposite.

I opened the door. Faint voices were coming from Kitty's room, so I hurried down the stairs. In the hall I stopped for a minute at that showcase. There was the space where the rifle had been, and there was the little saucer that had contained the three stubby cartridges. They had gone, but the little slip of white cardboard still had its explanatory notice.

> The rifle with which Emile Krantz killed Madame
> Decroy and her daughter at Lille.
> July 27th, 1938

I went on to the workshop; gave a quick tap at the door and entered. Lang was at his usual place beneath the window, and so busy was he at his typewriter that he didn't hear my knock or my entry. I coughed and he looked round. Then he gave his usual shy smile and got to his feet.

"Be a good fellow and do something for me," I said. "I have an appointment here with Inspector Goodman. Just ring the station and see if he's on his way. If not, tell him I want him urgently."

I had walked across to his machine.

"You type at a terrific speed," I said. "Don't you make mis-takes?"

"Sometimes," he said. "But not when I'm wound up as I am now. It's only when you're stumped for words that you're liable to be wool-gathering."

"Just my experience," I said. "Do that little job for me, will you? I'll be back in a couple of minutes to hear the result."

I nipped out by the front door and went round the house in search of Richard, and I was thinking how perfectly normal everything had been in that workshop. Never a sign of fluster on the part of Lang, and a complete absorption in his work. Not that Martin hadn't killed himself. Still, it was just as well to make sure just where people had been at the time of the firing of the shot.

I went through the gate to the walled garden and the greenhouses, but there was no sign of Richard there. An elderly gardener was working fairly near and I hollered to him. He said I might find him in the garage.

He was there sure enough, and he was deep in one of his fits of abstraction. I watched him as he stood there with his back to me, arms before him on the carpenter's bench, and then I gave a loud cough and went in. He seemed to blink his eyes for a moment before he recognized me, and then he gave me that gentle smile of his.

"No work for you today, sir, I'm afraid."

"What are you doing yourself?" I asked him.

He showed me. He had used up most of his small keg of putty and what was left was a bit hard, so he was remaking it with linseed oil and rubbing it to the right consistency with his hands.

"Not much in my line," I told him with a smile, added that I'd be seeing him later, and then hurried back to the house. Goodman's car had just drawn up and he and Lang were in the hall.

"Here *is* Mr. Travers," Lang said. "I was just going to report, sir, that the Inspector was on his way."

I took Goodman into Chaice's room and told him what I knew and what I'd done. Just as he was about to telephone for his doctor, in came Daine.

"Sorry," he said. "I was only going to telephone."

Kitty had come round and had told Constance what had happened. Then Constance had collapsed. Mrs. Edwards had got her to bed, and now Daine wanted to get the doctor to have a look at both the women. Then it happened that the Chaice doctor was Goodman's man. Goodman got him while Daine waited, and then the three of us went upstairs.

Kitty was sitting in a chair by the window. She had been crying, and it was a relief, perhaps, that she had.

"How are you feeling now, my dear?" Daine asked her and put an arm round her shoulder.

"I'm all right," she said, and gave a last dab at her eyes.

"Think you could answer a simple question or two?" I smiled at her.

She said she could, so I asked her just what had happened. It was a perfectly simple account. In Constance's room there had been a sudden shortage of material, but Mrs. Edwards had said she had a lot of odds and ends in her room and perhaps there'd be something there. So she and Constance had gone off to that room and Kitty had gone to her bedroom intending to have a private try-on of an almost completed dress. Then she heard a sudden crack like a shot. It had come from Martin's room, so she went to explore. She remembered seeing him lying back in the chair with the bullet hole in his head, and then she shrieked. That was all she remembered till she came to in her room.

"Just one other question," I said. "When you first looked in that room the window was closed?"

"It *was* closed," she said. "I remember now that I thought how stuffy he was, going to sleep with the window shut."

We left her there with the injunction to lie quiet till the doctor had seen her, and then we went to Martin's room. Goodman wanted Daine and me to compare times before he did any looking around.

"Did either of you gentlemen hear the shot?" he wanted to know.

"I did," Daine said. "Mind you, I didn't know then what it was, but I heard something like a sharp crack. I didn't mention the matter because it wasn't exactly an opportune time." He smiled rather sheepishly as he looked at me. "We happened to be having a friendly argument as to who should use the lavatory first."

"That's right," I said. "There wasn't exactly an argument. An unspoken one, if you like."

"And then you both heard the shriek?"

We explained all that, but what we couldn't do was calculate the precise moment at which the shot had been fired. It was while Daine and I stood in the corridor before the lavatory, that much was certain, and the nearest we could arrive at a time was five minutes past two.

Goodman took a note or two, then had a good look round while we stayed by the door. He agreed that Martin had been writing, and he also drew out the sheet of paper and read it before replacing it.

"Requiem. That's a funeral poem, isn't it?"

"Is that what he was writing?" cut in Daine.

"That was the title," Goodman told him. "A bit beyond me, though. And it wasn't finished."

"Might I have a look at it?" Daine asked.

Goodman drew it out and held it for him. Daine put on those reading spectacles of his and read it. Then he shrugged his shoulders. Then he looked bewilderingly at me.

"What was he doing? Writing it for himself?"

"Lord knows!" I said. "But if he was, then it might have been his final comment on the futility of a life he was just about to end." Then I gave a shrug of the shoulders. "Not that I necessarily agree with that explanation."

Goodman stepped over to the gun.

"I see," he said, and looked back at where the string ended. "When he pulled the string, the fact that it went back through the swivel made it pull the trigger. But where was the stock of the gun fastened to?"

I said I didn't know, unless it had been held in some way between the doors of the wardrobe.

"We'll test that later," he said. "But first I'd just like to see the other rooms. Where you two gentlemen were, and so on."

He locked the door behind him and pocketed the key. A couple of minutes and he had a good idea of the scene which I'd described. Daine had been looking a bit worried.

"Would you mind coming in my room for a moment, Inspector? You, too, Travers."

"I don't know how this is going to work out," he began, and none too confidently. "What I mean is, I don't know whether he shot himself or someone else shot him. If it was someone else, then there's something I ought to tell you."

He added that he was a busy man and getting in more and more of a muddle with his work on account of what had happened. So he'd rather volunteer a statement and save subsequent questioning if the facts came to light. What he then told Goodman was about Martin and the manuscript and how he'd intended to string him along. The Inspector might think it sharp practice, he added, but there it was. And it also, in a way, gave him a sort of profit out of Martin's death.

"I don't think you need worry about that, sir," Goodman told him. "You had nothing to do with the actual shooting, so why worry. Unless"—he frowned for a moment—"unless he found out what you intended to do, and that dispirited him, so to speak, and led him to killing himself."

"Oh, no," said Daine grimly. "When I have in mind business of the sort I've described to you, nobody finds out. It's in here," and he tapped his skull. "I mentioned it to Mr. Travers, but that amounts to the same thing."

"That's true," I said. "I'd never have mentioned it, least of all to Martin."

"Well, we won't keep you further, Mr. Daine," Goodman said. "Thank you very much for what you've done."

He and I went down to Chaice's room again, where he did some telephoning: I strolled out politely to the hall, but I couldn't help knowing that he was talking to Marney-Hope. It was five minutes before he called me in, but first I showed him where the rifle had come from.

"Three shells, were there?"

"Either three or four," I said.

"Then they should be in the magazine," he said, and closed the door of the room.

"Tell me confidentially," he said, "and before our people get here to test for prints and so on. Did he kill himself, or didn't he?"

"You know as much as I do," I told him. "The only thing that struck me as strange was that he should have shot himself, in the act, as it were, of writing, and in the very chair."

He nodded. "And the fact that the poem was unfinished?"

"I wouldn't place too much reliance on that," I said. "Those futurist poets, or whatever they call themselves, do queer things. Leaving the poem unfinished may have been intended as a kind of symbol. And the pencil hadn't trailed off as if he'd been shot while the pencil was actually in contact with the paper. Also there weren't any corrections, so we can take what he wrote as the final copy."

"I see that," he said. "And he hadn't seemed depressed to you?"

"Far from it. After he put that fast one across Daine—as he thought he had—he seemed to me to be absolutely cock-a-hoop. And another thing. It's a purely personal impression, by the way. I told you how this house was saturated with Austin Chaice's work, and how he dominated it, and how work dominated him. I think Martin had inherited something of the same kind. He was just as mad about his own kind of work as his father was about his. But he couldn't dominate anybody, and he couldn't even get anybody, except perhaps Mr. Chaice, to regard him and his work as anything but waste of time. That led to his nervous repressions, and may have ended in mania. After all," I added, and rather feebly, "the law assumes madness in the case of suicide."

"It's a damn good argument," he told me, and I thought he was being far too generous. I'd have liked to go over it all again and to have put it more clearly.

"But let's look at that other side again," he was going on. "We can't do anything till Smith gets here. Suppose, then, he was shot. It seems to me that only two people could have done it—or three."

I told him what I'd done about Lang and Richard Chaice. Either could have nipped up those stairs and done the shooting for all I knew. Then I asked him who was the third.

"Not Mrs. Chaice," he said. "She'd gone with the housekeeper to—"

"It may need checking," I reminded him. "She might have made some excuse and left the housekeeper's room."

"That's so," he said. "But Kitty is the one I was thinking of. Mind you," he added quickly, "I don't say she's the type. But she might have done the shooting and then the shrieking."

"There's no denying the *might*," I said. "But one thing we do know now. We know someone who didn't do any shooting, and that's our friend G. H. Preston."

"I wouldn't be so sure, sir," he told me surprisingly. "After all, we don't know where he is. He might still be here in Beechingford."

Just then a car was heard outside. It was the doctor, a mild-looking, philosophic sort of chap, as many doctors are. At least he told us his first duty was to the living, and he'd have a look at the two ladies and then join us in Martin's room. Before he was hardly upstairs, two more cars arrived. One was the Chief's and the other Sergeant Smith with what's often called the menagerie—two camera men and some oddments.

Marney-Hope looked worried.

"A damn bad business," he told us as we went upstairs. "Bad for the town. The wrong sort of publicity."

He stood just inside the door with me while the photographs were being taken. I had a good look at Martin's face. It showed neither frightened anticipation nor surprise. There was a pallor that made the eyes more dark, perhaps, but to me it was merely the face of Martin calmly asleep. Not that one can gather much from faces.

The doctor came in, but there was nothing he could do. The time of death was established already, and all he could say was that death had been instantaneous. Goodman asked him to be good enough to get the ambulance along. The sooner the bullet was extracted and checked with the gun, the better. Then we waited till Smith had gone over the gun for prints. There seemed to be few, but in the right places. Goodman ejected the spent shell and said there were two more still in the breech. I had been giving a running commentary: telling Marney-Hope where the gun came from and so on.

"That's all we can do now," Goodman said, and Smith helped him lay the body on the bed. Then, while the gun was being photographed, he went through the pockets and made an inventory. The wallet looked as if it might be interesting, for it had two letters from publishers to whom that manuscript had been submitted.

Another ten minutes and the room was clear except for the three of us.

"Well, what is it?" Marney-Hope said. "Suicide or what?"

"Can't say, sir," Goodman told him frankly. "It all depends on whether or not he could have kept the gun rigid while he pulled the string."

We went over to the wardrobe and had a look. First it was agreed that if Martin had placed the gun, then he had placed it parallel with the floor and on an exact level with his head. Next we took his actual pose, a half-right turn towards the door, and so calculated that the gun must have rested on the second shelf of the wardrobe with the doors partially closed to hold it in place. As we didn't want to mess up the gun with prints, we substituted a pincushion from the dressing-table which was about the thickness of the stock.

But it just couldn't be done. When we closed the twin doors there was nothing to hold them in place against the pincushion. If the doors had been a tight fit, then it might have been different, but they weren't. And there was nothing on the shelves sufficiently solid to have been packed against the sides of the gun stock to hold it firmly enough to resist the pull of the string.

"And yet it came out and fell on the floor," the Chief said.

"Not necessarily," Goodman said. "My idea is it never was held anywhere." He smiled rather grimly. "Unless it was by the one who shot him."

"Yes, but if someone came to that door and shot him, why did he leave the gun there? It's common sense that he'd have gone off like a streak and taken the gun with him."

"I see your point, sir," I said. "He daren't have risked coming in the room and laying that gun down where it was found. But wait a minute," I said. "Why the string then? Surely there wasn't any need for the string? If he was shot, then the one who shot him pulled the trigger."

"I don't get you," Marney-Hope said.

"It boils down to this," I told him. "Since there was that string on the gun, then either Martin Chaice committed suicide or else the gun was planted to give the impression that he committed suicide. The string proves it."

"That's just it," said Goodman and then frowned. "There's just one other possibility. He might have been experimenting in some way. An idea for a story, or something. Then the gun went off before he expected. Or he forgot it was loaded."

"I don't want to be difficult," I said, "but while that might apply to some people, it couldn't apply to Martin Chaice. He loathed detective fiction. The last thing he'd do would be to experiment with a gun."

The ambulance came and the body was taken away. Goodman came upstairs again and the arguments went round and round and got us nowhere. Marney-Hope said he would have to go, and I suggested that he should send that gun to the Yard so that an expert could determine if the prints were consistent with the use to which Martin had presumably put it. Marney-Hope said it was a good idea and he'd see to it himself.

It was then about four o'clock. I had the drawing-room to myself for tea. Harris was in a terrible state of dither.

"What's going to happen, sir?" he said to me. "Are we all going to be murdered in our beds?"

I told him he was talking rubbish and he must pull himself together. Martin had committed suicide, and that was all there was to it. Bad enough, but a long way off murder.

"It's the women, sir," Harris said, and mopped his brow. "And it's a judgment on the house, sir, if you ask me. All this writing about murders. Nothing but murders."

Before I'd eaten more than a few mouthfuls in came, or rather looked, Orford Lang.

"Is it true, sir, about Martin?" His eyes were bulging. Harris had obviously just taken in his tea and spread around a little more gloom.

"That he's committed suicide—yes," I said.

His eyes bulged again, and then he closed the door and I got on with my tea. I'd almost finished when the door opened again and in came Richard. He looked upset too.

"Is it true, Mr. Travers, about Martin?" There was something infinitely pathetic about the way he asked that simple question.

"Who told you?" I asked him.

"Mr. Lang," he said.

"Yes. It is true. It's a bad business, Richard, but it's true."

He shook his head, and I thought for a moment he was going to relapse into one of those fits of abstraction. Then he said a queer thing. I can see him now as he stood there, slowly shaking his head again.

"There was nothing I could do. . . . The other, yes. . . . But not him."

I went over to him. There was something he knew, and at all costs I had to know what it was.

"Listen, Richard," I said, and my hand was gently on his shoulder. "If there's anything you know about Martin's death, or Austin's, it's your duty to tell me."

"But I knew nothing," he said. "Nothing at all till Mr. Lang told me." He was slowly moving back. "And now, if you'll excuse me, sir, I'll be getting back to my work."

I grasped his arm.

"Listen, Richard," I said again. "The other day you told me there was something you knew. Something you might have told Austin before he died. If you hadn't thought you were mis-chief-making. What was it you could have told him?"

"Nothing," he told me, and his voice had an unexpected as-perity. He shook his head again and the tone became milder. "You mustn't listen to all I say, sir. I'm absent-minded some-times and I mix things up." He nodded to himself. "That's it. I mix things up."

Then he was gone. I didn't feel like any more tea, and I was thinking that all that was needed now was for Daine to come in and ask a few questions. So I went upstairs and had a wholly unnecessary bath. I lingered it out, and just when I had finished dressing, Harris came up to tell me that Inspector Goodman would like to see me downstairs.

Goodman had his car and wanted me to go down town for a conference with the Chief. The Chief had the wind up, he said, and thought things had gone too far for the Beechingford police to handle.

The rest of that evening was a nightmare of argument and indecision. It was eight o'clock before Marney-Hope made up his mind to call in the Yard. Dinner was over when I got back to Lovelands, but Harris found something for me. At about a quarter to ten I was called to the telephone. It was George Wharton. His tone was dry and official.

"You're catching the ten o'clock tomorrow morning," I said. "If it will help, I'll come up by the eight from here and we can come down together."

"Might be an idea," he said.

"And another thing, George. If you'd like to read through my notes beforehand, I can get them through to you tonight."

"Make it my private address," he said. "I'm going there now." I rang Goodman, and by the time the notes had been collected it was half-past ten. I looked in the drawing-room and everyone seemed to have gone to bed. The house had an eerie and empty silence that suddenly gave me the horrors, and at once I went up too. And, for one of the few times in my life, I turned the key of my bedroom door.

PART III

CHAPTER XI
WHARTON LOOKS ROUND

I HAD COME by an early train because it was necessary for me to look in at my flat and fetch a few things that I might be needing, for there was no telling how long I might now be detained at Beechingford. At the flat I had breakfast, for I had not wished to upset too much the normal routine at Lovelands, what with Constance upstairs in a case of real or feigned collapse, and Kitty and Daine with that cremation in front of them.

I got back to the station fairly early and thought I'd try to get a *Times*. But there wasn't one, and I was running my eye over the latest books when the bookstall assistant sidled up expectantly.

"Got anything by Austin Chaice?" I asked.

"Nothing at all, sir," he told me, and smiled tolerantly. "We didn't have many in stock, and this murder business made a rush on them. But here's something very good, sir."

I have learned to be suspicious of the recommendations of most sellers of books. Maybe I am wrong, but I still rather suspect I have bought in my time a good few volumes that might otherwise have gone on cluttering up the stock.

"How do you know it's good?" I asked.

"I've read it myself, sir. And one or two of our regulars have said so too."

I had a look at it—*The Frozen Alibi*, by Langford Orr. I didn't want the book, but there are times when I lack moral courage. Or maybe the assistant was a good salesman; at any rate I bought it, and thought rather guiltily that there was eight and sixpence squander-bugged. Then I went off to place myself strategically for the arrival of Wharton.

In a couple of minutes he was coming through the barrier, and he was well on time. It had taken me a moment or two to recognise him, for instead of the overcoat with the velvet collar, he was wearing what looked like a brand-new grey one. But the rest was much about the same. There was the leather bag with its ancient labels; there was the hunch of the shoulders and the same vastly protuberant moustache. And there he was darting looks this way and that from under his monumental eyebrows, and doubtless telling himself that not a soul suspected he was looking at a real live Superintendent straight from Scotland Yard. When he caught sight of me his face puckered with geniality.

"Here you are, then. Got me a seat?"

I told him I'd done better still—got what looked like being a first-class compartment to ourselves. And so it was to prove, not that there had been anything to boast about. The train was only a glorified local, and when it pulled out it must have been nine-tenths empty.

"Mind if I hang on to those notes of yours?" he asked me.

I told him he could keep them as long as he liked. I almost tapped my skull with one of Daine's gestures to show I had their contents well in mind. What I did ask was whether they'd been any use. He told me, with a deprecatory pursing of the lips, that notes were all very well, but there was nothing like seeing things for one's self.

"Too early to ask if you've got any ideas?"

He glared at me at that. Then his look altered.

"Couldn't be one of these tontine cases, could it?" He didn't ask me if I knew what a tontine was, but gave himself the trouble of an explanation. "You know, where the survivor takes all."

"In this case you mean that Constance Chaice would take all?"

"More or less," he said, with a wave of the hand that was intended to indicate vagueness. "First Chaice is murdered and that puts the money into circulation. Then this Martin Chaice is done in and there's another little ten thousand put in the kitty."

"In other words, you're wondering who's going to be the next."

He temporised. "Well, I suppose it's an idea that has occurred to you?"

I dodged the question with what I thought considerable subtlety by asking if the dangers he anticipated weren't the main reason for the calling in of the Yard.

It was only then that I realised a subtlety of his own. Why had he mentioned Martin Chaice's murder?

"Anything definite about that gun that was sent up?" I asked him.

He said the experts hadn't made up their minds, and then he was asking rather too quickly if I really thought as much of Inspector Goodman as my notes had made out. You see the tortuousness of a mind which can suspect that even one's private notes may possibly be faked. What I did protest was that that would be like cheating at patience.

"Well, I've asked for his services," George said. "We don't want that Chief Constable round our necks, but we might have to use his men."

"A good idea," I said, but what I was wondering was how Goodman would react to George. Rather like the simian-looking man in *Punch* who told the Zoo attendant that he was just tickled to death at being about to see the chimpanzee, but hadn't dreamt of wondering what the chimp would think of him. Then as I shifted in my corner I felt something hard in my pocket, and I pulled it out.

"What's that?" asked George, suspicious at once.

"Just a book I bought," I said, and then I stopped short. Then I passed it over to him. "See anything unusual about it?" He pursed his lips till they were visible under the moustache. "Can't say I do."

"What about the author's name?"

"Langford Orr." He looked a bit annoyed. "Conveys nothing to me."

"Try it as a Spoonerism," I said.

"A Spoonerism?" Then I saw he had it. "Orford Lang. Chaice's secretary!"

"That's it," I said. "And do you recall an occasion when there was a discussion at the dinner-table and—"

"Let me think it out for myself," he told me impatiently. "A discussion at the dinner-table. Chaice said he could write a detective story round anybody. Round this Lang. Hinted that Lang had broken an agreement and had published a book on his own, and that gave him a motive for murder."

"That's it," I said. "I thought it was merely a hypothesis, made up on the spur of the moment. Apparently it wasn't."

"Then we've got something," George said, wagging the book at me. Then his eyes opened still wider. "Wait a minute, though. Isn't this the Lang you suspected of having an intrigue with Mrs. Chaice—as you called it?"

"The very same."

George gave that look which I've often called his Colosseum one: the sort of leer that must have come over the face of one of Nero's lions at the sight of a particularly plump Christian. Then he said nothing for a good few moments, and then he was producing those notes of mine from his bag and consulting them.

"I thought I wasn't wrong," he suddenly announced. "Chaice gave two instances that night. He said Daine had a motive too. Daine had—"

"No, no, no," I cut in. "Chaice didn't say anybody had done anything. It remained hypothesis. And I think he quoted Daine so as to bring in Lang. Daine's was very definitely a hypothetical case, and it was a cloak for telling Lang about breaking that contract."

"There's nothing about that here," he said, rapping his knuckles on my notes. "Besides, why shouldn't he have found out that Daine had been doing him down?"

"It's all in the notes," I told him patiently. "If a client is as shrewd a business man as Chaice undoubtedly was, then Daine couldn't have swindled him."

"Have it your own way," he said, but made a note in his own book nevertheless. And then he had to approach it from another angle.

"Why couldn't this Daine have done the murders?"

"No reason at all," I said. "Provided you hadn't read my notes."

"No reason to lose your temper," he told me wheedlingly. "It's only a hypothesis."

"Then the answer is that he just couldn't," I said. "He has a perfect alibi for Chaice. As for Martin, Daine was never out of my sight. Mind you," I added, "I did have to take him into consideration. In our game we have to suspect our own mothers. I did wonder if Daine might somehow—somehow is what they call the operative word—have managed to shoot Martin through his bedroom window when he was in there, and just before he and I collided outside the lavatory. The question answered itself. Martin's windows were closed. You can't shoot through glass and leave no trace. Also I heard no shot. And how did Daine get the gun in the room?—assuming it was the same gun. And where was Daine's motive? He was handling Martin very well indeed. Even if he wasn't, that manuscript wasn't a sufficient motive."

"Then only that Richard Chaice is left," he told me surprisingly mildly. "What about him?" Then he actually chuckled. "I know what you're going to say. It's all in the notes."

I said he was wrong. What I was going to say was that he'd better be getting his things together, for this was Beechingford.

Marney-Hope was at the station with his car, and he had some surprising news for us. An arrest had been made in connection with that liquid-squirting, and in an unexpected way. A woman had got in touch with the police and had said that she'd smelt creosote on her lodger's overcoat. It was in a wardrobe where he kept it locked, but he didn't know she had a spare key. In a special silk-skin pocket of that overcoat the police found plenty of traces of creosote and a syringe. The man—an Eire Irishman—had been brought in from the factory where he worked, and only a few minutes ago he had made a confession.

"Those anonymous letters to Mrs. Chaice were fakes then," Wharton said.

"We've more or less known that the last day or two," Marney-Hope told him. "The business was still going on after Chaice's death."

Wharton shot a look at me, but I took care not to notice, even though something had happened which was not in the notes. Then we were at headquarters. I wasn't explicitly asked to go in, so I stayed in the car, and then went in search of Goodman.

He was having a cup of tea in his room, so I joined him. Over it I gave him certain guarded information about George and his methods. He seemed to understand; at least he grinned and said it took all sorts to make a world. Then the phone went. I guessed it would be the Chief asking for him, and maybe me too; but it wasn't.

"Ah! Good morning, Harris. . . . You don't say! . . . Wait a minute and I'll jot that down."

There were several 'yeses' and an assurance that the matter would be seen into, and then he rang off.

"Richard Chaice has gone!" he announced.

"You mean bolted?"

"Don't know what to call it," he said. "Old Harris wondered why he hadn't come in to the usual early breakfast, so he went along to the garage, but he wasn't there. Later on, when he had more time, he made more enquiries and nobody had seen anything of him that morning."

"What did he take with him?"

"Two bags he had and all his things. Not his tools. Everything in the garage is perfectly normal."

"Bed slept in?"

"Dammit, I forgot to ask him. Sort of took it for granted that he left this morning."

"This morning would have been a good time," I said. "You not there and I away. Daine and Kitty going up to town. Mrs. Chaice in bed."

The buzzer went then, and this time it was for the pair of us. Everything appeared to have been agreeably settled, and almost as soon as Goodman had been introduced, Wharton was saying with a specious reluctance that he supposed we'd have to be getting on with the job.

Goodman drove the car. George sat in front and I at the back. First we stopped at the Flagon, not a bad little inn-hotel within three hundred yards of the Harcourt Avenue bus stop, and there George expressed himself as satisfied with the room Goodman had reserved for him, and there he left his bag. Then we began the tour of inspection.

There's no need for details, but it was well after two o'clock when I at last got some lunch. George had to see for himself everything at No. 6, and all the time he was consulting those notes of mine, and with the attitude of one ready to pounce on the least omission. Then he had to go through the garden of No. 3, and so on to the summerhouse. Next came the annexe at Lovelands, with an inspection of the wire outside Daine's room. Then he saw the garage and what was left of the cord. Goodman assured him that it was the cord from which had been cut the piece that had strangled Chaice.

Then came the house itself. George's nickname at the Yard is 'the Old General', and though the name may have in it both admiration and affection as well as wrath, that tour of ours that late morning and early afternoon was worse than any General Inspection that the Army ever inflicted. Not that he wasn't right to see things for himself. It was the little bits of by-play that took up the time, and more than once Goodman caught my eye and winked.

The last thing George did was to see Harris. Once more Harris was all of a dither, especially when George froze him with one of his official stares.

"You don't *know* if he left last night? You knew if the bed had been slept in or not, didn't you?"

Harris ventured a quavering yes.

"Then he left this morning," George grumbled. "Hear any sound of a taxi?"

Harris had heard nothing. George nodded and then clapped the old boy on the shoulder. If there were more witnesses like Harris he'd be very pleased.

"Thank you, sir," said Harris, who was looking suspicious nevertheless.

"Mumbling old fool," George grunted when he'd gone. Then for an anxious moment we wondered if there was anything else he could possibly not have seen, but it was mercifully a false alarm. George took a look at his watch, said he was feeling a bit peckish, and he might as well be getting back to the Flagon. He also said that Goodman was to remind him to take all the keys, for he'd rather like to take another look at No. 6 on his own. Unless there was anything to the contrary, he'd meet me and Goodman at Lovelands at four o'clock.

I promptly rang for Harris and my lunch, and I took the precaution of ordering a cup of tea for a quarter to four. Then no sooner had my spoon dipped in the soup than Harris was telling me I was wanted on the telephone. When I asked who it was he said the gentleman wouldn't say, but he thought it was the gentleman who had questioned him about Mr. Richard. My heart sank as I said what I guessed might be a final farewell to that soup.

"Ah! There you are," George said. "About that disappearance of Richard Chaice. Did he take his ration book with him?"

I said, naturally, that I didn't know.

"Extraordinary how I have to think of everything," he told me, and not without a recognisable gratification. "Wherever he's gone, he's got to have a ration book, hasn't he? Even if he's thinking of staying at a hotel."

I said I'd make enquiries from whoever kept the books.

"You needn't ring me up," he said. "This afternoon will be soon enough. But if he hasn't taken the book, then you can bet he's intending to come back."

I returned to my almost cold soup. Harris came in with the next course and I mentioned the matter of the book. I don't know why, but the question seemed to catch him clean in the wind. Maybe he was thinking of another inquisition with Wharton and a charge of negligence.

"The book *has* gone, sir," he told me when he came back.

"Who keeps the books?" I asked him. "Mrs. Edwards?"

"Mrs. Edwards, sir," was his echo.

"She gave it to him?"

"No, sir. She hasn't any idea how it came to be missing."

"Maybe I'd better see her," I told him, and off went Harris with an obvious relief.

To Mrs. Edwards the whole thing was a mystery. She kept the ration books in a drawer, admittedly one to which everybody on the staff had access, and that went roughly for Daine's staff too. She was sure Mr. Richard would never have taken it, even if he had known where it was.

That was that, and I finished my meal. Then as I sat over my coffee I thought I'd have a look through that detective novel of Lang's. Then I realised that Wharton had never given it back to me. Maybe, then, he was thinking of Lang as the best immediate suspect; and if so, it would not be long before Lang learned something at first hand of the gentle art of questioning. That Wharton's artillery would soon be brought to bear I had no doubt. Like a good general, he had already made a rough survey of the ground, and at that very moment he was supplementing it with a more detailed and private inspection. Before the day was out he would have the details of those notes of mine fixed in his wily old brain, and things would begin to happen.

That, as I could tell myself, was why he had shown neither perturbation nor alarm at the sudden disappearance of Richard Chaice. All in good time, George was saying to himself. First fit Richard Chaice into the scheme of things, and then the significance of his disappearance could easily be assessed, and if then it were necessary to find him, found he would be.

I finished a pipe and was then at a loose end. It was true I had that book of Chaice's to finish, but somehow I didn't feel like reading. Then the thought of that book brought something back to my mind. Lang was finishing the two novels, but what about that manual of detection? If Lang was going to finish that too, then I had an interest in seeing that the information I'd given Chaice was properly used. And I ought to ensure that Lang implicitly understood that my name was in no case to be mentioned.

I tapped at the workshop door, and there was Lang typing away, as usual, for all he was worth.

"I don't want to disturb you," I began, and at once he was assuring me that he'd be glad to have a few minutes' rest.

"How are the books going?" I asked him. "Up to schedule?"

"Slightly ahead," he told me, and allowed himself to look pleased.

I broached the subject of the manual. Was I right in imagining that most of it had been written?

"Quite a lot—yes," he said. "Mr. Chaice was using a different method. A novel's written straight out. There may be modifications if new and better ideas happen to turn up, but generally it runs straight on."

"And the manual doesn't."

"That's right," he said. "Mr. Chaice wrote odd chapters as they occurred to him, irrespective of whether they made a sequence or not."

He saw I wasn't following any too well, and at once he was bringing out a paper from a filing cabinet.

"This is the complete outline of the book," he said, "as Mr. Chaice finally drafted it. I don't say it wouldn't have been further modified. For instance, we've already incorporated the information you gave Mr. Chaice. I'd just completed that on the day he was . . . the day he died."

This was the outline he showed me:

PART I

General Information
    (Poe, Gaboriau, Wilkie Collins, Conan Doyle)
New Scotland Yard
Method of Detection
    (a) Inductive
    (b) Deductive
    (c) Scientific
Toxicology and Medical Jurisprudence
    The Psychological Element
The Taking of Statements
Court Procedure

PART II

On Writing Generally
Murder as a Fine Art

He had been watching me critically while I read, and as soon as I'd finished he was pointing something out.

"I think I made what may sound like a mistake," he said. "This is the draft of both the editions, English and American. The same framework for both, if you follow me. But the American edition won't have purely English chapters, like the ones on Scotland Yard and Court Procedure, and other details have to be modified. Mr. Chaice got in touch with an American official some months ago and he's already got all the material. But the English book is virtually finished."

"What a stickler he was for accuracy!" I said. "I'll bet that he interviewed American detectives over here on service."

"To tell the truth, he did, sir. But the best way, don't you think?"

"Undoubtedly," I said. "But did I gather that the English version is practically finished? If so, I was merely going to suggest that you let me see the proofs when they come out."

"I'll make a note of it at once," he told me, and while he was doing so I asked what parts weren't actually completed.

"This one here, on the scientific method," he said, "and this one in Part II on the amateur detective."

"The scientific method ought to be easy," I pointed out. "There are no end of books one can consult."

"I don't know, sir," he said, and did a bit of frowning. "Will you keep it to yourself if I tell you something?"

"Most certainly."

"Well, it's rather hard to put into words," he said, "but there were some things about which Mr. Chaice would be extraordinarily secretive. I'd no idea what I was going to type till he gave me the rough manuscript or began dictating."

"Just what sort of things?"

"Well, this scientific method, for instance. I said what you just said, that there were reference books, and he rather snapped my head off. He said he was going to try certain things out at first hand. And the same with that chapter on the amateur detective." He paused for a moment. "I've wondered if he wasn't making some experiments on his own."

"What sort of experiments?" I persisted.

"I can't say, sir. Doing things at first hand, perhaps. Trying out theories personally."

"Like that famous typewriter business?"

"Well, yes, perhaps," he said, and actually flushed as if the episode had been a personal discredit. "He had very strong view of his own. Perhaps too strong. Remember that letter he wrote to *The Times* about a month ago about the use of disguise, after someone had said it was a very out-of-date method of—well, detection."

"I think I do remember it," I said. "But Chaice, if you ask me, was what they call an incurable romantic. He loved all that Gaboriau stuff. He saw himself as Lecoq . . ."

My voice rather trailed off there. I had been leaving the room and he had followed me courteously to the door, and just then there was the sound of a car. The door opened and in came Kitty and Daine. Both were looking tired.

"Hallo, Orford," she said, and gave him a wan smile.

"Hallo, Kitty."

I don't know if he smiled back, for at the moment she was smiling at me.

"A trying day you must have had," I told her.

"Just one of those things," she said. "But I'm dying for a cup of tea."

"Abominable food in town nowadays," Daine said. "I think I'd like some tea too."

"I'll see to it," Lang said, and was making a move at once. The three of us went up the stairs together. Kitty turned off into Constance's room, and Daine and I went on.

"Nothing happening here, I suppose," he asked me.

I told him about the arrival of Wharton, and we chatted while he had a wash. We were in his room, which was why I didn't hear the arrival of the second car, but as we went by Constance's door I heard voices, and I could have sworn that one of them was Wharton's. Then I saw Harris downstairs and he told me that Wharton and Goodman had arrived, and that Wharton had requested an interview with Mrs. Chaice. Constance had raised no objections, and after a minute or two she had rung down that she was ready.

Goodman was in Chaice's room. He had been setting things in motion to try to discover how Richard Chaice had got away from Lovelands with two suitcases—the same routine, in fact, that had been used in the case of the disappearing Preston. After we'd guessed at the questions Wharton was asking Constance Chaice, and why, Harris came in to say that tea was ready in the drawing-room and Mr. Wharton was there.

We found him installed on a large settee between Kitty and Lang. When he so pleased he could exhibit the most ingratiating of manners, and now he was obviously very much at home, though the least bit subdued, as befitted the occasion. He had managed, too, to spring the bombshell of Richard's disappearance on Kitty and Daine, and that was the topic of conversation as Goodman and I came in.

"The poor darling," Kitty said. "I'm sure he must be having one of those fits of his. Surely something can be done about him! Can't you do something, Orford?"

Wharton gently cleared his throat and relieved Lang of embarrassment.

"We'll find him, Miss Chaice. Don't you worry. Now I remember . . . " He was off on a quite interesting, if probably imaginative, case of amnesia he'd once been concerned with, and was contriving to make quite a good meal at the same time. Then he was asking Daine about books in wartime, and when at last he got reluctantly to his feet and said he'd have to be on the move, it was as if the room was losing a dear old family friend.

"I think your Mr. Wharton's an old dear," Kitty confided in me as he and Goodman went out. "And you really think he'll find Uncle Richard?"

"If he said so, you bet he will," I told her, and she gave me the most charming of smiles by way of thanks.

Wharton had turned off as if by chance to Chaice's room. I followed him there, and at once he was closing the door behind the three of us. A pause to wipe the last crumbs from his forest of moustache, and then he was giving a sigh.

"Well, I think that's all the preliminaries. I've seen everybody and everything. Now we'd better get to work."

He waved a hand aimlessly towards a couple of chairs, took the only easy one for himself and got out his notebook. Then he took his antiquated spectacles out of his case, made play with an accurate adjustment, and peered over their tops at the book.

"Those letters that were sent to the Yard," he said. "Never a print that's known to us."

Goodman gave a little grunt. I merely waited. George was staging some dramatic disclosure or else—in his own familiar phrase—my name was Robinson.

"In other words, this G. H. Preston isn't known to us," he went on. "If either of you can tell me, therefore, why he was so careful to avoid leaving fingerprints, I'll be delighted."

A somewhat whimsical look had accompanied the question. I said I had no idea. Goodman said nothing.

"So much for Preston," George said, "though I'll return to him later. But about that gun that Martin Chaice was shot with. The bullet came from it all right, so the medical evidence says. The only thing that's wrong is the gun itself."

He was now peering round at both of us. I thought it my duty to buy it.

"What *was* wrong with it?"

"The prints," he told us. "A beautiful lot of prints, and in the right places. Round the barrel and round the stock and a fingermark on the trigger. Unfortunately they weren't made by Martin Chaice."

I stared, so did Goodman.

"They were superimposed after death," Wharton went on, and his voice fell with a plummy kind of unction. "They were the marks someone thought might be the right kinds."

"They were faked?" asked Goodman.

"What else am I trying to tell you?" Wharton told him, and with a gentle patience. "To put it in plain English, Martin Chaice didn't commit suicide even if we find some way that gun might have been kept in place while he pulled the string. If you want me to put it even more simply, then Martin Chaice was murdered."

CHAPTER XII
LANG UNDER FIRE

WE MUST HAVE argued about the killing of Martin Chaice for best part of half an hour; the same old arguments, and round and round and back again in the same old way. Then Goodman came out with a perfectly new theory.

Imagine someone—Lang, for instance—wanting to work out something in connection with a detective novel; something that necessitated the use of that gun and a suicide. Well, he fastened the string and took the gun up to Martin's room, and asked if Martin would assist him in a little experiment. But in the course of that experiment the gun went off accidentally. The door was shut and no one heard the noise. Lang, or whoever it was, listened and then wiped off all the prints and then faked Martin's prints and put him in the chair as if he'd been writing, and then slipped downstairs.

"Sounds reasonable," Wharton said. "Depends on several things we shall have to prove sooner or later, so we might as well prove them now. If you'll get the gun out of the car, Goodman, I'll see Miss Chaice and get her to co-operate."

Inside ten minutes everything had been arranged. Kitty was to be in her room with the door slightly ajar as it had been at the moment she had heard the shot. I was to be at my bedroom door waiting for an imaginary Daine to emerge from the lavatory. Goodman was to be in the hall, and Wharton was to fire one of the two rounds into an old blanket, and he was giving none of us any idea how long we might have to wait.

I did just hear that shot when it finally went off, but I had to confess that I shouldn't have heard it if I hadn't been keyed up to listen. Goodman said much the same thing. Kitty said she had heard it exactly as she had heard it that vital afternoon. It was more like a crack than a shot.

Wharton was questioning her in her room, for the sight of Martin's room might have been too much of an upset. As it was, she was showing no distress at all. Wharton had a way with women, and he had somehow contrived to make the whole thing not only impersonal but interesting. When he came to his next questions he was on much thinner ice.

"From the time you heard that crack, Miss Chaice, till the time you actually were in the room—how long was it, do you think?"

"About a minute or two."

"Why are you so sure?" Wharton wanted to know.

"Well, I sort of went on with what I was doing, and then I began to wonder what it had been. Then I thought I'd have a look."

Wharton took out his watch.

"Just stand where you did that afternoon," he told her. "When I say 'Go!' that's the shot. You move off when you think you moved off."

The interval turned out to be about one minute only. Wharton had another question ready.

"Now the window, Miss Chaice. You're dead sure it was shut?"

"Quite sure," she said.

Wharton nodded. "Only one more question then, and I want you to think very carefully. Did you or did you not see the gun that fired the shot?"

"I did," she said, and Wharton looked disappointed. "I can't think how, but I do remember seeing a gun." She shook her head. "I can't explain what it was like, really. It was all sort of vague. I remember Mr. Daine. Just sort of seeing him before I fainted clean away. And I remember the gun."

"You remember where it was?"

"I don't," she said, and shook her head again. "I know that when I came round again on the bed there, the first thing I remembered was Mr. Daine, and then something about a gun." She bit her lip and frowned, then shook her head quickly again. "No, I can't remember. I know I saw a gun and that's all."

"Well, we're very grateful to you," Wharton told her. "I've a daughter of my own, and I know what you've gone through. Take my advice now and have a real good rest."

"But I have to go back on Friday," she reminded him.

"Oh, no," Wharton told her. "No going back on Friday for you. You let me have the telephone number of your commanding officer and I'll get it fixed up."

He gave her a smile and a pat on the shoulder and out he went. We followed him down the stairs and into Chaice's room, where once more he locked the door behind us.

"Well, that's another theory gone," he told us.

"Why, sir?" ventured Goodman.

"Why?" Wharton treated him to one of his most ferocious glares. "Under a minute between the time the shot was fired and she was in the room. Could the prints have been faked in that time? Would anybody have had the nerve to try?"

"He had to have the nerve," I said boldly. "The proof of the pudding's in the eating. The gun *was* faked, and it was faked after the shot and not before."

"Leave it," he said, and waved an impatient hand. Then he was whipping round on us. "Have it your own way. Lang is the favourite for that theory of yours, Goodman. Very well then: we'll have Lang in here." Then he stopped Goodman at the door. "Wait a minute, though. There're several things I'd like to ask that gentleman. Better jot them down."

He made a quick note or two, and then from a capacious inner pocket produced *The Frozen Alibi*. A grimace at it, and he replaced it in his pocket and gave Goodman a sign to go ahead.

* * * * *

Lang's manner was always on the diffident side, and he showed no perturbation even at what I might call the magisterial appearance of the room. I had had to bring a chair from the hall and Wharton had moved the window table. On it was his notebook and a sheet of paper or two, and he had covered *The Frozen Alibi* with a newspaper. He had also donned those spectacles of his, and one day, I was telling myself, I'd really make sure if they were anything but the perfectly plain glass I'd long suspected them to be.

"Come in, Mr. Lang," said Wharton genially. "Take a seat there, if you don't mind."

He waited till the three of us were seated, then his look became official.

"I take it your job has made you familiar with the rules of evidence as approved by His Majesty's Judges of the King's Bench Division, and in particular Number One." Without waiting for a reply he began to recite. "'When a police officer is endeavouring to discover the author of a crime, there is no objection to his putting questions in respect thereof to any person or persons whether suspected or not, from whom he thinks useful information may be obtained.'"

He took a look over his glasses to assure himself that Lang had been duly impressed, and then permitted himself a slight smile. "You must decide for yourself under which category you come."

Lang licked his lips and tried an answering smile.

"And so to business," went on Wharton. "You're here to help us and we're here to help you. And first of all, something that may be related to the murder of Mr. Chaice on the Monday night. Your own relations with Mr. Chaice were always friendly?"

"Well, yes," Lang said, and snapped his eyes a bit. "I liked working for him. And I believe he was satisfied with me."

"Just as I imagined," Wharton told him, and looked round at Goodman and myself for confirmation. "But your own movements that night; say between nine and ten?"

"I really can't say now," Lang said, and just a bit anxiously. "I think I was just sort of pottering around."

"You saw nothing suspicious?"

"Nothing at all," Lang said firmly.

Wharton nodded and made a tick on his notes as if that item was disposed of.

"Now we come to yesterday afternoon," he went on. "You didn't hear the shot that killed Martin Chaice?"

"I hadn't the faintest idea there'd been a shot at all," Lang said, and far more animatedly. "I was absolutely engrossed in my work."

I cut in with the statement that I'd seen Lang within five minutes of the firing of the shot, and he'd been so busy that he hadn't heard me tap at the door.

I'd expected a glare but merely got a nod.

"So I believe," Wharton said, and consulted his notes. "In fact, Mr. Lang, would I be right in saying you didn't see Martin Chaice at all that morning? He had lunch in his room, I'm told."

"I did see him once," Lang said. "Not long after twelve."

"Indeed?"

"I'd just gone out for a breather. I often do, you know."

"Yes, yes," said Wharton impatiently.

"Well, I took a short stroll round by the annexe and back. That's what I usually do. That's when I saw Martin."

"You spoke to him?"

"I didn't actually. He came out of the garage just as I was coming round by the barn, so he was ahead of me. He went straight back to the house."

"You don't happen to know why he'd been to the garage?"

"I don't. I know he was carrying a piece of wood."

"Wood!" Wharton could not help staring. "What sort of wood?"

"I really can't say. A piece of planed wood, about this length. And about this thick. He was carrying it in his hand."

"About a foot long and an inch and a half square," said Wharton, making an entry in his book. "Not that it's likely to be important." He completed the note and then looked up. "You didn't go into the garage yourself?"

"I didn't," he said. "I know that Mr. Daine came out just as I passed."

Wharton sat back in his chair. I knew what he was wondering—if that piece of wood was a gadget for holding the rifle in place. Then he made a sign to Goodman who was nearest the door, and Goodman left the room.

"And that was the last time you saw Martin Chaice alive?" Wharton asked Lang.

"Yes, it was."

Wharton pursed his lips and made play with consulting his notebook.

"I suppose, by the way, that if you'd been in any difficulty about a book, you wouldn't have asked Martin Chaice for any help?"

"I don't think that would have been any use, sir," Lang told him with the suspicion of a smile.

Wharton put the imaginary case of someone doing a stunt with a gun. "Might such a person have asked Martin to assist?"

"I doubt it," Lang said. "I don't think Martin had any use for guns of any kind."

"A bit of a pacifist, was he?"

"Not really. After all, he had tried to get into one of the Services. I think he just didn't like guns."

"Or detective novels?"

Lang smiled naturally for the first time.

"He certainly didn't. When we talked shop it used to drive him positively frantic."

There was a tap at the door and in came Goodman with Daine. Wharton was all apologies and Daine wasn't taking them too graciously. Wharton explained about the wood and wondered if he'd heard any talk about it between Martin and his Uncle Richard.

"I didn't," Daine said tersely. "Whatever they'd been talking about, they'd finished when I got there. Martin hung around for a minute, and that's the last I saw of him."

"Did you actually see the piece of wood he was carrying?"

"I may have done," Daine admitted. "Wait a minute," and he frowned in thought. "No. I believe he did have a piece of wood, but that's all I can say."

"And you didn't hear even the tail-end of any conversation?"

"Yes, I think so," Daine said. "At least I mentioned the matter to Richard when Martin had gone. He'd been asking his uncle whether or not it was David who said all flesh was grass." Wharton stared. I ventured to explain.

"That poem he was writing," I said. "Requiem, he called it, on the theme that all flesh is grass."

"So that was it," said Wharton, and the smile was that of the lion who had missed his first snap at the plump Christian. "And would you mind telling us what you were seeing Richard Chaice about yourself? Just for the records," he added quickly.

"Not at all," Daine told him calmly. "That damned wireless my staff uses is a hell of a sight too loud. I've asked them to turn it lower, if they must use it, and they say something's gone wrong and they can't turn it lower. That's what I saw Richard about."

"And he fixed it?"

"That same afternoon."

"Well, that's all perfectly clear," Wharton said, and turned to us for confirmation. "We're very grateful, Mr. Daine, and very sorry to have had to trouble you."

"That's all right," said Daine, but he was still in a bit of a huff. Perhaps the sciatica helped to make him irritable, for he was limping a bit as he went out.

Wharton let out a deep breath, then fiddled with his notes again. Lang, I suspected, was now about to be put through it, and I wasn't far wrong.

"Now I have to come to a far more personal matter," Wharton began again, and gave Lang a look that was distinctly grim. "I have here the report of a conversation that took place at Mr. Chaice's dinner table. A discussion or argument might be a better description. In the course of that argument Mr. Chaice virtually accused you of breaking a contract and—something which we have to consider seriously—of having definite reasons for— shall we say?—wishing him dead."

Lang's face went the colour of a tomato. Then he was giving me a reproachful look. I cut in quickly.

"You should know how things are in a murder case, Lang. Everything has to be reported, whether it has a bearing on the case or not. And if you are innocent, then what have you got to worry about?"

"Exactly," said Wharton pontifically, but the look over the spectacle tops was suspicious enough nevertheless.

"I *am* innocent," Lang said, rather feebly. "I didn't break any contract."

"But you wrote a book?"

"Yes, but in my own time. I actually wrote it when I was on holiday last year."

"This book?" The rabbit came from the hat, but Wharton had got the trick badly mistimed.

"Yes," said Lang, and moistened his lips as he glanced at the jacket.

"Would you mind my seeing a copy of your contract with Mr. Chaice?"

"There isn't a copy."

"You mean?"

"Well, it was only a verbal contract."

"Really?" There was scepticism in the tone. "And supposing we accept that statement, why should Mr. Chaice have accused you of breaking it? Breaking the implied clause, that is, that all your time was to be given to him."

"But there wasn't such a clause," insisted Lang, and now he was getting still more red in the face. "There was nothing mentioned between me and Mr. Chaice about his having the sole use of my time. That was implied, I admit, but never to the extent that I couldn't do what I liked with my leisure." He shook his head and then thought of something else. "Mind you, I did think Mr. Chaice wouldn't like me to publish under my own name, and that's why I chose a pseudonym."

"But one he could easily see through," I suggested.

"That was the idea," he said. "It was a sort of challenge. Well, not a challenge exactly. It seemed to me to put everything right."

"And he did find out about that book?"

"Well, I thought he had found out when he mentioned it that night in the argument. Now I'm not so sure. I think he may have been guessing."

"Why do you say that?"

"Well, he never mentioned it to me again. He didn't say, 'I saw an advertisement of that book of yours', or anything." Wharton gave a grunt or two and referred to his notes again. "Excuse me harping on that agreement, but just how did you come to work for Mr. Chaice? Tell us all about it, and about yourself."

That proved rather heavy going for Lang, though I had far more respect for him when Wharton had finally winkled the information out of him. Lang had left Cambridge after the death of his father. He had then stayed at home with his mother and had written a couple of detective novels. He had also got a commission in the Territorials, and on the outbreak of war he was called up. In the November he was in France, and on a patrol he was shot through the belly. The following March he was invalided out, but he went on with his writing. Then his mother died, and about the same time his agent heard somehow from Daine that Chaice was looking for a secretary with special qualifications. The agent must have taken action, because Chaice himself wrote. Terms were discussed at the first appointment and Lang was duly engaged. He admitted that he had expected to gain more out of the job than the salary. The experience was unique, and he had intended to keep the job only till he felt himself qualified to return to his old job with very real hopes of success.

"That seems very fair and reasonable," Wharton said largely. "We can take it, I think, that Mr. Chaice was talking very much with his tongue in his cheek when he made the writing of that book a reason for murder."

"That was his way," Lang said. "He loved saying things that disturbed people. In fact, he had a strong sadistic strain, if you know what I mean."

"I know what you mean all right," Wharton told him enigmatically, and was once more making play with fingering his notes.

"You got on very well with everybody here?" was his next question.

For some reason or other Lang's face flushed again.

"Well, I hope so," he told Wharton diffidently.

"You got on well with Mrs. Chaice?"

"I think so. She was always quite nice."

"But not too nice?"

Lang shot a look at him.

"Which brings me to another matter," Wharton went on. "I have here certain information about the Friday night preceding the murder. Where were you that night, Mr. Lang? Say from a quarter-past nine till a quarter to ten."

Lang had been hit clean in the wind. Then he was stammering that the question was hardly fair.

"And why not?" asked Wharton belligerently.

"Well, it's a long time ago. I can't be expected to remember everything I did on every night."

"Ah well," said Wharton with a sigh. "We must try to fix that night in your memory. The Friday night, I said. The night that Mr. Travers arrived, which might have helped you to recall it."

"I remember now."

"Capital!" said Wharton. "If that's so, you may remember that at about a quarter-past nine you were on the veranda of the summerhouse, making love to a certain lady."

He gave a kind of avuncular peer over his spectacle tops, and waited.

"And suppose I deny that," blurted out Lang.

"Entirely a matter of opinion," said Wharton imperturbably. "You might, of course, be asked the same question in a public court, and on oath."

Lang shook his head and said nothing.

"You won't tell us who the lady was?"

"I deny I was with a lady at all."

"Then you *were* on that veranda."

Lang had been too late for that trap, but the shake of his head showed he wasn't falling into any more.

"She was a lady who took a considerable interest in your affairs," went on Wharton. He, too, had a sadistic vein, and I always hated him when he baited a witness as he was now about to bait Lang. "She was doubtless very concerned to hear that Mr. Chaice knew about your meeting her. What were the exact words? 'He knows. I tell you he knows.'"

"It wasn't that at all," blurted Lang again. "It wasn't about any meeting. It was about him knowing about the book."

"Truth will out," said Wharton with a look at Goodman and myself. "And so you *were* on the veranda of the summerhouse with a lady! And you still won't tell us who the lady was?" Lang sat grim and immovable. Wharton sighed.

"Like me to tell you all about it?"

I rather stared and so did Goodman. Lang made no sign. "These are the facts," said Wharton, taking off his spectacles and wagging them at Lang. "Miss Chaice—perhaps I'd better her Kitty—rang her father that afternoon and said a friend was bringing her home and she wouldn't be in till about ten o'clock, which was when she did actually arrive. But meanwhile she'd arranged with you—the friend being non-existent—to come to Beechingford by a train which would get her to the summerhouse about an hour before that. There she met you, and later she went to the house as if she'd just arrived. A deception, but perhaps pardonable. Am I right?"

"Well, yes," said Lang, though he couldn't meet Wharton's eyes.

"You see the folly of not telling the truth and the whole truth?" Wharton asked him mildly. Then he leaned forward, and the tone was almost a snarl. "What else is there you're keeping to yourself?"

"Nothing. Nothing," Lang told him. "I've told you everything I know."

I saw a peculiar expression come over Wharton's face, and I guessed he was about to change his tactics. When he spoke next his tone was even conciliatory.

"Mr. Chaice would have objected to your marrying his daughter?"

"I don't know," Lang said, and moistened his lips.

"But you both suspected the fact?"

"Well, perhaps we did."

"He might have forbidden Kitty to marry you?"

"We wouldn't have changed our minds if he had," Lang told him stoutly. "We both had money put by. I could have made a decent living somehow."

"Then why didn't you broach the matter to him?"

"We were going to," Lang said, and then shook his head. "If you want the whole truth, we decided on that Friday night to tell him about it before Kitty—Miss Chaice—went back from leave."

Wharton got to his feet.

"Well, I may be satisfied and I may not," he said. Then his tone took on a positive unction. "Between ourselves, I think you're very fortunate. I have a daughter of my own and perhaps I've got a sentimental streak. But some people in my position wouldn't look at it that way. They'd say that you only exchanged one motive for another."

He left it at that, and for the very good reason that he'd already driven a wagon and horses through that first rule on the taking of evidence. Then he was looking round at Goodman and me.

"Meanwhile are there any other questions?"

Meanwhile was the operative word as far as Lang was concerned, and a nasty one at that. I tried to put the wretched Lang at ease.

"There is one thing I'm sure Mr. Lang could be very helpful over. Did you know, Lang, that Mr. Chaice was intending to write a play?"

His surprise seemed genuine enough.

"He even boasted to me," I went on, "that it'd be on in town before Christmas. *Mr. Polegate*, he was calling it. Know anything at all about it?"

"Not a thing."

"You never saw any rough draft or anything?"

"Never."

"Then one other question," I said. "Can you give any reason why Mr. Chaice used to go to that summerhouse and why he put it out of bounds for everyone else?"

"I can only give you the reason he gave me," he said, "and that was that he found it what he called sympathetic. He got ideas when he was there and he could think things out."

"You know the interior of that summerhouse?"

"Very well indeed."

"Then do you really think anyone could get ideas there better than one could get them, say, in a room like this?"

"I don't," he said. "But no one can judge about a matter like that. Some places are definitely sympathetic and some aren't. I've experienced that for myself."

"You actually saw him go there?" asked Goodman.

"Several times," Lang told him. "Generally of a morning, soon after breakfast. He'd take paper with him."

"Why didn't he keep paper there?" asked Wharton.

Lang couldn't say, but he supposed Chaice would have kept paper there if he'd wished to.

"And how long did he usually stay there?" I asked.

"It varied," Lang said. "Sometimes as long as an hour. I couldn't always tell, though. I mean, I had my own work to get on with, and Mr. Chaice didn't always come back to the work-shop. He might have come back here."

That seemed to be all the questions.

"Thanks for what you've told us, Mr. Lang," Wharton said. "I may have to see you again. Unless there's anything else you'd like to tell us now."

Lang said there wasn't, and then he sidled out. I gave the high sign that I had to go to the cloakroom and I overtook Lang in the hall. I wasn't being specious. It was just that I reckoned myself as good a judge of character as Wharton, and I was pretty sure Lang had had nothing to do with either of the murders.

"Sorry you had such a rough time, Lang," I told him. "But I shouldn't worry about Superintendent Wharton if I were you. His bark is very much worse than his bite."

"Thanks," he said, and just the least bit frigidly.

"And if I were you, I'd tell Kitty all about it," I said. "Two heads are better than one, even if they're sheeps' heads, as my old nurse used to say."

"I think I will," he said, unbending a little.

"And tell me, just between ourselves, and now it's all over," I added, "did you get any good material out of that interview?" He said he had, and even managed a smile.

I got back to Chaice's room to be greeted by the most ferocious glare that Wharton had ever given me.

"An intrigue with Mrs. Chaice!" he told me scathingly. "Where were your eyes?"

"Even I can't see in the dark," I told him.

"I'm not talking about the dark, I'm talking about this afternoon. That couple making eyes at each other under your very nose and you couldn't see it."

"Well, you saw it, George, and everything's fine," I said, for I was damned if I was going to let him stage a curtain and take half a dozen bows in front of Goodman. "And very good work too. And now what?"

He muttered a few inaudibilities and then rounded on me again. Did I imagine Lang was in the clear?

"I don't see that he had a motive, if that's what you mean," I said.

"Well, I do," he said. "For all we know he may have mentioned Chaice's daughter to Chaice himself, and been told where he got off. And not only that. Once Chaice was dead he could marry the daughter, and there'd be a nice little wedding present of seven thousand five hundred."

"All right," I said obstinately. "He killed Chaice. And what about Martin?"

"There was no hocus-pocus about that shot," he said, and I didn't see any connection with my question. "The shot that Kitty heard was the shot that killed him. The medical evidence proves it and so does everything else. Lang is the only one who could have got clear if she'd caught him in Martin's room. He could have told her he'd heard the shot and had come up to investigate. And she'd have believed him. Or if he told her to, she'd have kept her mouth shut about him."

"The first part—yes," I said. "The second part—decidedly no. Kitty Chaice wouldn't keep her mouth shut to conceal a thing like that."

"What about that piece of wood, sir, that he got from his uncle?" asked Goodman, a bit worried, I think, at those minor squabbles between George and myself. "Where does it fit in?"

"Don't know," George said. "It's nowhere in the room, so the murderer may have taken it away with him." He pursed his lips reflectively and then added that there wasn't any proof that the piece of wood had ever been in the bedroom at all.

"Even if it was," he said, "and if it was some sort of gadget for holding the gun, that doesn't affect things. Martin never handled that gun unless the murderer wiped off the prints and then put his dead fingers round the gun to fake others, and that's damn nonsense."

"The sooner we get our hands on Richard Chaice, the better," Goodman remarked feelingly.

"Which reminds me," I said, and told Wharton about the ration book. Wharton said he'd go and see Mrs. Edwards for himself, and he'd be back in a couple of minutes.

The door closed on him. Goodman lighted a cigarette and I filled my pipe.

"Having a good time?" I asked him.

"You can't very well be dull when he's around," he told me with a nod in the direction Wharton had gone.

CHAPTER XIII
THINGS HAPPEN

WHARTON WAS ON the job early the following morning, and the rendezvous was in Martin's room. Wharton was in none too good a humour. For some reason or other, as he was to tell me later, he had expected the Beechingford Case to be an easy one, and now that things were turning out to be far more complicated than he had imagined, he was getting a bit impatient. That Goodman had no news whatever of either Preston or Richard Chaice was an added irritation. People didn't vanish into thin air, was Wharton's trite rejoinder when Goodman said his men were doing all they could.

We met in Martin's room, as I said, and the first thing Wharton wanted was a time check. I had to be Martin and Wharton was the murderer, with Goodman holding the stop-watch. Wharton went through the motions of firing the rifle through the slit of the partly opened door, and at once I had to pull him up.

"When we made that test with Kitty, the rifle was fired inside the room. Surely if it was fired outside the room the sound would have been much louder?"

George claimed, pigheadedly, I thought, that there'd have been no real difference. We could have fired much farther through the door, and Martin, engrossed in his writing, would never have noticed. In any case he didn't propose to make any new test with Kitty. Only one of those foreign shells was left, and it had to be kept in reserve.

So we began all over again. The shot was presumably fired and Wharton nipped in. He'd explained that his hands were gloved, and when he'd closed the door and stuck the handy chair against it, he began pressing my fingers round parts of the gun. Then the gun was placed where we found it, the chair was removed from the door and, after he'd given a quick listen, he was announcing that he'd nipped out, and how long had the whole thing taken?

"Just about a minute, sir," Goodman said.

"Good enough," said Wharton. "That puts Lang back on the spot. Any questions?"

"You didn't move the chair in which I was sitting," I said. "You ought to have hoisted it and me round so that I almost faced the door. Otherwise the shot would have entered the right side of the head and not the left."

"Why not the other way about?" he told me. "Why shouldn't he have been sitting facing the door, and then the murderer moved the chair more round to the window?"

"But if the murdered man faced the door, then surely he'd have noticed the barrel of that rifle being insinuated through the opening?"

George said it was immaterial. Then I asked why he had put the chair against the door.

"Why?" he said, and glared. "So that no one could get in, of course. If someone *had* come to the door, they'd have found they couldn't get in. Supposing—and it's a hundred to one against it—they'd have asked Martin what the noise was, he could have given a rough imitation of Martin's voice. Simply blurted, 'Nothing,' or something like that. If they merely tried the door and then went away, then he could have slipped out."

I could have accused George of extemporising, but it wouldn't have been worth while.

"There we are then," he said, "if there are no more questions. That minute fits in with what we learned from Miss Chaice. And it was at least three minutes before you checked up on Lang."

There was no comment and he went on as if talking to himself.

"There can't be any other answer. From what you've told me about Richard Chaice, he isn't the man, and he didn't have a motive. Mrs. Chaice is out of it. That's why I saw that Mrs. Edwards about the ration book. I thought it might be a good opportunity to go into Mrs. Chaice's alibi."

"Just what motive had Lang for killing Martin?" I had to ask.

"What motive? The best of all motives. Martin saw him kill Chaice. Well, not kill him, perhaps, but bringing the body into that room."

That sounded reasonable; far more so than the premises on which it had been built.

"And Martin had begun to blackmail him," I said, and then had an idea. "I think I see how he could have done it. If Daine hadn't ostensibly swallowed that yarn about Chaice wanting Martin's poems published, then Martin would have forced Lang to swear he'd actually heard Chaice promise to have them published."

George was pleased at that. He'd have Lang on the carpet again, he said. Not too soon. Let him have a day or so's rope.

Make him think he was in the clear, and then spring the trap. And meanwhile some further evidence might crop up.

I wasn't feeling any too happy. Why I had had to go and present Wharton with that blackmail theory, I didn't know, and after my overnight assurance to Lang that he would have no more worries. And I still refused to believe that Lang could really have killed either Chaice or Martin. If I was wrong, then, as I told myself, I'd have to revise all my ideas on character and personality.

"Where next then, George?" was what I said.

"Harcourt Avenue," he told us. "I had an idea last night and I'd like to work it out."

We traipsed all over No. 6 from bedrooms to scullery and so to the dining-room. There George delivered himself of something that was most unusual for him.

"I don't know what you two are like," he said, "but when I'm in this house I feel I've got something on the tip of my tongue, if you know what I mean. Just the least little bit of luck and we'd know all this Preston business like a flash. And we'd be cursing ourselves because we hadn't seen it before."

Goodman and I nodded solemnly.

"Now the point I was coming to," George went on. "Preston made a good job of removing from this house everything that might have told us what sort of a man he really was: his business or occupation, for instance, and what friends he had, or relations, and where he came from. You agree?"

We duly agreed.

"Then answer me this," George said. "If he took incredible pains to remove all his fingerprints, why did he? There's no record of him at the Yard?"

"But he spoke with a suspicion of a foreign accent," I said. "Maybe Paris or America had his prints."

"That's an idea," he said. "We might do worse than try New York. But wait a minute. Which of the prints we've got are those of Preston? The envelope prints are no use. They've been handled by all sorts of people. And there weren't any prints on the actual letters except Chaice's on the letter he wrote."

"What it amounts to, sir, is that Preston either removed all his own prints from the letters or else took care to handle them with gloves on," Goodman said.

"That's it," Wharton said. "But there's something far more important to it than that. Every personal trace of Preston has been eliminated from this house. You agree? And extraordinary pains were taken to do it. You agree again?"

We agreed.

"Then answer me this," said Wharton, and not without a note of triumph. "Why were those letters left behind *if* it wasn't deliberately?"

That was a first-rate piece of deduction, and I said so.

"Right," said George, and was producing those letters from his wallet. "Let's try to find out why he didn't take the letters away."

We had a real good look at them, and various questions arose. Goodman said he had made enquiries from the electric light people and they had not filed Preston's letter to them because he had since written to say he didn't want to hire an electric kettle after all. As for the letter to the glass people, it might perhaps be in their files, though heaven knows who might have handled it. About the letter to the local stationers ordering the *Philatelist*, Goodman said the stationers hadn't kept it, since no business had arisen.

"Where exactly is their shop?" asked Wharton. "What I mean is, why should he write a letter when he was in town every day?"

Goodman said the shop was not in the main street. It was true it was the best stationers in the town, but it lay beyond the route Preston would have taken to the station.

"That leaves us with Chaice's letter," George said. "Did anybody ask Lang if Preston's letter had been filed?"

I said I had enquired in a roundabout way and Goodman added that he'd put the question to Lang direct, and Lang had had no knowledge of any letter from or to Preston.

We talked a bit more and then that line of enquiry petered out.

"And yet I never felt more in my life that something's staring us in the face with regard to these letters," George said scowlingly as he put them back in his wallet. "And this house too. There's something right under our eyes if only we could see it."

Then suddenly, as a sort of obstinate challenge to circumstances, he said he'd stay on in the house for a bit. Goodman might get back to the town and see how the Richard Chaice enquiry was getting on.

"Two people disappear and into thin air," Wharton said exasperatedly. "It can't happen, I tell you. It just can't happen."

"What about me?" I asked.

"You hang around Lovelands and keep your eyes and ears open," George said. "Unless anything turns up, I'll be along there this afternoon."

I was pretty sure nothing would turn up, which shows how far I was to be wrong. But it wasn't a morning for optimisms. It wasn't a morning at all, if it comes to that, for it wasn't far off lunch-time. And it was raining as if we were in for a solid week of wet. A cold remorseless rain it was, that made one want to blaspheme the weather, and Beechingford, and everything connected with the Case. Lunch wasn't any too cheerful either. Kitty and Lang were out, so the parlourmaid told me. It was she who saw to my lunch, and I couldn't help wondering if Harris was avoiding me. It was even the parlourmaid who brought me, with my coffee, the message that Mrs. Chaice would like to see me in a few minutes if I could spare the time.

I'd expected to find a Constance limp and wan, but found nothing of the kind. It was true she was what one might call reclining on the chesterfield beneath the window, but she was fully dressed and she greeted me with the cheerfullest of smiles.

"Darling! How nice to see you again!"

I reciprocated, as they say in the best circles; and, after all, it didn't cost me anything.

"So glad all this tiresome business is nearly over," she said.

I pretended to realise that I hadn't seen her since Martin's death.

"Wasn't it dreadful?" she said, and tried to shudder. "But it had to come. A very neurotic type, don't you think? You never know what they're going to do."

"Aren't you taking it very much for granted that he committed suicide?" I said.

"But what else could it have been?"

"It could have been murder." I pointed out gently.

"Nonsense!" She gave her little gurgle of a laugh. "You're trying to frighten me. How could it have been anything else but suicide?" She added a "Poor Martin!" maybe by way of epitaph, and that was that. At least, it was where I preferred to leave it.

"You seemed to be about the only real companion he had," I remarked.

"Sheer pity, my dear," she told me. "He and Austin didn't get on very well together." She sighed. "Poor Austin. He *had* got most frightfully difficult."

Her forehead puckered.

"Strictly between ourselves, I'm sure there must have been insanity somewhere in the family. Look at Richard."

"Yes," I said lamely. "You knew he'd left Lovelands, by the way?"

"Harris told me," she said. "We think he's probably gone back to some friends in town. He'll be writing when he wants money or something."

"Now, now," I said reprovingly. "That wasn't a nice thing to say."

"Perhaps it wasn't," she said. "Forgive me, darling, and don't let's talk about it any more. Let's talk about ourselves." Then, with a kind of wide-eyed simplicity, "When are you going back to town?"

That was a facer. Somehow, too, I was realising that here was the one question for which I had been invited to that room.

"Anxious to get rid of me?" I asked flippantly.

"Of course not! Only it's this way, darling. I simply must get away from everything; if not, I'll go positively batty and shriek."

"A holiday might do you good," I ventured.

She patted my hand.

"Darling, I knew you'd understand. And it was perfectly adorable of you to stay on and be a . . . what was it we called it? Being . . ."

"A cushion."

She laughed. "That's it. A cushion. But, darling, you don't have to go on being a cushion." Then she paused. "Unless—"

"Unless what?"

"I don't know how to put it," she said frowningly. "But you'll understand what I mean. It's so awkward having the police and people all over the house. Harris was quite in a state about it. Everybody in the kitchen's on edge too. And you simply can't get servants these days."

"What you'd like me to do is hurry the police up and get them out of the house."

"In a way, yes. And why *should* they be in the house, darling? But perhaps they won't be, after you've gone back to town."

"When are you proposing to go for your holiday?" I asked bluntly.

"On Monday, darling. Not a holiday really. Just a few days in town."

I thought quickly. Two more clear days in which quite a lot of things might happen.

"What about my going to town with you? I could see you across London, and so on."

"Darling, how sweet of you!" But there'd been disappointment all the same. She'd expected me to go before the Monday.

"See you about the details later," I said. "Meanwhile, if it would help things in the kitchen, I can go to the Flagon."

"Darling, I wouldn't dream of it!" And, in almost the same breath, "Do they make one really comfortable at the Flagon?"

"Very comfortable indeed," I said, and quickly. "See you at dinner tonight?"

"Perhaps," she told me archly, and with that I made my exit.

And I had plenty to think about as I made my way down the stairs. I recalled a previous visit to Constance's room, and how I'd been sure that she'd had ideas about Austin's murder. Now she was anxious for the police enquiry to end, and, above all, to get me out of the house. And I was damned if I was going to be winkled out of the house. She was the hostess and might ask me point-blank to leave, and then I'd certainly have to go. But I wouldn't go unless. I'd just blandly ignore that afternoon's conversation and cling on to my last two or three days. And I'd cling on longer than that if I hadn't found out just why she was so anxious for me to go.

I'd got to the point of wondering who it was that she wanted to shield from the police enquiry, and if that someone was herself, when I heard a car draw up outside. I supposed it was Wharton or Goodman, but it wasn't. It was Kitty and Lang.

They were laughing away and talking as they came into the hall. But there was a silence at the sight of me. Lang said he'd just nip into the workshop. Kitty gave me a smile, but it wasn't her usual one. I wondered if Lang had been giving a bad report about me, and then I decided her sudden seriousness was only a reaction. After all, I might have thought the gaiety unwarranted in view of what had happened.

"Haven't I got to congratulate you, young lady?" I said, and held out my hand.

She blushed delightfully and couldn't get a word.

"I think you'll make an excellent couple," I said. "Let me know when the real day arrives."

"It won't be for a long while yet," she told me. "Unless I volunteer for overseas."

"Well, you must let me know," I said. "Had a good time down town?"

"Not really good," she said. "Had my hair done and had lunch down town. A dreadful lunch."

"That reminds me," I said, and felt in my pocket. "Make-up easily obtainable these days?"

"Heavens, no!" she said. "It's frightful stuff and awfully hard to get."

"Then here's a present for you," I said. "Something I found. Pretty massive too."

I handed her the lipstick I'd found in the summerhouse. She took a look at it, squinted at it and then laughed.

"But this isn't lipstick. It's a grease-paint!"

"Good heavens!" I said. "Shows what I know about lipstick. But are you sure?"

"But look," she said, and showed me the writing on the blue paper binding round the bottom. "It's Leichner's. They're quite the best people. Look—Carmine No. 2. Besides, it's a much fatter stick than lipstick."

"Ah well," I said. "Another good deed gone astray."

But she laughed when I held out my hand for it.

"I'm certainly not giving you it back. It's a godsend." Then her expression changed. "Was it . . . daddy's?"

"Maybe," I said. "I found it in the summerhouse."

"How on earth did it get there?" Her forehead wrinkled. Then she nodded. "Probably some outdoor theatricals while I was away. Daddy did have a make-up box, I know."

"Well, I may see you later," was my goodbye, and as she'd gone on upstairs I opened the front door and had a look at the weather. It was still raining and the skies were leaden. Not the weather for outdoor theatricals, I thought to myself, and in no particular context. And fancy my mistaking grease-paint for lipstick.

I was probably shaking a regretful head over that when I turned back to the hall. I do know I was startled when Lang suddenly spoke at my elbow.

"Someone wants you on the phone, Mr. Travers. I think it's Mr. Wharton."

I went into the workshop to take the call. It was George right enough.

"Is Harris about?" he asked, and it seemed rather urgently.

"I think so," I said. "Do you want him on the phone?"

"No, no, no," he told me quickly. "Have him on tap. I want to talk to him in about ten minutes."

"Something happened?"

"Yes," he said. "We've got a line on Richard Chaice."

All George would tell me when he arrived was that Goodman had found out how Richard Chaice and his luggage had reached Beechingford Station. He did say that we ought to have suspected that Harris had had a hand in the disappearance. Who else could have taken the ration book from the drawer where Mrs. Edwards kept it? And hadn't Harris and Richard Chaice been like two bugs in a rug? I said I wouldn't go so far as that, but I knew that Harris often spent his afternoons in the garage.

Harris was sent for, but George didn't waste time over display.

"There's some information we think you can give us," was how he began.

"Indeed, sir?" said Harris, and cast a wary eye at me.

"Yes," said Wharton, and held his pencil poised over the notebook. "We just want Mr. Richard Chaice's present address, that's all."

"His address, sir?" Harris was pretending to be hard of hearing.

"That's all," said Wharton blandly.

"But how could I know his address, sir?"

"How could he know the address?" Wharton said to me, and his smile was that of the lion who'd made a second unsuccessful snap at a Christian. Then he gave Harris one of his special glares. I expected Harris's pendulous cheeks to start wobbling, but the old boy was keeping himself well in hand.

"Are you going to give me the address, or aren't you?" Wharton fired at him.

"Even if I knew the address, sir, I'm not at liberty to disclose it," Harris told him, with what I might call a watchful dignity. "As a servant of the family, sir—"

"Servant of the family be damned!" exploded Wharton. "Ever slept in a police cell?"

Harris gave an involuntary shudder.

"Because that's where you'll be unless you—" He broke off to change the phraseology. "Put it this way, and don't give me any more of the old family servant stuff. As far as I'm concerned you're an ordinary plain citizen who's withholding vital evidence."

He gave a grunt or two.

"Who was chauffeur here before the man who's now away?"

"A Mr. Stapley, sir."

"Mr. Stapley!" said Wharton sneeringly. "Over the telephone you called him Tom. And he's blown the gaff. When he left his employment here on account of ill health, he started a little greengrocery business, and Mr. Chaice gave him the money to buy a little van. That's the van you asked him to bring to the side gate at half-past six in the morning. You helped to carry the luggage. You shook hands with Richard Chaice and said you'd be letting him know this and that." He got to his feet and his eyes were narrowing as he took a step towards Harris. "Now will you tell us where he is, or do we have to take you away?"

Harris drew back a step and his shoulders shrugged in a cringe.

"Well, sir—"

"Well, sir, nothing!" Wharton told him grimly. "What is that address?"

Harris gave a preliminary licking of the lips, then said, almost inaudibly, that it was 24, Ransom Road, Hanford Rise. Wharton gave a quick glance at his watch.

"On the telephone, is it?"

"No, sir."

"Then don't try any monkey business with telegrams," Wharton told him. "And now tell me this. Why did Mr. Chaice leave Lovelands, and why did it have to be so secretly?"

Harris shook his head, took a deep breath and then decided that he might as well give in.

"The information will be in confidence, sir?"

"Damn it, what do you think we are? Of course it will be in confidence."

"Of course, sir," echoed Harris. "And you wanted to know why he left."

"Do I have to ask every question twice?"

"No, sir." His voice lowered. "Well, it was really because of the mistress, sir. I think she rather objected to having him here, and Mr. Richard was aware of it. In the late master's time, sir, things were different, if I may put it like that."

"I know," Wharton told him. "He thought she'd make things awkward for him, so he decided to go on his own account. But why the secrecy?"

"Well, sir, he didn't want any trouble."

Wharton gave him a look, pursed his lips to a smile of incredulity and said the excuse was as good as any.

"And who's he gone to at Hanford Rise?"

"His late wife's sister, sir. She's a widow, I understand, sir, and she's often asked him to live with her."

"He's gone there permanently, has he?"

"That I can't say, sir. It would have depended on what happened here."

"All right," said Wharton, and put the notebook in his pocket. "Make Mr. Travers a large packet of sandwiches, and if you've got a thermos, fill it with hot coffee. The bigger the better. And sweeten it."

"Poor old Harris," I had to say when the door closed on him. "He made a good fight of it, George."

"He's not a bad old boy," Wharton admitted now the battle was over. "A good job he owned up or we might have been in queer street."

Stapley, it appeared, had carried Richard Chaice's luggage to the platform, and had had no idea of the station to which his passenger had booked. Nor had Goodman been able to get any information from the booking clerk.

"How long will it take you to get to Hanford Rise?" George asked me.

There was a motoring map among the books and I had a look. It was a cross-country journey and I said I might make it in a couple of hours. But only if George sat behind and didn't keep making noises at what he considered the taking of chances. That, I should say, is when I do anything approaching thirty miles an hour. George himself drives with both hands firmly on the wheel, and on a very straight stretch on a summer day has been known to touch twenty-five.

He telephoned to Goodman while we were waiting, and in another quarter of an hour we were off. The rain was still coming steadily down, but that wasn't worrying me. With any luck at all we should be in Hanford Rise well before dusk, but what I wasn't looking forward to was the return journey on an unknown road. The only thing that cheered me up was the wondering just what it was that we should get out of Richard Chaice, and, above all, what had been the reason Martin had given for taking that piece of wood.

CHAPTER XIV
DISCOVERY

I WONDERED WHY George had insisted, after all, on sitting in front, but I was not to know the reason till we were more than halfway to Hanford Rise.

"Making pretty good time, aren't we?" he suddenly said. "Might as well have those sandwiches."

I knew then why he had asked Harris to make up a big package, and why it was a quart thermos. George insisted, too, that we should pull up for a quarter of an hour's breather, though he didn't do too much breathing. While I was trying unavailingly to get my proper share of that combined tea and supper, I was telling him about my interview with Constance Chaice.

"How *could* she be mixed up with it?" he wanted to know. Then he was giving me a look. "You aren't implying she instigated her husband's murder!"

"Not to such an extent that she'd incriminate herself," I said. "Constance is an extremely clever woman as far as her own interests are concerned."

"She struck me as a bit of a fool," George said.

"Maybe," I said. "But she's been fool enough to have had three husbands and to have come off uncommonly well out of each of the deals. And one fact remains, George, and you've got to take my word for it—that she was doing her best to get me out of the house. And the police too."

"You are the police, aren't you?"

I said he was begging the question, and he was. That's the worst of George. When I initiate a theory—and Heaven knows I'm apt enough at that—George treats it with either contempt or complete disregard. But he keeps it well in mind, and if it turns out a winner, then in less than no time the theory has become his own, and himself the only begetter.

But he didn't seem inclined to follow that particular theory up, so I tried to create a little comic relief by telling him how I'd been deceived over the lipstick. All he had to say was that I'd mentioned nothing in my notes about finding any lipstick, or grease-paint or whatever it was. Then, as he wiped that voluminous moustache and handed me back the empty thermos, he was asking if we were going to stay there all night.

As we came through Uxbridge the rain ceased, and by the time we reached the common at Hanford Rise a final watery sun was setting. A pedestrian put us on our way to Ransom Road, and in a couple of minutes we found it. The house at which we drew up was a little detached villa with a small front garden. Just beyond it was a narrow side road, and I moved the car on and parked it there.

A woman of about fifty came to the door. She was fluffy-looking and stout, and on the wrist that held open the door were at least three bangles.

"Mr. Chaice in?" asked Wharton.

She gave us a quick look.

"What did you want him for?"

"We don't," said Wharton pleasantly. "What we would like is a word with you. Mrs. Smith, isn't it?"

"Roper's the name," she told us.

"Of course." said Wharton, and looked at me as if I'd bungled things. "If you could spare us a minute, Mrs. Roper, we'd be much obliged."

"You don't want to sell me something, because if—"

"Nothing of the sort," said Wharton largely. "As a matter of fact we might be coming about Mr. Austin Chaice's will. You know, Mr. Richard Chaice's brother."

"Oh, that," she said, and her eyes bulged expectantly. Then she was making a gesture for silence and showing us into a room just off the tiny hall. It was a room stuffy with knick-knacks and photographs.

"We don't want to disturb Richard," she confided. "He went to the ironmonger's this morning and got himself a catalogue of carpenter's tools. I think he's going to be such a help in the house. Excuse me while I do the black-out."

The black-out curtains were drawn and she switched on the light.

"Wasn't it rather risky letting him come from Beechingford all alone?" Wharton asked.

"Oh, Mr. Harris fixed that," she told us. "I met him at the junction. Not that he really couldn't have come by himself. He's just a bit absent-minded at times, that's all. But wait a minute. Perhaps you'd like to see my poor sister's photograph—the one who died in Canada. I had to take it down because I thought it might upset him."

We duly inspected the photograph, and then Wharton said Mrs. Roper was a woman of understanding and tact who could put two and two together. She'd know, for instance, why Richard had left Lovelands.

"It was that woman, that Mrs. Chaice," she said. "A stuck-up hussy, if you ask me. Not that Richard has said much."

Wharton nodded knowingly.

"Well, perhaps we'd better have a word with him," he said, rubbing his chin and pursing his lips. "We ought to be alone with him really?"

He had looked at me, and I said we ought. I added that Mrs. Roper would understand.

"Perhaps you'll tell him there's two gentlemen to see him," Wharton said. "We'll be seeing you afterwards perhaps."

"In the dining-room," she said. "I've got a nice little fire for him. It's been such a wretched day, and poor dear, he does want some comfort."

She gave us a confidential nod as she led the way out.

"Two gentlemen to see you, Richard," she was calling. Wharton moved me ahead of him and pushed me on. I was in the room before Richard knew it, and when he saw me it was as if he saw a ghost.

"I'll just give the fire a bit of a poke," Mrs. Roper said. She did so lingeringly, and as lingeringly retired.

"How are you, Richard?" I said, and held out my hand.

He took it limply, and his look was that of a schoolboy caught in some escapade.

"You've come to see me, Mr. Travers?" was all he could say.

"And this is Superintendent Wharton of Scotland Yard," I said.

He shot Wharton a look, then his mouth gaped.

"There's nothing wrong, is there, sir, at Lovelands?"

"Nothing whatever," Wharton told him confidentially. "Everybody's well, and very worried about you."

He smiled at that. Wharton waved him back to his seat and drew one up for himself.

"You've got to come back, you know. Everybody wants you to come back."

"No, sir, I shan't do that," he said. "I think I shall be very comfortable here. Millie's been asking me to come for years."

"What about Kitty?"

"Kitty's a good girl," he said, and nodded to himself.

"She's engaged," Wharton told him. "Going to marry that Mr. Lang."

"I knew it," he said. "They didn't think I knew it, but I did. I see all sorts of things, Mr. Warford, that people don't think I do."

Wharton didn't bother to correct the name. His voice lowered as he hurried in with his question.

"So I believe. Mr. Travers here told me there were things you'd noticed and which you'd have told your late brother, if you hadn't thought they'd make mischief. Don't you think, now you've left Lovelands, you might tell us what they were?"

"No, sir, I shan't do that," Richard told him quietly. "Let the dead past bury the past; that's the best way in this life."

"Yes, but suppose the information might lead to the discovery of your brother's murderer?"

"That wouldn't make me change my mind," he said, and gently shook his head. "Taking one life, sir, won't bring back another."

I think Wharton knew he could never be forced, and I think, too, that he had already that other scheme in mind which he was soon to put up to Mrs. Roper.

"Perhaps you're right," he said. "But there one little question I'm sure you won't mind answering for us. About Martin. He saw you in the garage the morning he shot himself. What did he come for?"

"Let me see now," he said, and looked contemplatively at the ceiling. Then his face lit up. "It was about a quotation from the Bible, sir. Something he wanted for one of those poems of his."

"He asked you if that quotation about all flesh being grass came from the Psalms?" I put in.

"That was it, sir. And I told him." Then he was giving us a look so whimsical that I almost laughed. "I hope I was right."

"You were right," I told him, and smiled. "But after that, didn't he want you to give him a piece of wood?"

"Yes, sir, he did." He shook his head regretfully. "That's something I should have done before I came away. He'd asked before to attend to that window of his, but I'd forgotten or else I'd been too busy."

I didn't dare look at Wharton. All I could do was wait, and then at last I had to prompt him.

"Something was wrong with the window?"

"Yes, sir," he told me at once. "The sash cord was broken, and I'd promised to repair it."

"You mean he couldn't open the window," cut in Wharton. "That's right, sir. Well, he could open it, but it wouldn't stay open. That's why he wanted the piece of wood."

Five minutes later we were saying goodbye to him. Though he persisted that he would never return to Lovelands, I knew his heart was there, and we promised that we'd deliver faithfully all his messages. Wharton wouldn't let him see us to the door.

Mrs. Roper was in the hall waiting for us. Wharton made a motion for silence and drew her into the sitting-room again.

"Is there a neighbour whose telephone you could use?" he asked her.

She said there was a Mrs. Somebody-or-other at Rosecot whose telephone she often used, and while she was telling us that her lips were licking with expectation and the lipstick was smearing across her chin.

"If you weren't a woman of real tact and common sense, Mrs. Roper, I wouldn't be asking you to help us," Wharton said. "Mr. Travers here agrees with me, especially as it may affect the amount Richard Chaice receives under his brother's will."

"Anything I can do—"

"I knew it," Wharton said hastily. "I told Mr. Travers that we were lucky to find someone here like you."

He expounded the scheme, and he revealed his identity. Mr. Chaice wasn't the sort from whom vital information could be extracted, but she could do the extracting for us. There was something that he'd discovered at Lovelands that he ought to have told his brother, and which might have prevented that brother's death. Mrs. Roper could perhaps extract that information from him. It would have to be done guardedly, and along certain lines which he would himself suggest.

It was a good quarter of an hour later when we left. Wharton and I said nothing till we were back in the car. Then he asked if there hadn't been a pub at the common just short of the fork. How I was feeling he didn't know, but he could do with a beer.

There was a car park in front of the pub, and there we left the car. The saloon bar was almost empty and we had a corner to ourselves. I ordered two half-pints, and Wharton said I'd better make his a pint. Then we got our heads together.

"Well, where are we now?" George began.

"That's what I've been trying to puzzle out," I told him. "All I can see is that we're in a bigger muddle than we were before. I don't mean about the piece of wood. That's simple. Martin wasn't sitting at that window with the window shut. The window was open, but the one who shot him took away the piece of wood and shut the window. Which leaves us where we were before. Who did the shooting?"

"And it complicates that timing we did," George said. "I worked it out just as quickly as the murderer must have done, and I took a good minute. It'd have been more if I'd had to shut that window and pocket the wood. And he daren't have shut the window loudly."

He glanced at his watch and closed his eyes as if going mentally through the motions. Another glance at the watch and he was shaking his head.

, "Well over half a minute. And that window wasn't easy to get at. The chair was close up against it."

"Perhaps Kitty was longer than she thought," I suggested.

"You can't argue like that," he told me reprovingly. "Either you trust a witness or you don't. She made it about a minute. That's sixty seconds, and when you count in seconds, thirty more seconds are the hell of a way out."

We agreed to leave it. There'd be plenty of time for thought on the way home. But George wasn't in any hurry, and as I'd finished my beer I called for another.

"Obstinate old cuss, that Richard Chaice," George remarked. "Wonder if that Mrs. Roper will worm what we want out of him?"

I said I thought she would. And I offered to bet that before long Richard would get back to Lovelands. If not, his sister-in-law would mother him to death.

It was amazing how near we were at that moment to having the solution to a couple of murders. One little twist to that conversation and we'd have seen the things that were right under our noses, but the conversation didn't take that particular turn. A stranger came up, for one thing, and asked if either of us would care to make a four in a game of darts. George, who fancies himself at the game, promptly got to his feet. He had a couple of games and won them both, and he even offered to buy me another drink. I said it was pretty late and we ought to be making a move.

The stars were out, but it wasn't too light, when we set off again. George was hunched up in the seat beside me, and I was driving carefully and trying to remember just where it was in Uxbridge that I turned left. By chance I hit the correct spot, and perhaps it was that that made me relax and do a bit of thinking on my own account. Then I thought of something that made me chuckle.

"What's tickling your fancy?" George asked grumpily.

"Just thinking of Mrs. Roper," I said. "Did you notice how she was licking her lips like a cat, and smearing that lipstick all over her chin. I bet she had a fit when she saw herself in the glass."

"Old fools of women, dolling themselves up!" George said and relapsed into his corner.

When he next spoke, and that would be about fifteen minutes later, his tone had so changed that he startled me.

"You mistake lipstick for grease-paint?"

I didn't quite gather what he meant, unless it was some reference to Mrs. Roper.

"Not that," he said. "That grease-paint you found in the summerhouse and thought it was lipstick."

"Oh, that," I said. "I told you about that."

He gave a grunt, then began filling his pipe. There was only the sound of his puffing till we were running into Pinner. Just as we came to that open space that looks like a village green he was suddenly asking me to stop the car.

"The pubs are all shut now," I told him. "It's well after ten."

As soon as I pulled up he was getting out. I thought he wanted to stretch his legs and I got out too. The stars were still shining and a young moon was rising away to our left. It was a grand night after the day we'd had, and it was a night I was long to remember.

"Let's walk a yard or two," George said. "There's something I want to put up to you."

I lighted my pipe, but before we'd gone half a dozen yards he was stopping me.

"Listen to this," he said, "and tell me if I'm right. *There never was anybody of the name of H. Preston!*"

I stared at him.

"But there was!"

"Have it your own way," he said, "but I say there wasn't. What's more, I think I can prove it. I say there wasn't a G. H. Preston, and this is why. *G. H. Preston was Austin Chaice!*"

I took off my glasses and began polishing them, and as I blinked away I began to see things for myself.

"You're right, George," I said. "You're dead plumb right."

"Well, let's hear how you'd prove it."

"Well, that was why he used that grease-paint," I said. "I think he had a make-up box in the summerhouse, and when the man I disturbed that night cleared away all the make-up apparatus and the false whiskers he didn't know that Carmine Number 2 had dropped on the floor."

"Yes. Go on," he told me impatiently.

"That's why Chaice used to go to that summerhouse," I said. "He'd do a quick make-up—unless it was for some special occasion, as when he called on himself or saw the house agents—and then he'd slip out the back way to the lane and on to the back door of Number 6. Then he'd show himself for the benefit of the neighbours."

"Yes, but why did he do it?"

I said it was a long story. Chaice had that passion for verisimilitude, and he was very much of an exhibitionist. He'd got a lot of publicity out of the typewriter affair and he'd proved himself right. The creation of G. H. Preston was a kind of improvement along the same lines. For one thing, he was about to write a play which he was calling *Mr. Polegate*, and undoubtedly that play would deal with a case of double identity and be worked out in accordance with his own experiences at Number 6. I said Chaice had actually told me that his play was to deal with a double identity, but he'd refused to give further details.

"And another thing," I said. "He was writing that manual of detection. Lang told me he'd stopped short at three different sections, one of which dealt with disguises. I'd say he was waiting to incorporate his experiences in those three sections. What a kick he'd have got out of writing something like this:

'It's the fashion nowadays to decry the use of disguises, but let me give you a personal experience.' Then he'd have related how he fooled not only the house agents but even his own secretary. Can't you see him gloating as he dictated that to Lang?"

"He must have been barmy," George told me with a grunt.

"I think he ultimately would have been," I told him. "But you didn't know him as I did. You can't get into the hide of another man by reading somebody else's notes."

"Right," said George. "Let's get on the move again. We can talk the rest of this over in the car."

What he was soon wanting to know was how the discovery helped us. He had ideas, he said, but he'd like to hear mine first. All I could say was that it looked as if we'd solved one murder, though we'd never be able to prove it.

"Chaice's murder?"

"Yes," I said. "Everything goes to prove that Martin murdered him."

"All right," he said, a bit testily. "Let's hear your reasons."

As I began to expound them they sounded more and more convincing. Martin had owned to me that he had followed his father, and ostensibly to discover if he really had anything to do with the liquid-squirting. Chaice became aware of his clumsy efforts and led him a dance. Nevertheless, when Martin said he had always lost his father, that might have been deliberate lying. Maybe Martin had seen him enter the back or front of Number 6. After all, Chaice would boldly enter by the front gate in order to let any chance neighbour see him.

"Now take the Monday when Chaice was killed," I said. "I had been induced by Constance Chaice and Martin to lend a hand in following Chaice if he went out that night. Then Martin went sick, and, as I said in the notes, I think the sickness was a fake. What was intended was that Daine and I should do the following while Martin had a good alibi. What he did, as soon as his father had left, was to slip downstairs. He may have followed the three of us. He may have been the running man that Pymme saw at Number 3. But what he almost certainly did do was to catch up with his father when he was nearing the house and crack him on the skull and then finish him off. As I said, he had a perfect alibi. If necessary, he might have got Constance to add to the proof that he'd never left his room."

"You realise that you're making her a pretty cold-blooded murderess?"

"Not necessarily," I said. "She mayn't have been aware of how she was being used. Or she might have suspected, and pretended she didn't. But haven't I been insisting lately that she knows a hell of a sight more about things than we'd imagined? And why was she getting nervy about me and the police still being in the house?"

George said there was a lot in that, but it'd take the very devil of a lot of proving.

"Unless we can tie it up with Martin's own murder."

"Yes," he said. "And I don't see how Mrs. Roper's going to help us there. Even if she does worm something out of Richard Chaice, it may turn out to be something connected with Austin's murder, not Martin's. In fact, it's almost certain to be."

We more or less left it at that, and at once found ourselves getting back to G. H. Preston. George was even more of the opinion that Chaice was as near mad as makes no difference.

"When he went to Number 6 that Monday night he actually knocked at his own door. Daine heard him talking to an imaginary somebody inside. Then he came out and said good night to the same imaginary character. If that isn't lunacy, what is?"

"Not at all," I said. "Everything was done for the benefit of anyone going by. Take a secret service agent, for example, or even one of our own men who has to assume a wholly new personality to get himself into the confidence of a suspect. What's the golden rule if it isn't that you don't *pretend* to be the character? You *are* that character, and it's just as important to know it when you think you're alone as when you're not. And you bet your life Chaice would have put all that in his book."

"You class those letters we found under the same heading?"

"Undoubtedly," I said. "The show piece was that letter he wrote to himself."

Then I had a brainwave.

"I think I've got something, George. What we haven't thought about is the logical end of G. H. Preston."

"You mean?"

"This," I said. "I think the time had practically arrived when Chaice would wish to finish Preston off. How, I don't know, but it'd have been something spectacular. Something that would have made a stir in the local Press. Maybe in the London papers too. But it would have been something that brought the police to Number 6 in search of Preston. They'd have found the letter. They'd have interviewed Chaice, who'd have had the time of his life spinning yarns with his tongue in his cheek. Then at the right moment he'd have let the whole cat out of the bag. Magnificent publicity—especially for his forthcoming play."

"That's it, for a fiver," George said, and then was asking if we weren't near Beechingford.

We were, and it was not a long way off midnight. George said he'd stop at the police station in case a message might have come in from Mrs. Roper. I could drive myself home and leave the car at Lovelands. Then he changed his mind and told me to wait.

There wasn't any message, so I drove him to the Flagon, and left the car there.

"What about the morning?" I asked him.

He thought for a bit, and then said he'd be at Number 6 at about ten o'clock. I pushed off on foot. Harris had given me a key, and I found a message on the mat to the effect that a thermos of coffee was in the dining-room. There were sandwiches too, and the remains of an apple tart.

When I'd finished that meal I was too awake for bed, so I lighted my pipe and did some more thinking. It was about one in the morning when I made my way out towards bed. In the hall my hat and coat lay where I'd carelessly thrown them on the table, and the sight of them there grieved my sense of tidiness. So I picked them up, intending to hang them on a peg outside the cloakroom, and for some reason or other I happened to notice the table drawer.

Then I suddenly thought of something. I thought of something else, and then all at once I had my glasses in my hands and was blinking away as I polished them. From that table drawer my thoughts had ranged to that rubber-tired wheelbarrow that had been propped against the back of the summerhouse, and then they ranged still farther afield. A minute or two later I was going upstairs. But I was going very slowly; in fact I hardly knew I was going at all. Gaps there might be, and far too many, and yet the general pattern was clear. I knew, and yet I didn't quite know.

It was a long time before I fell asleep. When I woke there were still too many gaps, but of the main pattern I had never been more certain. I knew, for instance, who had killed Austin Chaice, and though I didn't know how, I thought I knew who had killed Martin.

CHAPTER XV
ALL THE ANSWERS

I was very late for breakfast that morning. Daine had finished his, and when he looked into my room I was only just getting out of bed. I told him in confidence about Richard, and he, too, was of the opinion that it would not be long before he was back at Lovelands.

"You never know," I said enigmatically, and at once he was giving me a questioning look.

I closed the door after having had a look along the corridor. "Can you keep something under your hat?"

"I think so," he told me.

"I oughtn't to let out even a hint," I said. "There'd be the devil to pay if Wharton knew I'd said a thing. But the fact is, I don't think I shall be here after today. I might even get away tonight."

"You mean the job's finished?"

"As good as, and that's all I can say."

He nodded to himself, and then had to try a question. "Suppose you couldn't give me an idea who did it?"

"That's more than my job's worth," I said, and shook my head. "What I might do is give you a hint, and for God's sake don't ever mention it, even when it all comes out."

Then I shook my head again.

"I oughtn't to tell you really, but you'll have to draw your own conclusions. The answer really is, 'Why did Richard bolt?'"

His eyes opened wide.

"So he *was* mad, was he?"

"You're getting nothing more out of me," I said, and began to hustle him out of the room. Then he thought of something.

"If you're likely to be going, why not sign that agreement? It's been waiting for your signature."

I met him again in the hall after breakfast. Harris, by the way, had not appeared, and doubtless he was now terrified of a new encounter with Wharton. It was a Saturday and Daine's staff were away, but we found the agreement and the covering letter at the bottom of one of his trays. I signed and he signed, and, as I was going out, I said I'd post the letter and get the matter finished.

It was about a quarter to ten, but before I set out for Number 6 I took a quick look through the workshop door. Lang was busy typing, but not with his face to the window. He was facing Kitty, who was settled comfortably in a chair and knitting what looked like a jumper sleeve. The pair actually looked pleased to see me.

"Don't move," I told them. "I only looked in to tell Kitty her Uncle Richard was well."

She was tremendously thrilled to hear he'd been located, and to hear my opinion that he'd probably return.

"You write him a letter," I told her. "Give him all the little details of news and make him homesick."

She said she'd do it at once. Lang brought me a piece of paper on which to write the address, and he was wanting to know why Richard had gone away. I was giving away no more information. All I did say was that he'd thought he was a bit of a nuisance. Then I made my exit, and was hurrying off to Number 6. But not by the back lane. I went out by the front gate as if I was really bound for the town.

*   *   *   *   *

More pieces were already fitting into the puzzle, and before the morning was out that jigsaw was almost entire. Not that we had an interesting morning. Goodman had obviously been staggered at Wharton's revelation about Preston, though he could contribute little to that evidence of double identity. But Wharton had done some telephoning and had a few more facts.

That question of the beard, for instance. A beard takes some fixing, and even an experienced actor like Chaice would have had to make a remarkably good job of it to have faced the light of full day. For an ordinary visit, as to Mrs. Pymme, it wouldn't have mattered so much, or on those occasions when he showed himself at Number 6 for the purpose of satisfying either neighbours or passers-by. But Wharton had rung up both the house agents and Lang. Each had confirmed that the mornings of Preston's visits had been dark and rainy. In Morland's office there had been artificial light, and at Lovelands no light but the dim one of nature. An added confirmation was that when Preston called at Lovelands Chaice had not been there.

Well, we spent the whole morning at Number 6 and the summerhouse, and for the sole reason, apparently, of Wharton's notes. A General's inspection was nothing to it. We were expected to get ideas, or he would find his own and then he'd write them down. And everything was now around the theory that Martin Chaice had killed his father. The motive was centred round that manuscript, and I gathered that in the background was Constance Chaice, with a question-mark.

But I was glad when George said he'd like to spend the afternoon thinking things out. In any case, Mrs. Roper had promised to ring before six o'clock whether she had information or not. So I said I'd take a holiday too, and I'd have lunch in town for a change. So we dropped George at the Flagon, and Goodman took me on to the station, where I rang Harris and said I mightn't be in all day. But I might be leaving that night and would he pack my bag in case.

I hung up before he could ask any questions, and then I went off in search of lunch. There was a matinee every afternoon at the big cinema, and two o'clock found me in the stalls. It was an appalling programme, but I hadn't gone there to see the pictures. I was there in hiding, as it were, and because I still wanted to do some thinking.

It was nearly five o'clock when I came out, and at once I went in search of tea. I lingered it out, and it was nearly six o'clock when I made my way to the police station. Now I had all the answers, or so I thought. Goodman, I was told, had gone to the Flagon, so I asked if I might use the telephone.

It was Daine whom I called, and I had to wait a minute or two before he was on the line.

"Hallo, Daine," I said. "I'd like to confirm, still in confidence, that I'm leaving tonight."

"Harris said something about it," he told me.

"Well, something has occurred to me," I said. "I'd like your opinion about something. All this business down here has given me a few ideas and I'd like to make use of them."

"What sort of ideas?"

"Well, I think I could write a damn good detective story about them. Well, not about them exactly. What I mean is that they've given me ideas which I think I could use. I'd like to put the ideas up to you."

"But you've never written a detective story."

"I know I haven't. But I did write *Kensington Gore*."

"Yes," he said, a bit reluctantly, I thought.

"What I don't want to do when I get back to town is to start something I can't finish. Now you're an authority. Perhaps *the* authority. . . . No, don't protest, my dear fellow. You *are* the authority. You couldn't have been associated with Chaice all these years without knowing everything that matters. In any case, the question is, will you do it?"

"Well, if you feel that way about it."

"That's damn good of you, Daine," I said feelingly. "Even if you do stand to make something out of it. Half-past eight suit you? In Chaice's room? I'm dining in town, by the way."

So that was settled, and I telephoned Wharton. He and Goodman were at the Flagon, and Wharton seemed pretty annoyed that I hadn't called him up before. When I asked if any-thing had happened he said that nothing had, except a message from Mrs. Roper. When I asked what the message was, he said it would keep till I got to the Flagon.

I looked into the drawing-room at Lovelands. Daine had just finished his coffee and was waiting for me. I thought he might suggest that we stay there, but he didn't. It was he who said we might as well get on with our chat, especially as I might be wanting to get away.

In Chaice's room I had a look back into the hall and then turned the key in the lock.

"We don't want to be disturbed," I said, and passed him my cigarette case. He said he'd have a pipe, so I filled up too.

"Made an arrest yet?" he asked me.

"You know how things are," I told him. "You don't make an arrest nowadays till the whole thing's been talked over with the Public Prosecutor. If you know where your man is, you can always collect him."

"That where Wharton is now?"

"That's right," I said unblushingly. "He and Goodman. I'm only a hanger-on."

"You're too modest," he told me. "But about this book of yours."

"Oh yes," I said, and produced some notes I'd made. And I had to shake my head. "This is going to be rather difficult. I hope you won't think I'm being personal."

"How do you mean?"

"Well, I'd rather like to put my plot in a hypothetical way. Assume, for instance, that you're the villain of the piece. Build the whole story round the murder of Chaice and Martin, but disguise the scene and the characters."

"I see that," he said, "but I don't see the point of making me what you call the villain."

"That's what I was trying to apologise for," I said. "I know there are crooks among every class, and any member of that class oughtn't to take it personally if I pick a crook—a murderer, if you like—from that class. In fact," I said with a new apologetic smile, "I want to build my story round the supposition that a literary agent was the murderer. To make it easier for us two to follow, I'm making him you."

He was gripping the pipe stem pretty tight and looking me clean in the eye.

"You're not proposing to bring me into this story of yours?"

"My dear fellow, I've just told you I'm not. The whole thing's supposition."

"Of course," he told me, and not too graciously, and: "Well, tell me what you're proposing to write."

"I knew you'd see the point," I said, and spread out my notes. "But I ought to explain, too, that everybody else is imaginary. Chaice, for instance, and Martin. We don't want people reading the book and saying, 'Oh, but this is just like that Austin Chaice murder.'"

"Certainly we don't."

"Right-ho then," I said. "I'll get on with it. Here's the rough plot. There's an author like Chaice, an agent like yourself, and a son and a wife and so on. Most of them are red-herrings, so we can confine ourselves to what I might call the solution of the murders."

"More than one murder?"

"That's it. The author and his son. Just like Chaice and Martin, only disguised. Let me make myself more clear. If Richard Chaice did the murders, then it doesn't matter so much about my making Chaice and Martin a bit more true to life. Or the agent, for that matter. After all, the reading public couldn't connect with the murders. If anybody should happen to say, 'This is rather like those murders at Beechingford', then they'd soon changing their minds, since my book gives quite a different solution. And, as I said, the setting will be disguised."

He didn't know why I was stalling for time, even if he did think I was talking a lot of preliminary blether.

"Sorry to be so prolix," I said, "but here's the plot. I'll use the actual names of Chaice and Martin and Daine because that will make it more easy for you to follow.

"We start, then, with an author, Austin Chaice, who's a bit of a paranoiac. He has an absolute craze for the accuracy of his local colour and would rather write of personal experience than anything else. Now he's going to write a play, among other things, which involves a case of double identity. He happens to have been an actor himself, and that gives him the idea of himself assuming another identity. A house of which he's the ground landlord happens to be vacant, so he hires it under the name of G. H. Preston."

"I suppose none of this is true?" he broke in.

"It happens that it *is* true," I said. "We discovered it only yesterday. Chaice used to use that out-of-bounds summerhouse as his dressing-room. He kept his make-up box there. By the way, a rather interesting thing will happen in my book about that. I happened to be near that summerhouse one night and I saw a crack of light. The murderer, and that's you, remember," I said with a smile, "was in the act of removing the make-up box and false whiskers and cheek pads and so on, then I happened to stumble and he got away. Unfortunately for him, he left behind a stick of grease-paint which gave us a clue."

"Wait a minute," he said exasperatedly. "Am I to take it that there wasn't a G. H. Preston?"

"That's it," I said. "And that's not fiction but fact. G. H. Preston was Austin Chaice."

"I can't believe it," he said. I shrugged my shoulders.

"Believe it or not, it's true. When I'm allowed to unload some of the facts I'll give you more details. But to get on with my plot. Chaice loved all that disguise stuff. It was like playing at Indians. I can still hear him chuckling to himself after he'd taken in Lang, and that chap at the house agents'.

"Oh, yes, and you come in too. Chaice—my Chaice—always consulted his literary agent about everything. After all, they'd been associated for years and the agent always read his manuscripts personally. So the agent must have been a pretty ingenious cove too. And, of course, when Chaice put up that double identity stunt, the agent—sorry about that—let's call him you. When Chaice put up that scheme you daren't put him off it. So long as he didn't make a fool of himself as he did over that typewriter business, you didn't mind what he did. And you intended to keep an eye on him. For instance, whereas you two used often to play chess at night at the house, now you took the chess things to Number 6, and you two used to play there instead. Rather a good point I've got there," I said. "When those chess things were returned and put in the table drawer in the hall the murderer gave himself away."

I looked up to find his eyes on mine and with a grim intensity.

"Think it's all right so far?" I asked.

"Carry on," he told me. "We haven't really got to your plot yet."

"Sorry," I said. "I'm afraid I've been a bit long-winded. But about your motive for killing Chaice. We've got to have a motive. I've thought of two. Remember that night when Chaice started an argument here about everybody being a potential murder story, and quoting you as having rigged his accounts, and how Lang said there couldn't be a dishonest literary agent unless the client was a fool? Well, I thought how an agent might swindle a client, if he wasn't above a bit of simple forgery. It's true that a client can get information at first-hand from his publisher about his sales, but only from an English publisher. He wouldn't get the information these days from the owners of foreign rights.

"In Chaice's case those rights must have amounted to a considerable sum, especially in Switzerland where the exchange is favourable from an English author's point of view. Still, that's only a detail. And in my story, of course, I shall make it clear that Chaice wasn't *hinting* about you. He was giving you the straight tip that he'd found you out. That gives us a motive for the murder.

"The other motive is also based partly on fact. There'll be someone in the story like Richard Chaice, who also does a bolt after the murder. It turns out that he bolted because he didn't want to be questioned. He didn't believe in capital punishment, shall we say. That's why he didn't want to tell the police that he knew for some time that you'd been carrying on with Constance. And he didn't tell Austin because he didn't want to make trouble."

Daine got to his feet.

"All this is beginning to sound in—well, I'll be frank—in very bad taste."

"You're too touchy," I told him. "What you can't get into your head is that it's all supposition."

He didn't say anything, but only knocked out his pipe.

"Besides," I said, "I do want you to hear how the murders were done. Everything else can be altered to avoid even a suspicion of what you called bad taste, but the murder methods are really original."

"All right," he said. "But do get to the point."

I thought for a moment he was going to put his glasses on, but he didn't. I should have hated talking to him with those eyes of his behind the glasses.

"We'll come straight to the first murder," I said. "To save time, let the circumstances be the very same ones that prevailed on that Monday night. You've written two anonymous letters to Constance about her husband being concerned with that liquid-squirting. You foster the plan to have Austin followed and you induce Constance to get me to help Martin. In my book you've warned Chaice that Martin suspects something, and so Chaice amuses himself by throwing Martin off the scent. What you'd decided—always, of course, in my book—was to arrange with Chaice for you and him to go to Number 6 that night. You'd be there first and you'd kill him in the house. Then you thought of a better scheme. You induced Constance to get Martin to pretend to be sick, and then she was to get me to persuade you to accompany me. You pretended to be reluctant, but you did it. And no wonder. Since you were always under my eye, you would have a perfect alibi. And, if necessary, you could turn suspicion on Martin.

"And so to the actual night. Either then, or some time before, you'd wheeled up to the back premises of Number 6 that rubber-tired wheelbarrow that stands behind the summerhouse, and we'll see why in a minute. Chaice left here and we followed him to No. 6. He went up to the door as Chaice, visiting his friend or acquaintance there, Preston. He knocked at the door because you—already there, he supposed—would admit him as what a passer-by would assume to be Preston.

"Then it was suggested that we should watch both doors, and you chose the back. I suggest in my book that you entered by the back door, stunned Chaice and then strangled him. You didn't shoot him because the shot would have been heard, and you didn't stab him because blood might have been left on the floor. Then you got the body outside and came back to me and reported that Chaice was talking to somebody—Preston presumably—in the house. Then you put the body in the barrow and covered it with the piece of tarpaulin and took it to the summerhouse gate. You may have wheeled it or carried it to the house, and then you had to get back hurriedly to Number 6. You were, in fact, Pymme's running man.

"Next you came out of the house wearing Chaice's hat and cape and you took a short cut across the grass so as to be well away from where I was watching. You imitated Chaice's quick little mincing steps and I followed you to Number 3, where you nipped through, along the lane and so to this room where you replaced the hat and cape. Then you got back to Number 6. There you were when I came back, and you'd obviously been there all the time. When we came home you deliberately went out of the way so as to prove your ignorance of the district and to give more time for the discovery of the body. And that's about all. What do you think of it so far? Pretty ingenious, don't you think?"

I knew I had him. He daren't deny, for that would have shown a knowledge of things of which he was presumably ignorant. And he daren't go out of the room in a pretended rage, for he simply had to hear what else I knew. My question was intended to exasperate him: to get him to make some admission in a sudden panic or fit of temper. But he was still too wily for that.

"I've heard worse," he said, but the hands were shaking as he began filling his pipe again.

"Glad you like it," I said, "and sorry to be so long-winded. But about the motive for the second murder. I've made Martin either see you bring the body here or else seeing you put it in this room. So what I say is that he approached you the following morning and blackmailed you. You and he weren't talking in your room, you may remember, but outside. That is what gave me the idea. Not only did he insist that you should publish his book, but later, after the reading of the will, he boasted that he could get a job at five hundred a year whenever he liked, you, presumably, supplying the job. You, in my book, gave me the excuse, for publishing the book, that Martin had said his father had given orders to that effect.

"But you weren't sitting pretty any longer. That visit of Martin's altered the whole complexion of things. You might be Chaice's literary executor, and so in a position not only to cover up any manipulation of the accounts but also to manipulate any posthumous pickings, and later still you could make your financial position impregnable by marrying the lady; but now all that wasn't worth a red cent since Martin had your neck in his fingers, like this. So Martin had to go.

"It was lucky you found out about the window and were in the garage when Martin asked about the piece of wood. You saw that piece of wood and at once you hit on what looked like a fool-proof scheme. While Martin was at the bathing-pool you went up to his bedroom and tied a piece of string to the lower id of the piece of wood that propped the window open. You knew it was there because you reconnoitred from your bedroom window. I don't know quite how I shall make you get the other end of that string into the lavatory window which you'd opened for the purpose. It was only a short distance and it wouldn't have to be a particularly good shot. The side curtain, by the way, hid both wood and string, and you attached your end of the string to an old nail just outside the lavatory window.

"The premature discovery of the string wouldn't, however, have involved risk to yourself. In fact, the way you were going to work the whole scheme involved no risk. But what happened afterwards was very simple. You manoeuvred me upstairs. You went into your bedroom and took a look out of your window, and there was Martin, sitting at his open window writing. You had pretended a nasty twinge of sciatica, and when you put the gun under your coat that sciatica would have made any awkwardness look like a natural lameness.

"Then you went first into the lavatory, with gloves in your pocket. You just raised the lavatory window with its frosted glass, and at the very moment after you'd pulled the chain you shot Martin. Not a difficult shot from that short range, and you got him clean above the left temple. In the same three or four seconds you jerked away the wood, and the noise of the lavatory flush drowned both sounds. It's a very noisy flush, by the way. You had your gloves on and you hauled in the wood and pocketed it and the string, and slipped the gun under your coat again. Then you came out of the lavatory and I went in. You waited outside, and I could hear you there all the time.

"Even if Kitty hadn't heard the crack of the falling window—a noise she mistook for the crack of the gun—you'd have been running no risk. You were outside the lavatory and I could have heard you there. And we two were going to your room to sign that agreement, and you'd have contrived to keep me there till the body was found. I'd have sworn that you were never out of my sight. I know you'd have had to slip back the catch of the window and deposit the gun, but you could have done that by keeping me in the hall while you made an excuse to run up and see either Constance or Kitty. I'd still have sworn that you hadn't done the shooting because I'd not have heard the sound of a shot.

"But Kitty's scream made things easier. You nipped along while I was still *in extremis* in the lavatory, and there was Kitty in a faint. She went off just as you got in, and, strangely enough, she remembers your taking out the gun. I know that was bluff in a way, but that must have been what had happened.

"Then you turned the chair and Martin in it so as to face the wrong way for a shot through the window, and you hastily pressed his fingers round the gun and placed that too, and you fastened the catch of the window. When I got there you were trying to bring Kitty round. And that's about all," I said. "Except perhaps one thing I forgot to mention: that you took Chaice's keys. They admitted you to the summerhouse, and they might have opened a safe in which Chaice kept his accounts or something that connected him too closely with G. H. Preston. You had your own key, of course, to Number 6. After we were all asleep that night it was easy for you to slip out of the house and go back to Number 6 and do a bit of tidying up. And you left the letters where they'd be found."

I took a deep breath and put the notes back in my pocket.

"There we are then, Daine. That's the outline of my proposed plot. What's your opinion?"

He slowly got to his feet, knocked out his pipe, and then his hands thrust deep into his pockets. I thought he had put them there so that I shouldn't see them trembling, but I was wrong. But I didn't like his look, and I drew back in my chair.

"Wharton and Goodman are in town, you said?"

His voice was shaking.

"That's right," I said.

"You haven't told them this ridiculous story?"

"You're not calling this book of mine ridiculous?" I protested.

His eyes narrowed.

"Travers, you've always been just a bit too clever or else not quite clever enough."

"Admitted," I said. "And what about it?"

A hand came out of a pocket and then I saw the gun. It was a heavy Webley, and it looked to me like a young cannon. And yet it somehow didn't frighten me. It was a curiously impersonal sort of gun—at least at that first moment.

"Give me those notes, will you?"

"But why?"

"Give me those notes!"

"Very well," I said. "If you feel that way about it."

He rammed them into his pocket and then told me to get to my feet.

"Now put your hands up and turn round!"

"This is damn preposterous."

"Do as I tell you," he said, and then I felt that gun in my back. That was when I was scared. It isn't pleasant to feel potential death against your spine.

"I don't think I'd do anything foolish with that gun," I told him. "You know Sergeant Smith?"

"Who's he?"

"He's the sergeant who first came here with Goodman," I said, and was trying to squint over my shoulder. "He's the fastest thing at shorthand that ever was."

"Yes?" The gun was firm as ever at my back.

"Well, if you look at that telephone you'll see it isn't connected. It's acting as a receiver for Sergeant Smith who's in the workshop taking down every word that's said in this room. So even if you dodge the rope for Chaice and Martin, you won't dodge it for killing me."

"Blast you, Travers!"

I don't know if it was fury or panic or hate that brought those words. In fact I only just heard the words, and I heard nothing else. For while he was spluttering them he must have struck my skull with the butt of that Webley. I faintly remember a terrific sear of pain and then I went down like a poleaxed bullock. One other thing I do faintly remember as I was in that infinitesimal part of a second before the passing out: that I'd been a fool and a coward to have mentioned Smith.

When I came to I was lying on my back on the floor of that room. A cushion had been placed under my head and somebody had been slopping water over me. When I moved, my head felt as if someone had been at it with an axe. Wharton was looking down at me, face all concern.

"How are you now? Feeling all right?"

"Parts of me," I said, and began hoisting myself up. Then the head began to swim.

"The doctor ought to be here at any minute."

"I'm all right," I said testily. "I don't want any doctor."

"Take it steady," he admonished me. "You're damn lucky to be alive. But why the devil didn't you let Smith know he had that gun?"

"Blast you, don't make me talk," I said. "It hurts my head."

I blinked for a minute, decided my glasses were all right, then said I'd mentioned the gun as soon as I could. Then I had a sudden alarm.

"He didn't get Smith, did he?"

"Not he," Wharton said. "Goodman collared him as soon as he was out of that door. Tried to shoot himself, but only Goodman through the shoulder. Nothing very serious. Then I chipped in."

It hurt my head, but I had to smile at that. George chipping in with his fourteen stone.

"Well, that's that," I said, and George began helping me to a chair. "But what about Constance?"

"Nothing doing yet," he told me cautiously. "We'll wait to see if Daine blows the gaff."

Then he asked what about a drink, and a stiff one. I didn't object. Then, as I leaned forward and gingerly felt my head, Lang looked round the door.

"May I come in, sir?"

"Why not?" I told him.

He smiled a bit sheepishly, and then was asking me if it was true about Daine.

"If you mean, did he do the murders—yes."

"My God. You just can't believe it," he said. "Not that I ever liked him very much."

He shook his head, and the mere sight of a shaking head made me wince.

"Puts me in a spot, though," he went on. "If there's no literary executor, then I'm out of work."

"You should worry," I told him. "I'll bet you a pound to a penny you're offered the job. If you think you can do it."

"You bet I can do it," he said, and then he hesitated. "Perhaps, sir, you'd help me out some time, with advice and all that."

I was wishing he'd either go away or shut up. At that moment I had no use for anybody, for my head had begun to ache like hell.

"Advice?" I said, and grunted, but he still didn't seem inclined to go.

"Some advice I might give you," I said. "You're getting married, aren't you?"

"Well, I hope so, sir."

"Then buy yourself a house that's number six in the road."

I think he thought I'd suddenly gone barmy. Perhaps his question was designed to humour me.

"Number six, sir? Why? Is it supposed to be lucky?"

"You'll never know how lucky it's been for you," I told him, and then, thank heaven, Wharton came in with that drink.

THE END